"DEBORAH STEPPED FORWARD TO CENTER STAGE AND TOOK A DEEP BREATH . . .

"Here she was in the Los Angeles Arena, listening to the orchestra's introduction mix with the roar of the crowd. Deborah felt as if God's abundant blessings were pouring directly on her at that very moment.

"It wasn't difficult for the words to flow from her soul. She closed her eyes and sang to the Lord, telling Him with her song that she loved Him, she worshiped Him, she praised Him. She bent over and held her hand against her waist as the words flowed from her: 'I'm lost without you . . . so don't ever go away . . .'

"It was only when Lavelle took her hand for them to take a bow that she remembered where she was."

—from SINGSATION

"Need a little good news in your novels? Look no further."

—*Essence*

Singsation

Jacquelin Thomas

WARNER BOOKS

An AOL Time Warner Company

Walk Worthy Press

West Bloomfield, Michigan

This book is a work of fiction. Names, characters, places, and incidents are the product of the author's imagination or are used fictitiously. Any resemblance to actual events, locales, or persons, living or dead, is coincidental.

Copyright © 2001 by Jacquelin Thomas
Reading Group Guide copyright © 2003 by Warner Books, Inc., with Walk Worthy Press
All rights reserved.

Originally published in hardcover by Warner Books, Inc., with Walk Worthy Press
Walk Worthy Press, 33290 West Fourteen Mile Road, #482,
West Bloomfield, MI 48322

Real Believers, Real Life, Real Answers in the Living God™

Warner Books, Inc., 1271 Avenue of the Americas, New York, NY 10020
Visit our Web sites at www.twbookmark.com
                        www.walkworthypress.net

An AOL Time Warner Company

Printed in the United States of America

Originally published in hardcover by Warner Books, Inc.

First Trade Printing: April 2003

10 9 8 7 6 5 4 3 2 1

The Library of Congress has cataloged the hardcover edition as follows:

Thomas, Jacquelin.
    Singsation / Jacquelin Thomas.
       p. cm.
    ISBN 0-446-52798-X
    1. Afro-American women—Fiction.   2. Rhythm and blues music—Fiction.
  3. Women singers—Fiction.   4. Young women—Fiction.   5. Georgia—Fiction.   I. Title.
  PS3570.H5637 S5 2001
  813'.54—dc21

                                                                    00-050343

ISBN 0-446-67886-4 (pbk.)

Cover type by Carolle Nay
Cover photo by Franco Accornero

This book is dedicated to

ALEXX DAYE

You are a very gifted singer and songwriter.
Glorify God in all that you do.
May this book uplift and encourage you.

ACKNOWLEDGMENTS

My Heavenly Father: Thank You for this gift. I accept it and will use my talent to glorify You.

My family: Thank you all for being so patient and understanding while I worked on this project. I've been truly blessed.

Deirdre M. Knight: Thank you for being the voice of reason and for being supportive of my decision to write Christian fiction.

Denise Stinson: Thank you for having this vision, and for allowing me to give voice to stories that glorify God.

Pastor Alvin Smith: Thank you for being such a wonderful mentor. It was your teaching of God's word that brought me to this point.

Pastor Kenneth Grant and Shirley: Words cannot express the way I feel about the two of you. It is truly a blessing to have you both in my life and as members of my extended family.

Greg Moore: One of the most talented musicians of all

time. Thank you for taking time out of your busy schedule to answer all of my questions regarding the music industry.

Victoria Christopher Murray: My wonderful and caring friend. None of this would be possible if not for your support and encouragement. Thank you for being there and for understanding. I thank you for being who you are, but mostly, I thank God for bringing you into my life.

CHAPTER 1

BEING ONSTAGE WAS EXHILARATING. THE OVAL-shaped Mecca was choked beyond capacity with screaming men and women chanting her name. Like a sponge, she soaked up their adoration, then granted them a single smile.

A hush fell over the stadium, and anticipation thickened the air. Deborah Anne ran her right hand along her purple sequined gown, and waited for just the right moment.

She gave an almost undetectable twist of her hand, and the orchestra played the first note. Deborah Anne spread her arms and began her song. The applause was deafening, but not enough to drown out her voice. She was wrapped in a silken cocoon of euphoria, and the notes flowed from deep within her soul.

Closing her eyes, she sang the final note, holding it for several seconds as the crowd roared. She stood still, not moving a muscle, allowing the moment to settle. Then she opened her eyes.

A ray of sun sprinkled through the stained-glass window depicting the Madonna and hit Deborah Anne's eyes. She squinted through the polite applause as she looked over the congregation of seventy-nine parishioners who sat on the wooden benches of Mountain Baptist Church.

She was still standing, stuck in place, and it took a subtle nod from her mother before Deborah Anne returned to the choir stand.

A moment later, Deacon Miller stood. "Please turn to Psalm 90:17 for today's scripture reading."

As Deborah Anne flipped through the worn pages of her burgundy-covered Bible, she scolded herself. "I don't know why I do that," she whispered under her breath. She often let her mind wander too far—daydreaming of stadiums packed with adoring fans, thrilled to hear just a single note from her. She shook her head. She had told herself many times that whatever God had in store would be good enough.

She used the church bulletin as a fan, hoping her heart would stop racing so she could pay attention to Deacon Miller's reading of the scriptures.

As the deacon read the words aloud, Deborah Anne scanned the faces of her family and friends, many of whom had attended Mountain Baptist Church for as long as she had walked the earth. Her eyes moved to the second row, and she smiled at Alfreda Dobson, known as Mother to all who knew her.

Mother was the oldest woman in the church—and in all of Villa Rica, for that matter. She sat with her petite frame held tall, like a queen on her throne.

Mother Dobson smiled and nodded ever so slightly, before Deborah Anne shifted her gaze to look at the young man sitting next to her. She frowned, not recognizing the face.

When the young man's lips spread into a wide grin, Deborah Anne coughed, and let her eyes fall to the Bible in her lap.

The Deacon was speaking. "In each of us is a talent that comes from God above. How we express this varies from person to person. But the most important thing is that we can never forget the source. Some people think that they are free to do what they want without thinking about God at all."

Slowly, Deborah Anne lifted her eyes again, but dropped them quickly when she saw that the stranger was still looking at her. She turned slightly in her seat, pretending to focus on Deacon Miller, but from the corner of her eye she glanced again at Mother Dobson and her guest. He was handsome—cute, really. His chestnut-colored skin and baby-face features made him look barely twenty-one.

A few seconds later, Deborah Anne realized who he was and stared at him outright. Triage Blue.

Everyone in Villa Rica knew about Triage Blue. He was one of the most successful rappers in the country, and now a big screen star. But most important, Triage Blue was one of Mother Dobson's thirty-two grandchildren, and Mother Dobson bragged about him every chance she got.

"My grandson performed for the President at the inauguration," the matriarch had proudly announced to everyone she knew.

Deborah Anne glanced at the young man again. That was definitely Triage Blue. She'd seen enough photographs of him in the tabloids to recognize him. Mother Dobson had also reminded her recently that she had actually met Triage many years before his rise to success. It was one summer about twenty years ago—when they were both about seven or eight—when his family was visiting Villa Rica from Chicago.

"Now before we turn to Pastor Duncan," Deacon Miller began, "I would like to acknowledge our visitor."

After a nudge from his grandmother, Triage stood and smiled shyly.

"Well, well." Deacon Miller beamed. "I believe we have Mother Dobson's grandson visiting with us today. Brother Waters is here from California."

Triage nodded as the congregation clapped. Before he returned to his seat, he looked at Deborah Anne again and smiled.

"We welcome you back to Mountain Baptist Church and want you to know that we're all proud of you. Now I can't say that I'm one who knows all of your music, but my girls can't get enough of you."

Deborah Anne held back a giggle as she watched Deacon Miller's three teenage daughters slide lower into their front-pew seats.

"Keep making us and your grandmother proud, Brother Waters."

Deborah Anne lowered her head to her chest, but strained her eyes upward so she could continue watching Triage.

It wasn't until Pastor Duncan's bass voice rang through the small church that Deborah Anne allowed her eyes to return to the altar. She hadn't even realized that the pastor had taken his place.

"Today's sermon is taken from the twenty-fifth chapter of Matthew," Pastor Duncan boomed, and took a handkerchief to wipe the sweat that dripped from his brow, even though

he'd only uttered ten words. "From the fourteenth to the thir-
tieth verse—the parable of the talents."

Deborah Anne sat up. One of her favorite stories.

"A talent in Jesus' time was a sum of money that was worth
two years' wages. But it is no coincidence that this term for
money is what we use today to describe the gifts that the
Lord has given us. Whether it is a *talented* singer or athlete,
a *talented* businessman or even a preacher man . . ." Pastor
Duncan sang. He paused until the chuckles faded.

"Whatever the talent is," Pastor Duncan continued, "it has
been given by God, not to be wasted. . . ."

Deborah Anne ran her hand down her neck.

"But the gifts that God has blessed you with cannot be
used in just any old way. No! Your gift must be used for *His*
purpose. Your gift must be used for *His* glory. Your gift must
be used to serve *Him*. . . ."

Deborah Anne closed her eyes and let Pastor Duncan's
voice fade into the background as she prayed. *Lord, help me
to know how I'm to use this gift You've blessed me with,* she
prayed silently. *Show me what You want me to do.*

Pastor Duncan continued talk-singing and strutting, admonishing them all to take inventory deep inside. "Most of
you know what gift He gave you. Some of you will be wondering to your graves. But if you pray for wisdom, God will
be faithful and just. He'll answer you. He'll show you the
way!"

Pastor Duncan slid into his seat, and Deborah Anne joined
the rest of the congregation, rising to her feet with shouts of
"Amen" and "Hallelujah."

She vowed to do exactly what Pastor Duncan urged. She
knew what her gift was, and she was going to find how

she should use it. In prayer, she'd find her answer. When she looked up, the first person she saw was Triage Blue, still smiling at her.

❧

Deborah Anne gathered up her Bible, then lifted her choir robe, preparing to step from the stand. But before she could get down the five steps, Deacon Miller stopped her.

"Sister Deborah Anne, that was a fine song you lifted to the Lord today. Mighty fine."

She smiled. "Thank you, Deacon."

"I know your mother and father are proud of the gift that God has blessed you with."

Deborah Anne shifted from one foot to the other and looked over her shoulder.

"I'm sorry, am I keeping you from something?"

She whipped her head around. "Oh no, I . . . was just looking for my mother."

"She's at the front door talking to Mother Dobson."

"Thank you," Deborah Anne said before she carefully made her way down the aisle toward the front doors. She paused every few steps, smiling and kissing people who praised her at every turn. Though it was just a few minutes, it seemed like an hour passed before she finally made it to the door.

"Baby, you did good today." Virginia kissed her daughter and handed her her coat. "I'm so proud of you."

"Yessiree, sugar," Mother Dobson added. "You have the voice of an angel."

"Thank you, Mother Dobson." Deborah Anne leaned over

to kiss Mother Dobson's weathered cheek. Over her shoulder, Deborah Anne could see a group of young girls, squealing as they circled Triage.

"Would you look at my grandson?" Mother Dobson exclaimed. "And look at those fast girls, all over him." With a single turn and one tap of her cane, she called, "Milton, can you come over here?"

After signing one last church bulletin, Triage came quickly toward his grandmother and the Peterson women.

Before Mother Dobson could say a word, he extended his hand to Deborah Anne. "Hello, I'm Triage Blue." He squeezed her hand in his.

"I'm Deborah Anne Peterson," she said forcefully, though her knees were weak. Triage Blue is holding my hand! she screamed inside.

"Boy, you ain't in Hollywood now. Your mama named you Milton. Leave that Triage stuff back there. Anyway," Mother Dobson said, shaking her head and introducing Triage to Virginia, "this is Deborah Anne's mother, Mrs. Peterson."

"Nice to meet you, ma'am."

"Mrs. Peterson used to watch your mama when I worked for the Wiltons." Mother Dobson paused, and a frown spread across her face. "Or was I working for old Mrs. Mattie King back then?"

Virginia took Triage's hand. "When you speak to your mother, please tell her that I asked after her."

Triage nodded and glanced again at Deborah Anne.

"Well, come on, honey." Virginia nudged Deborah Anne. "I know your daddy is waiting in the car, and it's a bit chilly out here."

Virginia took Mother Dobson's elbow and helped her down

the stairs. Deborah Anne and Triage followed, lingering a few steps behind.

"Forget that Milton stuff—call me Triage." He grinned, but kept his voice low.

Deborah Anne looked at him sideways. "I guess you look like a Triage more than a Milton. How did you get that name—Triage, I mean?"

Triage chuckled. "During college I worked in the ER at Cedars-Sinai because I wanted to be a doctor. But I still needed to make some extra money. So I did a little rapping on the side at nightclubs and parties. The music took over my life, and I decided to name myself Triage for all that it represented. And Blue, well, that's not so interesting. That's just my favorite color." He laughed.

She smiled up at him. His six-foot frame towered over her by at least four inches. His closely cropped hair made him look boyish, and it was hard to believe that he was a year older than she was.

"So what are you doing in town?" Deborah Anne asked.

"Just spending time with my grandmother. I have a concert in Atlanta next weekend. I love coming here; not that many people know who I am."

"It doesn't look that way to me," Deborah Anne teased, as she nodded toward a group of girls standing by the church giggling and pointing toward them. "Are you enjoying your vacation?"

"What vacation?" Triage raised his eyebrows in mock surprise. "I've whitewashed a fence and painted three rooms. I get up every morning before dawn to feed the chickens. Hanging with Grandma is no day at the beach."

Deborah Anne laughed. "You may never come back."

"Oh, I'll be back." He gave her a long glance. "Girl, you know something? You can sing! I've heard a lot of people tackle 'His Eyes Are on the Sparrow,' but you tore it up."

She grinned widely. A compliment from Triage was worth more than all the accolades she received in church. "Thank you."

"Ever thought about singing professionally?"

"I think of nothing else. But I don't know how to be discovered in Villa Rica."

"Maybe you don't have to do anything. Maybe I just discovered you."

"Yeah, right," she said, kicking a pebble as they got closer to the car where her parents were chatting with Mother Dobson.

"I'm serious. I have a friend who's auditioning backup singers in LA right now. Lavelle Roberts. You've heard of him, right?"

She stopped. "Please don't kid me."

"I'm serious," he said, stopping next to her. "All you have to do is send him a copy of a tape with a note that I recommended you. You have a tape?"

She nodded. "My cousin Bubba has a friend with a studio, so I've got several tapes."

"And you've got the voice."

"Do you think he'll like me?"

"If he has an ear, he will. You sound as good as the singers he has now. Anyway," he said, leaning closer to her, "it's about who you know in this business, and now you know me."

Deborah Anne stopped in front of her parents' car. She shoved her hands deep into her coat pockets.

"Well, come on, Milton." Mother Dobson tapped her cane twice, and Triage took her elbow.

"Thank you, Triage," Deborah Anne said sincerely. "I really mean that."

"It's no big deal." Just as Mother Dobson and Triage stepped away, he said, "Deborah Anne, can I give you a call while I'm here?"

"I'd like that." She grinned.

Before Deborah Anne got into the backseat of her parents' Lincoln Continental, she could hear Mother Dobson muttering, "What was Deborah Anne thanking you for?"

Deborah Anne smiled. If Mother only knew.

"Deborah Anne, what did you do with the lace tablecloth?" Virginia yelled from the kitchen.

"It's in the bottom drawer of the buffet, Mama," Deborah Anne replied as she entered the dining room. "I'll get it."

Virginia was still wearing the gray knit suit she'd worn to church, but Deborah Anne had already changed into her favorite T-shirt and denim overalls and had pulled her thick black hair into a ponytail.

"Mama, why don't you go change?" Deborah Anne said as she spread the tablecloth across the dining room table. Even with the large oak table set for twelve, they'd still have to set up a couple of card tables along the wall to accommodate all the relatives who came by every Sunday. "People will start arriving soon." Deborah Anne had barely finished saying it when she heard voices on the porch. "See, I think that's Aunt Bird and Uncle Moses now."

As Virginia scurried down the hall to her bedroom, Deborah Anne opened the front door.

"Girl, you sure sounded good in church this morning," Aunt Bird drawled. "One day, somebody's going to come and take you away from us."

Deborah Anne only smiled, knowing that she had to wait for the right moment to tell everyone her news. Before she could close the front door, her cousins Willetta, Pauline, and Maxine arrived.

Though they were first cousins, Willetta and Deborah Anne were also best friends. Born only four months apart, they'd lived next door to each other all of their lives.

"Girl, get in here. I've got something to tell you." Deborah Anne grabbed Willetta's hand and pulled her into the dining room, away from the other relatives who were starting to arrive in groups.

While the living room filled with loud talk and laughter, Deborah Anne kept her voice low.

"Help me set the table," she said, handing Willetta the wooden case holding the Sunday silver.

"So what's the big news?" Willetta whispered back.

Grinning widely, Deborah Anne gushed, "Girl, you missed it in church today. You'll never guess who was there." Before Willetta could respond, Deborah Anne announced, "Triage Blue!"

Willetta's mouth opened wide, and Deborah Anne laughed.

"Oh, no," Willetta groaned. "How could I have missed that? Did you meet him?"

Deborah Anne bobbed her head. "Yes, and Mama and Daddy did too!"

Maxine sauntered into the dining room. "What ya'll whispering about?"

Willetta was still holding her head in her hands. "Deborah Anne just told me that Triage Blue was at church this morning." Willetta glared at her sister. "Why didn't you tell me?"

Maxine's eyes grew round and wide. "He was at *our* church?"

"Yeah, girl." Deborah Anne laughed. "That's what you get for sneaking out before Deacon Miller introduced Pastor Duncan and his sermon."

Pauline plopped into the chair next to her sister. "I love his music."

Deborah Anne said, "Me too. I love that he's so popular, even though he doesn't use profanity or bash women, like some of those others."

"Yeah, and if you listen to the words, he's really talking about taking care of family and being true to yourself," Willetta said.

"Ooohhh!" Pauline moaned. "If I had stayed in church, I could've told everyone in school tomorrow that I met Triage Blue!"

"I bet that's the last time y'all will be sneaking out." Deborah Anne laughed.

The cousins continued laughing and talking about Triage Blue as Virginia and her sisters-in-law started moving the food onto the buffet table. Twenty minutes later, all eighteen Petersons were standing around the table, with Elijah Peterson at the head. Even as the smell of the macaroni and cheese and fried catfish wafted under their noses, Elijah, the oldest of the four Peterson brothers, made the family wait until every hand was held and every head was bowed.

"Heavenly Father," Elijah finally began. "We thank You for this food that we are about to receive. We thank You for the many blessings that You have bestowed on each of us and we want You to know, Lord, that we take none of it for granted."

As her father prayed, it took everything in her for Deborah Anne not to scream out her secret right then. But she knew she had to wait, and she was grateful when Elijah finally said, "Amen."

It took another twenty minutes for the Peterson clan to pass through the buffet and pile their plates high. It took only moments for the conversation to turn to Triage Blue.

"I can't believe I missed Triage Blue!" Deborah Anne's cousin Bubba said, as he stabbed his fork into a chicken leg. "If I'd known that he was going to be there, I would've been in church myself."

"Is that the only reason you can find for going to church, Bubba?" Elijah asked. "You know when the Lord comes back, some of his people gonna be in real trouble. Now, I ain't calling no names, Bubba. . . ."

The room filled with laughter as Bubba lowered his eyes and grinned. "I know, Uncle Eli, but I still wish that I'd seen Triage Blue," he said sheepishly. Then he raised his head. "Did you get to meet him, Deborah Anne?"

She nodded and took a deep breath. "Not only did I meet him, but he told me that he might know of a singing gig. Lavelle Roberts is looking for a backup singer, and I'm going to send in a tape." She stated this matter-of-factly, even though her heart was beating furiously.

An electrical shock seemed to sear through the room, silencing them all. Only the tick-tock of the grandfather clock in the living room filled the air. But it was the smile that fell from her father's face that Deborah Anne noticed the most.

Willetta was first to break the silence. "Deborah Anne, you didn't tell me that! You're going to sing with Lavelle? I love him!" Willetta held her hand over her chest.

Deborah Anne's heart continued to pound, but she kept her voice steady. "I don't have the job yet. Triage just suggested that I send in a tape, and I'm going to do it."

To Deborah Anne, it seemed the room parted like the Red Sea. On one side, her excited cousins jabbered about how their cousin was going to be famous; on the other, her aunts and uncles remained silent and waited for Elijah to speak.

Finally, Deborah Anne picked up a biscuit and slowly spread butter across the top. "So what do you think, Mama and Daddy?"

Virginia took her time, wiping her mouth with the corner of her napkin. "That sounds interesting, baby." Virginia's words came slowly. "But we don't know anything about it. Where exactly is this job?"

"In Los Angeles."

"Girl, you're going to Hollywood," Bubba bubbled. "I wanna go!"

"That's a long way from home," Uncle Moses said, eyeing Elijah, who remained silent, though his eyes hadn't left Deborah Anne's.

Deborah Anne smiled. "I'm just sending in a tape. We don't know what's going to happen. There are lots of talented women out there."

"None as talented as you, Deborah Anne," Maxine piped in. "My cousin is da bomb!"

"Well, nothing is going to happen until I talk it over with you and Daddy, Mama. And I'm going to pray about it a lot."

"Wouldn't that be exciting?" Aunt Bird smiled. "Our little Deborah Anne, a big-time singer."

Deborah Anne smiled at her aunt, grateful for the support and hopeful that the sea was beginning to close. "Remember, everyone, I'm only sending a tape."

"Well, all you can do is just wait and see what happens," said Virginia as she patted her daughter's hand. Then she changed the subject. "Has anyone heard about that big company that's supposed to be opening an office right here in Villa Rica? All the nurses are talking about it. People are saying there's going to be lots of new jobs, but a lot more traffic." Virginia spoke to no one in particular, but it was enough to take the focus from Deborah Anne, who exhaled, finally taking a bite from the biscuit she'd held in her hand.

She leaned back in her chair and let her mind drift. This was going to be her first real chance at her dream, but it was going to be a tough sell to her father. Deborah Anne knew that Elijah would never try to stop her. She was twenty-six years old—"grown folk," as her father was fond of saying. But still, she wanted to please him, and she wanted to please God even more. As Pastor Duncan had said this morning, everyone had to use the gift God gave them. This was how she'd use hers.

When she heard her father's voice, she looked up. He was smiling, deep in conversation with Uncle Moses. Deborah Anne smiled then too, knowing she'd jumped the first hurdle.

"Girl, I am so happy for you," Willetta whispered, and took her hand under the table. "You're going to get this job. I'm going to be praying for it. You know what the Bible says about when two agree."

Deborah Anne only smiled, but she didn't need to say a word for Willetta to know that she would be praying for exactly the same thing.

Deborah Anne squeezed her cousin's hand. "Thanks, girl. I'm going to need you on my side."

"Don't worry about me," Willetta said. "You've got God, and He's all you need."

CHAPTER 2

DEBORAH ANNE CLOSED THE DOOR BEHIND WIL-
letta and sighed. Finally. Everyone had stayed
much later tonight than usual. When the last of
her aunts and uncles left, her parents retired to
their bedroom. But Willetta stayed for almost two hours
longer, wanting to know every word that Triage had uttered.

Deborah Anne turned off the two bright living room lights
before scurrying silently over the tan carpet to her bedroom
at the opposite end of the house.

She quickly changed into her nightshirt, then got into bed
and leaned back against the stack of pillows. She closed her
eyes. Could her dream really be coming true? She allowed
herself to drown in the fantasy that she'd had ever since her
parents had taken her to see Patti LaBelle. When Patti belted
out "Somewhere Over the Rainbow," Deborah Anne knew
what she wanted to do.

The shrill sound of her telephone interrupted her reverie,

and she sucked her teeth. She knew it was Willetta. That girl was as excited as she was.

"May I speak with Deborah Anne, please?"

Even after only one meeting, she recognized his voice. "Hi, Triage."

"Hey, I hope I'm not calling too late, but I wanted to give you Lavelle's address. I've made a couple of calls, but you should still get your tape into the mail tomorrow."

Deborah Anne sat up and wrote down the information as Triage dictated it to her.

"Triage, I can't tell you how much I appreciate this," she thanked him again.

"Hey, I know how difficult it is in this business. Everyone needs help." He paused. "Plus, I have to take care of the daughter of the lady who baby-sat my mama!"

They laughed together.

"Well, if there is anything that I can do to return the favor, just let me know."

"How about going out with me tomorrow? We can grab a bite to eat or something. I haven't done much since I got here, and it'll be kinda nice to get out with someone who doesn't take her teeth out at night."

"That's terrible!" Deborah scolded him through her giggles. "But dinner sounds fine. I should be home by six."

Deborah Anne's smile was still wide when she hung up the phone and pulled back the bed covers. Before she got in, she knelt by the bed.

"Heavenly Father, I thank You for this day that You blessed me with. But most of all, Father, I thank You for this opportunity that You've brought my way. Please, Lord, You know my heart, You know my dreams. I've waited so long for something like this, and I pray that this is from You." She paused. Of course this was God, Deborah Anne thought. Didn't she find out about this in church? She grinned, then continued her prayer. "Thank You, Father, for this gift that You've given me, and I thank You in advance that I will get the call from Lavelle and I will be blessed with this dream."

She jumped into bed and pulled the covers over her, but a moment later, she got up. She opened her closet door, stood on her tiptoes, and pulled a box filled with tapes from the top shelf. She sorted through them, already knowing which one she would send. When she found it, she placed it inside her purse, then returned to bed for a night full of fantasy-filled dreams.

❧

"I can't believe you're still awake," Virginia said as she peered over her reading glasses at her husband.

Elijah grunted and flipped the television channel with the remote control, as he'd been doing for the last two hours.

Virginia closed her Bible and turned onto her side. "Come on, Eli, let's talk about it."

He remained silent.

"Okay," she said, sighing. "But this isn't going away. Deborah Anne is going to send in that tape, and with the way she can sing, and the recommendation from Milton, there's a good chance that she could get this job."

Elijah clicked off the television and ran his hand over his bald head. "It's just that I didn't think our baby would use her voice that way."

"Well, that's the first problem, honey. Deborah Anne isn't our baby anymore."

"You know what I mean. I've heard that man, Lavelle, and he does nothing to exalt the Lord."

Virginia sighed. "That's what I was thinking. But we've raised Deborah Anne right. We can't tell her not to do this."

Elijah stood and paced along the side of the bed. "I know. I stopped trying to tell grown folks what to do long ago." He sat on the edge of the bed with his back to his wife. "This just isn't what I imagined for her."

"I know, sweetheart," Virginia said, rubbing his back. "Why don't we just wait and see how this is going to play out? There may be nothing for us to worry about."

After a few moments, he nodded, then clicked off the light on his side of the bed. Virginia did the same, then lay back in his arms, but it was several hours before either fell asleep.

CHAPTER 3

DEBORAH ANNE PEEKED THROUGH THE HEAVY curtains at the front bay window for what had to be the third time in just ten minutes. As soon as she turned away, she heard footsteps coming up the porch steps.

She smoothed her pants suit down and waited for Triage to ring the doorbell. But when she opened the door, her face dropped in disappointment.

"Pauline, what are you doing here? Don't you have a Girl Scout meeting or something?"

"Very funny." Pauline laughed as she closed the door behind her. "I came here to see Triage Blue. Aunt Virginia told Mama that you were having dinner with him, and I want to get his autograph."

Deborah Anne's eyes opened wide. "No, Pauline. Please don't embarrass me this way. He probably already thinks we're country."

"So? He's as country as we are, even if he lives in LA."
She laughed.

Deborah Anne stubbornly shook her head. "No way. And
if he comes while you're still here, you're out the backdoor!"

Pauline sucked her teeth. "No, I'm not," she said, plopping
into the wide chair in front of the window. "I'm going to sit
right here until he signs this for me." She held up an index
card.

Deborah Anne tilted her head and looked at Pauline as if
she were crazy.

Her cousin's stance made Pauline believe that Deborah
Anne was serious. "Please," Pauline finally pleaded. "I'll be
the most popular girl in high school with that autograph.
Please!"

It was the begging that made her acquiesce. "All right, I'll
get it for you while we're at dinner."

Pauline grinned. "That's fine. Just tell him to sign it to his
best friend in the whole world and the finest woman he's ever
met."

Deborah Anne rolled her eyes. "Okay," she assented. "But
now do me a favor. Don't go running around town telling
everyone that Triage is here. He's trying to get some rest."

"All right. But everyone already knows that he's here,"
Pauline whined.

Just as Pauline stood, they heard a car in the driveway.
Pauline peeked through the window. "Oh, Deborah Anne, it's
him! Please let me meet him. I promise I won't do anything
to embarrass you." She held up her hand as if taking a vow.

Deborah Anne laughed. "Okay, open the door for me,
please."

Pauline kissed her cousin on the cheek before she ran to the door.

Deborah Anne stepped forward. "Hey, Triage. Come on in."

She introduced him to Pauline and was amused that suddenly her sixteen-year-old cousin acted like she met celebrities all day long. A moment after Pauline had scurried down the porch steps and over the lawn to her house, Deborah picked up her purse and coat, leading Triage out the door.

"This is nice," she said, as he helped her into the Ford Explorer. "But I'm surprised that you're not riding around in a limousine or something."

"Why would I do that?" he asked, as he put on glasses and pulled his cap over his forehead. He pulled out of the driveway and turned onto the main road. "I'm not trying to be noticed."

"If it were me, I'd be in a long limousine with a driver wearing a black suit and black hat and white shirt with a black tie—"

"Dang, girl, you've got this all figured out."

They laughed and chatted easily, as Triage followed Deborah's directions to her favorite restaurant in Carrollton.

Rapture was only half filled, as it was almost every Monday night. The young hostess led them through the restaurant. Deborah Anne was amused as the girl looked over her shoulder at Triage as if she recognized him but couldn't place the face.

"Would you mind if we had a table farther in the back?" Triage asked, motioning toward a corner booth.

"That section's closed."

Triage slowly pulled his wallet from his jacket. "Is there anything I can do to get it opened?"

The girl's eyes moved from his face to his hands, then back to his face again. "I know who you are!" Her surprise was etched in each word.

He held his finger to his lips. "I'm trying to keep it a secret," he whispered.

She nodded with a wide grin and led them to the table he'd requested. "I'll explain it to the manager." She stood at their table. "I can't believe that Triage Blue is actually in our restaurant."

"But we're going to keep it a secret, right?" He smiled.

She nodded and hurried away.

Triage looked at his watch. "In five minutes, there'll be twenty people standing at this table," he said, without a hint of annoyance. "I hope it's not going to bother you."

"Are you kidding? I dream of the day when people will rush me for my autograph. It must be awesome to have people love you and your music so much."

He twirled his glass of water. "In the beginning, it was cool, but it gets old quick. It's hard to go anywhere without being swamped by fans."

"Mr. Blue!" A short man with just a wisp of hair combed over his scalp rushed to their table. He took Triage's hand before he or Deborah Anne could say anything. "I'm Otis Newman, the manager. It's an honor to have you here."

Triage smiled and pulled his hand away from the man, who didn't seem able to let go. "Thank you, Mr. Newman. My friend tells me this is a real nice place." Triage motioned to Deborah, but Otis kept his eyes on Triage.

"Well, if there is anything I can do while you're here, just

let me know. Dinner is on us. Dessert too! If there is anything you need—"

"We need menus." Triage smiled.

"Oh, yes." Otis swung his head around and motioned to
the girl who had led them to the table. "Andrea will help
you." The man paused and looked down at his shoes for a
moment. "Mr. Blue, if it's not too much to ask, would you
mind signing an autograph before you leave?"

"No problem."

"It's not for me," Otis said quickly. "I've got two girls at
home who play your CDs constantly."

Triage nodded and took the menus from Andrea. He
handed one to Deborah Anne. Otis and Andrea continued
to stand by the table.

Triage pointed to the menus and said, "We'll need a few
minutes."

"Oh, of course." Otis coughed. "Andrea, take care of those
people who just came in," he said, as he led her from the
table.

"Is it always like that?" Deborah Anne chuckled.

Triage nodded and sighed. "Don't get me wrong, I'd be
nowhere without the fans, but sometimes, I'd like to just have
a nice dinner without any interruptions."

"You seem to handle it. I've heard of stars being rude to
people when they ask for an autograph or a picture."

"I try not to be that way, but I can understand how celebrities can go there. It's as if you lose all your privacy. Anyway,
what's good here?"

Deborah Anne suggested the grilled salmon, and Triage
agreed. Otis and Andrea hovered nearby, bringing them drinks
and, finally, dinner.

As Triage picked up his fork, Deborah Anne said, "Would you like to bless the food, or should I?"

He blinked and after a moment said, "Uh, no, I'll say it." He stammered and began, "Uh . . . thank You, Lord, for this food . . ." and then stopped, as if he didn't have anything else to say.

Deborah looked up at him. "Amen," she said. She picked up her fork. "I guess you don't say grace very often."

He shrugged. "I do forget most times, except of course when I'm with Grandma. You know, in her house, we thank the Lord for everything."

"Don't you think that's how it should be?" Deborah Anne asked, shoveling a few green peas onto her fork.

"Yeah, but you know, in this business and with my schedule, sometimes God doesn't get His due."

Deborah Anne put down her fork and sat back in her chair. "Well, you know I've got to ask you the question that all card-carrying Christians ask." She paused. "Are you saved? Do you have a personal relationship with God?"

"Oh yeah!" he exclaimed. "For a long time. It happened right here in Villa Rica with Grandma. As soon as she thought I was old enough to understand, I prayed for Jesus to come into my heart." With his fork, he cut a piece of the salmon. He continued, "Even though I'm a card-carrying Christian, I don't pull the card out of my wallet often enough." He smiled weakly, but Deborah Anne could hear the sadness in his voice.

"What do you mean?"

He shrugged. "I guess it's this business. It may sound like an excuse, but work takes over everything. Instead of going to church on Sundays, I find myself in the studio or on somebody's boat negotiating a new deal. Instead of reading my Bible when I wake up, I roll out of bed and jog five miles or go to the gym to make sure I'm in shape for the next video or movie. And don't even talk about touring. Road trips really keep me away from God."

Deborah Anne dropped her eyes.

"Go ahead and say it. I'm not really a Christian, right?"

She tilted her head. "You know you can't lose your relationship with God. Once you accept Him, He's always there."

"I know that, but I do feel bad because I've allowed this business to move me away from where I should be with the Lord."

Deborah Anne pursed her lips. "If I make it in this business, that'll never happen to me."

He raised his eyebrows.

"I'm sorry," her apology came quickly. "I don't mean to sound judgmental. It's just that no matter what, if I end up in the business, I'll do my best to maintain my walk with God."

Triage smiled. "I'm surprised that you're not trying to get a gospel deal."

She shook her head. "There's no money in that."

His eyebrows rose higher.

"I keep saying the wrong things," she said, pulling her napkin to her mouth. "I just meant that I don't think that's what I *have* to do. I think that I'll be able to serve the Lord better if I'm right in the middle of the world. That's what Jesus did."

"Well, if you think this is what Jesus would do, then you go for it, girl. Did you send in the tape?"

Her smile returned. "First thing this morning. My hands

were trembling when I gave the envelope to the postman. I've been hoping and praying for something like this to happen, but being a twenty-six-year-old police dispatcher, living in Villa Rica, wasn't doing much for my dream." She paused and bit her lip. "Triage, do you really think I have a shot at this?"

He nodded boldly. "I'm telling you, when Lavelle hears that tape, it's going to blow his mind. In fact, I'll give Lavelle a call in the morning."

Her eyes opened wide. "You'd do that for me?"

"Of course. I'm going to take care of you, girl."

Deborah Anne beamed. It seemed like her prayers were finally being answered. But just to be sure, she vowed to pray every chance she got.

🕊

They stayed in the restaurant until closing time. Then, at the stroke of ten, Otis and all of the other employees lined up at their table to get Triage's autograph. Deborah Anne stood to the side, enjoying the scene.

"I'm so sorry about this," Triage whispered to her between signings.

She waved her hand. "Don't worry about it."

As she watched him, she imagined herself returning to Rapture and receiving the same adulation. She sighed, content to watch it all from the sidelines—at least for now.

On the way home, they laughed about Otis and his crew.

"Otis told me those autographs were for his daughters, but then he had me sign two with his name on them."

"Oh, that reminds me, I almost forgot," Deborah Anne said as she pulled the card Pauline had given her from her coat pocket. "Do you think you have the energy to sign one more for my cousin Pauline?"

He laughed as Deborah Anne dictated the words just as Pauline had told her.

"You sound like Otis and his people."

Finally, he walked her to the front door. "Deborah Anne, I had a great time. Thanks for showing me something else besides Grandma's house."

She laughed. "I enjoyed it too. And it's the least I could do with all that you're doing for me."

"Hey, I'm leaving tomorrow, but how would you like to come to my concert in Atlanta on Friday? You'll be my guest, and you can even bring some friends along—not a whole crew, just a few folks."

"I'd love it!"

"Okay, I'll call you when I get to Atlanta." He kissed her gently on the cheek, and waited until she was in the house before trotting back down the porch steps.

She could hear the television coming from her parents' room, but it was too late to disturb them. Instead, she tiptoed to her own room and lay across her bed. "Oh, God," she said aloud. "Your Word says that You will give us the desires of our heart. Well, Lord, You know my greatest desire, after knowing You, is to sing. I want to do what You want me to do, Lord, though, if there is any way possible, please make this job with Lavelle come through."

In the silence of her bedroom, she let the words of her prayer sink in.

When she finally closed her eyes, her sleep was filled with

dreams of singing at sold-out concerts, draped in glamorous gowns, jewels dripping from her ears. Screaming fans mobbed her until her bodyguards finally whisked her away in a sleek black limousine.

CHAPTER 4

WILLETTA WAS SITTING ON THE PORCH STEPS when Deborah Anne pulled her Toyota into the driveway behind her father's Lincoln.

"Hey, girl, what are you doing out here?" Deborah Anne asked. "Daddy's home."

Willetta stood and dusted off her jeans. "I saw him, but he was just sitting in the den reading his Bible. I tell you, he should know that book by heart now. How many times has he read it cover to cover?"

Deborah Anne laughed. "Leave my daddy alone! He's prayed this family out of a whole lot of situations! God must be listening to him." She stopped in the den and kissed her father, and then she and Willetta went into her bedroom.

While Deborah Anne changed from her uniform into a Clark University sweatshirt and leggings, Willetta stretched out on the bed.

"You know why I'm here," Willetta said after they were

silent for a few minutes. She grinned. "How did your date go with Triage?"

"Girl, I told you before, it wasn't a date."

"I don't care what you call it. You went out with *Triage Blue,* and I want to know all the details!"

Deborah Anne grinned back. "There's nothing to tell. Triage and I are just friends. He said that I was just like a little sister to him." Deborah bounced onto the bed.

"Um-hmm." Willetta sounded doubtful.

"Really, all we talked about was my sending a tape to Lavelle."

Willetta's eyes widened with new excitement. "Did you send it in?"

Deborah Anne nodded. "Yesterday. Now all I have to do is wait. Triage said he was going to call Lavelle."

Willetta kicked her legs into the air. "My cousin is going to be a big-time famous singer."

"Don't get so excited," Deborah Anne warned. "There's a lot of pieces to this puzzle. First Lavelle and his people have to like my tape, and then there'll be an audition. I don't know what happens after that, but I know it won't be easy." Deborah Anne's words were for Willetta, but she spoke to her own heart as well. She'd barely been able to concentrate at work, as the dreams she'd had in her sleep carried over into her day.

"I don't care what you say, Deborah Anne. I'm going to keep praying about this for you." Willetta paused and stared at her cousin. "This is something that you want, right?"

"I can't tell you how much. But I'm trying to remain calm. I realize that there are a lot of women going for this."

"Yeah, but none of them are as good as my cousin!" Willetta laughed.

"Come on." Deborah Anne stood and walked to the door. "If you're going to sit here and grill me, you might as well help with dinner. Mama's going to be late, so it's just Daddy and me."

"I guess I have to hang out with my cousin while I have the chance." Willetta pouted. "Soon you'll be a big LA girl."

"Girl, you're crazy," Deborah Anne said as she threw a pillow at Willetta.

They went into the spacious kitchen, and Deborah Anne pulled out a large pan before she took the pork chops from the refrigerator. She handed Willetta a muffin tin.

"What do you want me to do with this?" Willetta grinned, tossing the tin onto the counter.

"You're not going to help?"

"Why should I? This is *your* dinner."

Deborah Anne put her hands on her hips. "Okay, but don't ask me anything about *my* backstage tickets to Triage's concert."

Willetta frowned. "What you talkin' 'bout?"

Deborah Anne turned her back to her cousin. "Well, Triage invited me, as his special guest, to his concert in Atlanta on Friday, and he said that I could bring a friend with me," she explained as she lifted the muffin tin from the counter. "But since I don't have any friends—"

Willetta snatched the tin from Deborah Anne. "Girl, move out my way! I have some muffins I've got to prepare."

As they laughed, Elijah came into the kitchen. "What's so funny in here?" Elijah asked as he pulled a soda from the refrigerator.

"Nothing, Daddy," Deborah Anne said, barely able to contain her giggles.

"We were just talking about Deborah Anne's job," Willetta added.

Elijah popped the soda can open, took a swig, then looked at the women through slitted eyes. "Um-hmm . . ."

Deborah Anne and Willetta broke into laughter.

"You girls are acting silly. Just let me know when dinner is ready."

"Deborah Anne, I hope you guys like muffins," Willetta said when Elijah's steps faded down the hallway, "because I'm about to make a whole bunch of them up in here!"

CHAPTER 5

THE APPLAUSE WAS DEAFENING. DEBORAH ANNE smiled from her backstage position behind the heavy scarlet velvet curtains. There had to be over twenty thousand people in the Civic Center audience cheering Triage as he danced across the stage.

"Deborah Anne, can you believe that we're really here?" Willetta whispered. "I hope you and Triage become close. I could really get used to this."

Deborah Anne only smiled, not trusting her voice. While Willetta clapped her hands and sang along with Triage, Deborah Anne only watched, holding her eyes to his every move. He strutted with a superstar's confidence, igniting the crowd's frenzy; the stage was his tabernacle. She weighed how he used his voice to draw excitement or to calm the crowd. It was fascinating.

His arms glistened with sweat. His sleeveless black muscle shirt and black jeans were damp from the heat of the lights and the fervor of his moves.

Finally, Deborah Anne broke her eyes away to glance at her watch. He'd been onstage for over an hour and would begin his finale soon.

Just as she thought that, she heard Triage say, "Now, ya'll know how I like to end my shows."

The applause sounded like thunder, the cheers like a lion's roar.

"I always pull someone onstage with me, and tonight, I have a special friend that I want to introduce y'all to."

Deborah Anne smiled, wondering who was going to be the person who would get a shot at fame, singing with Triage Blue.

"You guys are going to love her. This gal can sing," he said, as he strutted across the stage toward Willetta and Deborah Anne.

"Deborah Anne," Willetta whispered excitedly, "I think he's talking about you!"

Before she had a chance to respond, Triage came to where they were standing and took Deborah Anne's hand.

"No, Triage," Deborah Anne protested as she shook her head. "I can't do this."

"Do ya'll want to hear my friend, Deborah Anne?"

It was the applause that helped her to move forward, though her steps were still tentative.

"This is Deborah Anne Peterson. Remember her name, because this girl is going to be famous!"

Deborah Anne hoped she didn't look as silly as she felt. But the moment she heard Triage start a "Deborah Anne" chant, her fear dissipated.

"Deborah Anne, Deborah Anne, Deborah Anne . . ." Just like she'd imagined.

"What are we going to sing?" she whispered.

"Do you know 'Gotta Jam'?"

She nodded. "Yes, most of it."

"That's good enough, girl! Let's go," cried Triage as he motioned to the band and began clapping, encouraging the audience to join in.

Deborah Anne was glad Triage had chosen a song that was more melodious than most of his raps. She followed his lead, and after only a few moments they were harmonizing and gliding across the stage as if they'd been together forever.

The cheers heartened her, just like she imagined they would. She was born to sing.

At the end, the crowd yelled for both of them, as Triage led her backstage.

Triage kissed her cheek, telling her, "You did great. I'll be right back."

It wasn't until then that Deborah Anne breathed.

Willetta was still clapping. "Girl, you're a star! I think this is a sign that you're on your way!"

Still shaking with excitement, Deborah Anne hugged Willetta. "Oh my God. It was incredible."

Even the other women who were waiting backstage for Triage came over to congratulate Deborah Anne.

After Triage had taken his final bow, he ran off the stage and grabbed Deborah Anne. "I'd better watch out. You almost stole the show from me." He grinned.

"Triage, I can't believe you did that."

"Well, did you enjoy it?"

She nodded as if she were mute.

Triage's bodyguard tried to push him toward his dressing room as the backstage mob swarmed him.

"Wait a sec." He motioned to his guard.

"What are you guys going to do now?" he asked Deborah Anne.

"I don't know. We booked a room at the Ramada Inn around the corner so we wouldn't have to drive back so late."

Triage looked at his watch. "I was thinking about getting something to eat, but it's kind of late. What about getting together for breakfast in the morning?"

"That'll be great!"

He hugged Willetta, then Deborah Anne. "You were terrific. Lavelle is going to love you."

"Triage, thanks so much for tonight," Deborah Anne began, but before she could finish, his bodyguard had pulled him away.

Willetta and Deborah Anne left the auditorium through a back door and went to their car. By the time they made it to the hotel room, the adrenaline was fading and yawns were taking its place.

But even after they'd undressed, they stayed up talking until the beginning of a new day's light shone through the window. Only then did their eyes finally close.

CHAPTER 6

DEBORAH ANNE PUNCHED LAVELLE'S NAME INTO the computer and waited for his website to appear. She read through his biography and his group's history. She was engrossed in the tour information and so was startled by the voice behind her.

"I didn't even know you were here," Virginia said.

"Hi, Mama. I didn't hear you come in."

"I could tell." Virginia chuckled. "Whatever you're working on must be important." She kissed her daughter's cheek. "Where's your car?"

"Willetta borrowed it when we got back from Atlanta this afternoon. Uncle Moses took hers to the shop."

"So how was the concert?" Virginia asked as she smoothed her nurse's uniform and sat on the bed.

Deborah Anne stood up from the desk. "Mama, it was fantastic. I'd never been that close to the stage before, and . . ." She paused, grinning as she remembered the moment. "Triage pulled me onto the stage to sing with him."

39

Virginia smiled. "Really? I bet that was a thrill."

Deborah Anne sat next to her mother and took her hands. "Mama, it was just like I'd imagined. I was a little scared in the beginning, but only for a minute. Then I felt like I belonged there."

The front door slammed, and just seconds later, Elijah came into the room. "There're my girls! I'm glad you made it back safely." He smiled widely as Deborah Anne kissed him. "How was your little trip?"

"Eli, Deborah Anne was just telling me she sang onstage with Milton."

Elijah's smile seemed to narrow a bit. "Well, that must've been something."

"It was, Daddy." Deborah Anne noticed that her father's smile wasn't as bright as it had been, but at least it was still there. "I always knew that I wanted to do that, but I wasn't sure how I'd feel onstage."

"Baby, you're onstage just about every Sunday at church."

Deborah Anne scrunched her face, but then smiled when she noticed her father's stare. "Daddy, this was a real stage, with thousands of people watching me." Her eyes lit up with the excitement of the memory. "I know this is how I want to use what God gave me."

His smile totally disappeared. "Well, let me get out of this suit. I went with Pastor Duncan to the city meeting, and I'm ready to relax."

"Okay, honey," said Virginia. "I'll start dinner in a moment."

Deborah Anne waited until she heard her father close the bedroom door at the far end of the hallway. Then she whispered, "Mama, what's wrong with Daddy?"

Virginia shrugged. "Nothing."

"Come on, Mama. You saw the way Daddy changed when he found out I sang with Triage. And neither you nor Daddy has said anything about me sending in the tape. We have to talk about it sometime."

"All right." Virginia sighed. She ran her hand over her silver ponytail. "You know your father is very proud of you. He just thought that you were going to use that beautiful voice of yours to serve God."

"Oh, Mama. Daddy of all people should know that there are lots of ways to do that. I don't think Christians have to *always* be doing something 'Christian.' The way you and Daddy raised me, helped make me who I am, I'll be able to lift up God's name. I can make a big difference by singing with Lavelle or someone like him. I can bring more people to God that way."

"You sound so sure," Virginia said matter-of-factly.

Deborah nodded. "I am sure. It doesn't matter what I do; I'll always find a way to serve God. You won't have to worry about that, Mama. I promise, you and Daddy will be proud of me."

Virginia placed her palm against her daughter's cheek. "We're already proud of you, sweetheart. Your father just wants good things for you."

The shrill sound of the phone stopped Deborah Anne from responding.

"I'm going to get dinner ready." Virginia stood up.

Deborah Anne sighed as she picked up her phone. She hoped her parents realized that she was going to go through with this. If Lavelle Roberts ever called . . .

"Hello."

41

"May I speak with Deborah Peterson, please?"

She frowned, not recognizing the male voice. "This is Deborah speaking."

"Ms. Peterson, my name is Charles Wilson. I'm calling on behalf of Lavelle Roberts."

She dropped onto her bed. "Yes?" she said softly.

"We received your tape last week and would like you to come to Los Angeles for an audition."

Inside, she screamed, Oh my God! but with all the composure she could muster, she replied, "I'm surprised it's so soon."

"Well, we're speeding up the process. We're starting a U.S. tour in a couple of months and have to get ready. That's why we're hoping that you'll be able to come out by the end of next week. Do you want to check your calendar?"

For what? Deborah Anne thought. "Uh . . . no, next week will be fine."

Deborah Anne jotted down the information that Charles gave her, then she gave him her fax number at work just in case.

"We'll send your tickets and itinerary FedEx on Monday, so look for the package on Tuesday. I look forward to meeting you, Ms. Peterson."

"Please, call me Deborah A— . . . call me Deborah."

The moment they exchanged good-byes, Deborah Anne shrieked and ran into the kitchen.

"What is it, baby?" Virginia asked, as she tied an apron around her waist.

"Mama, you and Daddy cannot have any doubts, because everything's happening so quickly. All of my prayers are being answered."

"What are you talking about?"

Deborah Anne took a deep breath, trying to calm her shaking. "That phone call was from Lavelle Roberts. They want to fly me to Los Angeles for an audition."

Virginia put her hand on her chest, then smiled. "Well, baby, that's wonderful," she said, hugging her daughter and hoping her husband was ready for this news.

"They're making the arrangements and want me to fly out the end of next week."

"Will you be able to get the time off from work?"

Deborah Anne waved her hand in the air. "I have tons of time coming to me, but if I didn't have a day, it wouldn't matter. I'm going to LA. This is so exciting."

"What's the hoopla about now?" Elijah asked as he came into the kitchen.

"Daddy, I got the call! I'm going to Los Angeles for the audition."

Elijah looked at Deborah Anne for a long moment, then left the room.

"Oh, Mama."

"Now don't worry, baby. Your father will be just fine. Give him some time to digest this. You've got to admit it's so sudden."

Deborah Anne nodded.

"Let me finish dinner."

"You want some help?" Deborah Anne asked.

"No, you just enjoy this moment. You probably want to call Willetta or something."

Deborah Anne went back to her room and closed the door behind her. She jumped up and down, raising her hands in praise.

"Thank You, Father, thank You!" she said over and over again. It was all that she could say. Finally, she walked to the window and rested her head against the cool glass pane.

The late afternoon sun shone brilliantly on the backyard garden that Elijah worked on every weekend. There wasn't much color now, but as winter gradually gave way to spring, Deborah Anne could see the shifting of the seasons. The trees that had been bare just a few weeks ago were now stirring with new life. Colored shoots were pushing their way through the dirt—the signs of the roses, peonies, and coneflowers that Elijah had planted a few months ago. In just a few weeks, the yard would be alive with every hue of the rainbow.

Deborah Anne lay on her bed. Where would she be when the flowers finally bloomed? What would the Lord have in store for her?

She picked up her journal, wanting to record everything that she was feeling. Her hand moved quickly across the page.

> Careful, creative, loving hands
> You have, Lord—the greatest artist.
> You made such lovely things,
> Both Heaven and earth.
> I only have to look around
> To survey Your handiworks.
>
> Careful, creative, loving hands
> You have, Lord—the greatest artist.
> With Your great and wondrous hands
> You made man and woman.
> I only have to look around
> To see Your love revealed.

Careful, creative, loving hands
You have, Lord—the greatest artist.
There are no words that I can say
To Praise You, Lord of Love.
I only have to look around
To revel in Your Arms.

She pressed the pen against her lips as she thought, then smiled. "The Artist." That's what she'd call this.

Deborah Anne read the words once again, nodding in satisfaction. Closing her journal, she leaned back against the headboard. There was so much to think about, but one thing she was sure of—this was right. First, she'd met Triage in church, on the day Pastor Duncan was preaching about gifts and talents. Next, she'd sent the tape, and a few days later she found herself living her dream onstage with Triage. Now Lavelle's people had called her in less than a week. This couldn't be anything else but God. Of that she was sure. Now it was time to convince her parents.

CHAPTER 7

DEBORAH ANNE WAS WORKING HARD TO FINISH her paperwork. Even though she'd be in Los Angeles for only a day, she needed to take three days off from work. And with such short notice, she wanted all of her files to be in order.

Her phone rang, and Deborah Anne picked it up without looking away from the files in front of her. "Peterson," she answered in her work voice.

"Hey, Deborah Anne. I heard that you're coming my way."

"Triage!" she exclaimed, then lowered her voice so she wouldn't be heard over her cubicle wall. She knew he was in Los Angeles, having left the day after his Atlanta concert. "How did you find out?"

"I told you I was going to keep checking on you. I found out this morning."

"They called me on Saturday, and I'm leaving tomorrow morning. The audition is on Thursday."

"I know all the details." He laughed. "I had to make sure they were treating my girl right. So are you excited?"

She leaned back in her chair. "You have no idea. I haven't slept in days. Even Mama is excited, though Daddy is still moping a bit."

"He'll get over it once you start making the big bucks."

Deborah Anne sighed. "It's not about money for him. He just wants to make sure that I'm doing the right thing."

"I can understand that, but you're sure about this, right?"

"Oh, definitely," she said.

"Good, because I'm sure too. When I heard you sing in church, Deborah Anne, I was blown away. You left a big impression on me, and I know it'll be the same with Lavelle."

"I hope so. Do you think we'll get a chance to see you while we're out there?"

"Yeah, I'll pick you up at the airport. Who's coming with you?"

"My cousin Bubba. Mama wanted to come, but Bubba begged. I think if it were a longer trip, Mama would have, but when Bubba promised to be in church every Sunday, my parents decided to let him take the trip."

They laughed.

Deborah Anne gave Triage her flight information, then leaned back in her chair after she hung up the phone. In less than twenty-four hours, no matter what happened with this audition, her life would never be the same. She'd be leaving Georgia for the very first time, taking her first airplane trip, and, finally, meeting one of the biggest entertainers in the world. She forced these thoughts to the back of her mind, though, and returned to the files on her desk. There would be more than enough time to think once she was done.

Deborah Anne pressed against the back of the airline seat and gripped the armrests. She closed her eyes and muttered a prayer. She was still holding her breath when she felt the plane level off, and only then did she open her eyes.

"Are you all right, Deborah Anne?" Bubba asked.

She nodded. "It doesn't even feel like we're moving."

Bubba laughed, and his full cheeks jiggled. He handed her a magazine, but she shook her head, instead pulling the opened FedEx envelope from her briefcase. Lavelle's people had sent sheet music along with her tickets, and she'd been studying it for two days.

"Girl, you don't need to look at that stuff no more. Aunt Virginia told my mama you were at the piano all night." Bubba laughed.

"That's not true, but I just want to be prepared."

"Whatever." He turned back to the *Sports Illustrated* swimsuit edition.

Deborah Anne continued reading over the music until lunch was served. Minutes later, the main cabin became dark, and Deborah Anne put on the headphones for the movie, glad to have the distraction of Taye Diggs and the rest of the ensemble in *The Best Man*. By the time the plane began its descent, Deborah Anne felt like a flying pro.

They were sitting in the fourth row of the main cabin, so they got off the plane quickly. The moment they walked through the gate, they saw a tall, slender Black man, dressed in a black suit, white shirt, and black bow tie, holding a sign: "Deborah Anne Peterson."

"I'm Deborah A—. . . Deborah Peterson."

The man smiled and took her carry-on bag, laying it on a cart.

"I'm Bubba," her cousin said. "What's your name?"

"Anthony," the man replied, as he took Bubba's bag. "There's a car waiting for you outside."

Bubba and Deborah Anne looked at each other in amazement, and then followed Anthony down the long Delta terminal.

"I thought you said Triage was going to meet us," Bubba whispered, disappointment clearly in his voice.

"He probably had something to do. Don't worry, he has the hotel's number. He'll probably call us there. You'll get your chance to meet him."

Outside, the LA sun made Deborah Anne take off the new denim jacket that matched her jeans, and both she and Bubba put on their sunglasses.

"Welcome to Cali!" Bubba laughed with excitement.

They stood behind Anthony as he signaled to a sleek black car just a few feet away. Slowly, the car moved toward them.

"Hey, I like how they do it here," Bubba said. "Two chauffeurs."

When the limousine stopped, the window slowly lowered. Deborah Anne peeked inside. "Triage!"

He smiled, but put a finger over his lips. "Sshh, girl. I don't want anyone to know I'm here." He jumped from the front seat and rushed to open the door for them as Anthony put their bags into the trunk.

"I'm so glad to see you." Deborah smiled and scooted next to him in the backseat.

"What's wrong? Getting the jitters?" He put his arm around her shoulders.

Deborah Anne nodded. "I was confident, but now—"

"Ah, girl, you don't have anything to worry about."

"That's what I keep telling her." Bubba grinned. "My cousin can sing something fierce."

"Remember to tell me that on our way home, okay?" Deborah Anne laughed. "By the way, this is my cousin Bubba." Deborah Anne motioned to her cousin, and the two men shook hands. Anthony got into the front seat and slowly moved the car away from the curb. Traffic was Wednesday-afternoon light, so Anthony was able to pick up speed as they exited onto Century Boulevard.

"You guys aren't going to be here for too long, so I thought I'd take you to see some sights this afternoon. Are you up for it?" Both Deborah Anne and Bubba nodded as the limousine sped down LaCienega Boulevard.

Los Angeles, like Atlanta, was a blur of concrete to Deborah Anne. Somehow, she'd expected this city to be a little different. While they moved along, Triage pointed out everything from Magic Johnson's Starbucks to the Hollywood sign that Triage told them was a treat to see. "There's usually so much smog, we only get to see that sign five times a year." He laughed.

They pulled into the Beverly Hotel on Wilshire Boulevard, and Anthony waited while they checked in. Once they had the keys to the suite, they left their bags with the concierge and returned to the car, anxious to continue the tour.

As they moved slowly down Melrose, Deborah Anne and Bubba pointed to shops with window mannequins covered in clothes she'd never imagine anyone wearing. Bubba laughed at the groups of teenagers with pink, blue, and green spiked hair and various forms of body piercing.

"There's Spike Lee's store," Triage pointed out.

"Oh, man. Can we stop?" Bubba asked.

Triage nodded. "No problem, but I'm not getting out. I want to take it easy today."

Bubba asked Deborah Anne, "Are you coming?"

She shook her head. When Bubba ran into the store, Deborah Anne said, "I guess it's like this for you all the time. You can't go anywhere."

"Not without a bodyguard or a heavy disguise, though I have my secret place. But since I chose this life, I live with it."

Deborah Anne was thoughtfully quiet.

"Girl, don't let that bother you. There are more good parts to this business than bad."

"Believe me, I don't think it would bother me."

Bubba jumped back into the limo with a small plastic bag in his hand. "Man, I could get used to this."

Triage laughed. "You guys have got to be hungry by now. And you really should go to bed early, Deborah Anne," he said as he squeezed her hand. "You want to be in top shape for tomorrow."

"I'm always down for eating," Bubba said. "Where are we gonna go?" he asked.

"Why don't we eat in the hotel restaurant?" Triage suggested. "They have great food."

Within thirty minutes, they were sitting in the opulent Beverly Hotel restaurant. Deborah Anne instantly knew why Triage had recommended this place. From the moment they'd walked through the front door until they were seated at the crystal- and silver-covered table, she had counted at least five celebrities. Angela Bassett was sitting at the table across from them, and she waved at Triage. Even though the restaurant was filled, no one seemed to notice the stars. Everyone behaved as if they saw these people all the time—which they probably did.

Deborah Anne's eyes opened wide when she opened the menu. "Triage, this might be a bit outside our budget."

"You don't have to worry about that, Deborah Anne. All of your expenses are being taken care of."

"I know, but I don't want them to think that I just came here to spend all their money."

"You mean *they're* paying for everything?" Bubba asked, placing the bag from Spike Lee's store next to him.

Deborah Anne rolled her eyes, and Triage laughed.

"Man, I wish I could sing." Bubba shook his head.

A woman dressed in a sleek black knit dress came to their table. She smiled, then asked, "Are you ready to order?"

Deborah Anne raised her eyebrows. The woman wasn't dressed like a waitress, and she didn't have a pad. How is she going to remember it all? Deborah Anne wondered.

All three took Triage's recommendation and ordered the jumbo peppered shrimp, though Bubba added clam bisque and stuffed mushrooms to his order. They chatted about Villa Rica, their parents, and Mother Dobson as they enjoyed their delicious meal. As the conversation turned to the Lakers and the Laker Girls, Deborah Anne became quiet.

Triage reached across the table and squeezed Deborah Anne's hand, but kept talking to Bubba, who hadn't seemed to notice her sudden contemplative silence.

Through dessert, Bubba bombarded Triage with questions about his career, his music, and women.

"Man, I bet women are throwing themselves at you all the time!" Bubba said, his eyes glassy with envy.

"That gets old quick. I'm getting to the point where I'm thinking about my future—settling down and starting a family."

Bubba shook his head. "If I were in your shoes, I wouldn't get married at all. What would be the point?"

"Maybe Triage is more mature than you are, Bubba," Deborah Anne snapped. "Maybe he knows that the way God set this plan, men and women are supposed to be together."

Bubba waved Deborah Anne's words away. "Whatever. I'm just saying that with all the babes in LA, this is heaven enough for me."

Deborah Anne wanted to tell Bubba that no "babe" would want his country behind, but instead she wiped her mouth and placed her napkin on the table.

"I think you guys should be going up to your rooms now," Triage said.

"Why?" Bubba looked at his watch. "It's too early."

"It might be, but Deborah Anne's audition is pretty early. She should be well rested, especially with the jet lag and everything."

Bubba's eyes darted between Deborah Anne and Triage, and Deborah Anne could tell that her cousin was waiting for an invitation from Triage for just the two of them to hang out together. Deborah Anne nodded, agreeing with Triage. Bubba sulked as they all walked from the restaurant to the elevator.

As they waited, Triage hugged Deborah Anne and told her,

"You're going to do great tomorrow. I'll be here around seven-thirty. We can go over to The Nosh, and have breakfast before we go to the studio."

"I don't think I'm going to be hungry." Deborah Anne wrung her hands.

"*I* will be." Bubba laughed, the cheer returning to his voice. "So we'll be ready."

Triage shook Bubba's hand, then waited until the two got into the elevator.

Deborah Anne and Bubba were silent as the elevator rose to the seventeenth floor. They both gasped with pleasure when they opened the door to Deborah Anne's suite, which looked more like an expensive studio apartment than a hotel room. The hotel had already placed Deborah's bags on the luggage rack, and a bowl of fruit waited for her on a side table next to a luxurious-looking chaise lounge.

When Bubba finally closed his mouth, he said, "This is nice, but I still have to check everything out."

Deborah Anne frowned as Bubba got on his knees and peeked under the bed.

"What are you doing?"

Bubba didn't say a word as he walked into the bathroom, checked the shower, then returned to the bedroom. Finally, he said, "I read that you should do this in every hotel. You never know who might be lurking, and Uncle Eli would never forgive me if anything happened to you." He slid open the wide closet doors, checking both sides of the closet's interior. "Everything is clear."

"Well, thank you for protecting me." Deborah Anne grinned.

"No problem." He stuffed his hands in his jeans pockets

and shifted his feet. "Deborah Anne, you sure you want to go to bed *this* early?" he asked, hoping that Deborah Anne would agree to call Triage back. Bubba had been more than eager to accompany Deborah Anne on this trip because he'd had visions of LA nightclubs, shaking hands with celebrities, and hanging out with Triage.

"Bubba, if you want to go out, go on. I'm going to take Triage's advice and get some rest. I'm here for business, remember?"

After a few seconds, he said, "All right. Well, I guess I'll just watch some TV. Call me if you need me."

She kissed him on the cheek, then closed the door behind him.

As soon as she turned the lock, she wanted to call Bubba back. She thought she'd be happy to finally be alone, but now she realized too much thinking time loomed in front of her—time that she knew she'd spend speculating about tomorrow.

Deborah Anne went to the balcony window. She'd never been this high in a building before; this was the kind of place she'd seen only in magazines. It was dark now, but Deborah Anne could tell that the city had renewed life. Cars moved through the street beneath her window like it was the middle of the day. Lights glowed as brightly as a Christmas tree.

She looked at the king-size bed, but it really was too early to use it. She picked up her Bible and sank into the chaise in front of the window. She'd been studying Psalms, and turned to the 119th. The words were familiar to her, but tonight the 105th verse stood out in her mind: "Thy word is a lamp unto my feet, and a light unto my path."

With the Bible still lying open on her lap, she closed her

eyes. That was what she wanted to do—have God guide her through every part of her life.

"Please, Lord," she whispered. "I know this is of You. The way this has come together, I see Your hands all over this. Now please help me to do what I have to do. Light my path, Lord, so that I perform tomorrow in a way that glorifies You and this gift you've given me. I pray, Father, that I do well. This has been my dream, the desire of my heart, and I pray for You to guide my steps. . . ."

Deborah Anne reached up and turned off the floor lamp next to her, instantly turning the room into a quiet dark haven. She sat that way for hours, meditating, thinking, and spending time with the Lord.

CHAPTER 8

TRIAGE EXTENDED HIS HAND, HELPING DEBORAH
Anne from the car that had been sent to the hotel
by Lavelle. She tried to take steady steps, even
though every part of her was shaking. She knew
Triage could feel her sweaty palm, and she was grateful he
didn't mention it. She'd heard enough "It's going to be okay"s
and "You're going to be all right"s to last for the rest of her
life. From her parents to Willetta, and even Bubba, who was
waiting back at the hotel, everyone was sending her their
prayers. She was grateful for their concern, but this morning
she didn't want to talk much and hoped that everyone understood her silence.

She smiled stiffly when Triage held the studio door open.
He squeezed her hand. He signed them in at the security
desk, then led Deborah Anne down a long narrow hallway
to a door at the far end.

When Triage opened the door, Deborah Anne stepped into
a very large room with maple paneling and hardwood floors.

A stage lined with microphones was set up in the far corner of the studio.

The room was filled with people, but her eyes immediately focused on Lavelle, who was the first to come toward them. "Hey, Triage. What're you doing here?" he said.

"I told Charles I was coming down with Deborah Anne," Triage replied as they shook hands. "Lavelle, I want you to meet one of the best singers I've heard in a long time."

Lavelle's wide smile made Deborah Anne's shoulders relax. "That's quite a recommendation, young lady." He took her hand. "It's very nice to meet you."

She quickly took inventory of the man who held her future. He wasn't wearing one of his trademark sequined jackets. Instead, he wore jeans, a white shirt, and a navy blazer that hugged his large frame. His light brown eyes smiled under his thick eyebrows, and it took only a moment for Deborah to decide that she liked him. "It's nice to meet you, Lavelle." She wanted to tell him that she loved his music and videos, but she feared she'd sound like a gushing fan.

"Hi, I'm Vianca Lake." A petite woman came from behind Lavelle and extended her hand. "I'm one of the singers." She was dressed in a pair of black stretch pants and a matching midriff top. Very chic, very LA, and very much the thing that made Deborah Anne cringe and wish that she'd worn something else instead of her mid-calf-length navy wool suit.

"I'm Deborah A—Deborah Peterson."

"Come on, let me introduce you to the rest of the gang."

As she and Triage followed Lavelle, Triage whispered, "So you're Deborah now?"

She rolled her eyes at the smirk on his face. "I've always

preferred Deborah. My family just insisted on calling me Deborah Anne," she hissed.

"I see." He chuckled.

The next minutes were filled with introductions of far too many people for Deborah to remember their names.

"Where's Emerald?" Lavelle asked, looking annoyed as he scanned the room.

"Here I am. What do you want?"

Deborah turned to the voice and watched as a tall woman strolled toward them. She was model-thin, dressed in a black unitard and a sheer leopard-print jacket. It wasn't until she was right in front of them that Deborah realized her hair was a mass of micro-braids, pulled back into a long ponytail.

The woman shook Deborah's hand firmly. "I'm Emerald Taylor," she said, rolling her eyes at Lavelle. "I don't know what the fuss was about."

"I want everyone here for support." Deborah noticed Lavelle's sharp tone, but he smiled when he turned toward her. "Are you ready?"

Deborah looked at Triage, and he gave her a slight nod.

"Just go over there and tell Tyrone which song you're going to sing," instructed Lavelle as he pointed toward the stage.

The heels of her low pumps clicked against the floor as she took the twenty-foot walk. It was the silence behind her that made Deborah begin to tremble. How was she supposed to sing in front of all these people?

Tyrone smiled, and his shoulder-length brown locks swayed gently as he nodded reassuringly. "Which song?"

"'Born for You,'" she whispered.

His smile widened. "You want me to play it just like the sheet?"

She nodded, not really understanding his question. How else would he play it? I guess I have a lot to learn, she thought.

She stood behind the microphone.

"Just nod when you're ready," Tyrone whispered.

Deborah looked at the eyes focused on her, and she froze. There was no way she'd be able to perform in front of Lavelle Roberts and his entourage.

But this was the moment of her dream, so she had to do it. She closed her eyes and imagined that she was at Mountain Baptist Church, preparing to give praise to God. Deborah Anne could see the church's beautiful stained-glass windows as well as the smiling faces of its parishioners. These were the people who knew she could sing, and would never be disappointed with anything she did.

She opened her eyes and cleared her throat, nodding to Tyrone. She began. The words came easily, the rhythm was smooth, and she swayed to the beat, feeling each note, stroking each word. She lifted her arms and moved her hands, conducting the orchestra within her.

Her eyes were closed as she sang the last note and held it as long as her lungs allowed. It wasn't until she heard the clapping that her eyes snapped open.

Her vision was blurred, and she blinked several times to bring the group into focus. Triage led the applause, whistling to show his appreciation. When Lavelle stood and walked toward her, his smile was even wider than before.

"Deborah, that was just great! I don't know if I should love you or hate you. I don't want nobody who can sing the song better than me." His smile belied his words. The others echoed his approval, and Deborah breathed a sigh of relief.

Triage hugged her, then turned to Lavelle. "I told you, man. Isn't she something?"

Lavelle nodded. "Your tape does nothing for you. Listen, give me a moment. I'll be right back."

"Okay." Deborah blinked.

When Lavelle and five others left the room, Deborah asked Triage, "What's going on?"

"They went to the office to talk over a few things. He'll be right back."

She breathed deeply.

"Girl, you tore it up! I'm proud of you."

Deborah smiled. "I was scared at first, but then it just came naturally." She paused as she wrung her hands. "How long do you think it'll take him to let me know if he liked me? A week?"

Triage raised his eyebrows, but before he could utter a word, Lavelle walked back into the room.

"Deborah, we want to try a song with you, to see how you sound with us."

Her heart was thumping when she nodded.

She followed Lavelle's instructions like a zombie, taking her place on Vianca's left side, while Emerald was on Vianca's right. When the music began, she sang her part, grateful that Lavelle's steps were simple to follow, unlike many of the hip-hop steps she'd seen so many new artists perform. Thank God for rhythm and blues, was the last thought she had before the routine ended.

There was a moment of silence before Lavelle turned toward her. "Deborah, it's going to be a pleasure having you as part of the family."

For the second time in twenty-five minutes, she stood frozen on the stage.

Triage rushed to her side. "Congratulations, Deborah. I knew you could do this."

"I-I . . . don't understand," she stammered.

The confusion was clear on her face. "Girl, you did it; you got the job."

"Just like that? They don't have to call me back?"

"Girl, you've been in Corporate America for too long. It's not easy to find someone who will fit in with a group, and when you meet that person, you have to gobble them up before someone else does. Trust me, I know."

"Congratulations, and welcome to the group," Vianca drawled. "It'll be good to have a homegirl by my side."

"Are you from Georgia too?"

"No, girl. I'm from the real South—Birmingham."

"There'll be time enough for chitchat. Right now, Deborah, I need to go over some things with you and Charles."

She looked at Triage, and he motioned her forward, saying, "Go on, I'll wait for you out here."

Deborah tried to focus as Charles filled her in on the details. She would have to move to Los Angeles within the next few weeks; the fifty-one-city tour would begin in June; it would be divided into two parts because they would record an album in between. . . .

"Wait a minute," Charles said suddenly. "Deborah, no one has asked you if you are interested in all of this."

She raised her eyebrows. "You're kidding, right? Who wouldn't be? Yes!"

Lavelle and Charles laughed. "Well then, here's the offer. It'll take us a day or two to draw up the contract, but you'll start at eighty thousand dollars a year, which I know is low, but it's based on experience. . . ."

Deborah almost fell from her chair. If Charles thought that was low, what kind of money were the other singers making? She could show them some scanty salaries—just one look at her current pay stub, and he'd never use the word "low" again.

". . . and that's just about it. Any questions?"

Deborah just shook her head. "Everything sounds fine to me. What do we do now?"

Charles said, "There's nothing else right now, but you can call me anytime if you have any questions. You still have my number, right?"

She nodded, and extended her hand toward Lavelle. "Thank you so much for this opportunity."

He playfully pushed her hand away. "Girl, we're family now." He pulled her close, crushing her against his chest and rubbed his hand along her back. Deborah frowned and abruptly pulled away from him, but Lavelle just gave her a bemused smile.

"So we'll see you in a few weeks?" Lavelle licked his lips.

She nodded and quickly grabbed her purse. Charles led her back to the studio, while Lavelle stayed in the office.

Triage and Tyrone were the only ones left in the studio. "So is everything set?" Tyrone asked.

She nodded.

"We'll get that contract out to you in a few days," Charles said. "Welcome aboard."

Triage hugged her again. "I'm really happy for you, *Deborah*," he kidded. "You're going to love Lavelle. It's like a family here. He's not one to put distance between himself and the people he works with. He's approachable, one of those hands-on stars."

Deborah opened her mouth, then closed it. Maybe that's all it was with Lavelle—just an approachable, hands-on guy.

"Let's get out of here." Triage took Deborah's hand. "We'll pick up Bubba and your luggage, then have lunch before I take you to the airport."

As they walked past the office, Deborah and Triage could hear Lavelle and Charles talking behind the closed door.

"Do you want to say good-bye to Lavelle?"

"No," she said quickly. "We already did that. I just want to go out and celebrate!"

She pulled her lips into a smile, and pushed the scene with Lavelle from her mind. She'd just have to get used to it— things were done differently here. She was in show business now, and she needed to fall into line—as Steven, her supervisor, would say.

The car was waiting for them when they stepped outside. Deborah put on her sunglasses and yelled, "I got the job!"

Triage laughed. "Girl, you're just now getting it?"

She nodded. "I get it." She held her hands toward the sky. "Thank You, Lord."

Triage was still laughing as he helped her into the car.

CHAPTER 9

D EBORAH ANNE, WHY DON'T YOU SIT ON THIS trunk, and I'll snap it closed."

The bedroom was a field of chaos. Brown U-haul boxes of various sizes were stacked around them, and opened suitcases lay across her double bed.

Deborah Anne glanced at her mother. The way Virginia's eyes narrowed in concentration told her that her mother was serious. So she sat on the trunk, bouncing until it closed.

"I can't believe I have so much stuff."

"Baby, you're twenty-six years old and have lived in the same house your entire life. You're bound to have a lot of stuff." With her last words, Virginia flipped the last clasp. "That should do it."

The doorbell rang, and they both moaned.

"I thought I'd be finished with this by the time everyone got here."

Virginia looked at the clock, the only thing left on the dresser. "We still have some time. It's probably Willetta. I'll get the door, then finish up with the food. Make sure you put extra tape on those boxes," Virginia instructed.

Just a few minutes after Virginia walked out, Willetta came sulkily into the room. "I was hoping this was a dream, and that when I woke up, you wouldn't be going away."

Deborah Anne smiled. "I thought you wanted me to become rich and famous."

"I did. But I want you to do it right here in Villa Rica. What am I going to do without my best friend?"

They hugged.

"I wish you'd consider coming with me. We could get an apartment together, and you could be a manager at Lane Bryant out there. Or at any store, for that matter. Anyone would be blessed to have you."

"Girl, I can't just pick up and change my whole life." Willetta straddled the desk chair. "Plus, this is my home, and I don't want to leave Steven. He's still talking about getting married."

"He's been talking about that since forever." Deborah Anne threw a pillow at her cousin. When Willetta tossed it back, they laughed again.

Between two boxes stacked against the bed, Deborah Anne slid down into the small place and crossed her legs.

"I guess we knew this day would be coming soon, huh? A man has finally come between us."

Willetta scrunched her face. "Well, it ain't my man. It's yours—Lavelle Roberts."

Deborah Anne laughed. "Well, you can come visit me anytime." Her face became long with sorrow. "I'm really going to miss you, Willetta. Who am I going to spend all my time with? Who am I going to call late at night when I have a secret to tell or a problem to solve?"

"Girl, you don't need me anymore. You've got Triage Blue now." Willetta giggled. "Your new man."

Deborah Anne rolled her eyes. "First you call Lavelle my man, and now Triage. I keep telling you, Triage doesn't see me that way. Being with him is like being with your brother. But I'm glad that he'll be at least one person I'll know in LA. Vianca, one of the other singers in Lavelle's group, told me to call her as soon as I got there."

"And then there's all the other stars you'll meet. You'll forget about little ol' us, down here in Georgia." Willetta poked out her lip.

Deborah Anne's smile was rueful. "There's little chance of that."

The doorbell rang, and Deborah Anne blinked back the tears stinging her eyes. These weren't the first. She had cried every day for the last two weeks, hoping that she was doing the right thing. In her heart she knew she was, because not many people had such a clear path to their dreams. But it was still hard to leave all that she knew and loved behind, and so quickly too.

"You'd better get out there, Miss Guest-of-Honor." Willetta wiped a single tear from her eye.

"You go on and tell everyone I'll be out in a few minutes, Willetta. I feel a little sweaty and want to change my clothes."

"Okay, sweetie."

When they hugged, they held each other silently, fighting their emotions. Willetta didn't look back as she left the room, closing the door behind her. Deborah Anne looked around her bedroom. Its decor had changed over the years—from the pink canopy bed she had when she was a ribbons-and-bows-loving seven-year-old to the tie-dyed covered daybed she'd had as a teenager because she wanted her room to look like a college dormitory.

Now it looked like the bedroom of any twenty-six-year-old in Villa Rica living with her parents. She had bought the whitewashed furniture last year, when she and Willetta decided not to get their own apartment.

Deborah Anne chuckled—she couldn't count the number of times she'd thought about leaving home. But the discussions had never been more than mere chatter, never serious. She didn't have to leave home. She loved her parents, and though she knew it was difficult for them sometimes, they respected her privacy and treated her like an adult. Being close to them also gave Deborah Anne the opportunity to care for them. There were daily reminders that they were aging, and she wanted to be close, to provide anything they needed. It was probably the result of being an only child. There was never a good enough reason to leave—until now.

The sheer flowered curtains softly waved toward her, carried by the afternoon breeze. Deborah Anne sighed. In less than twenty-four hours, she and her mother would be on a plane heading toward her new home, following her dream.

"That's what I have to remember," she whispered. "The dream."

She took a deep breath, wiped her face, and went out to face her guests.

It seemed like almost everyone in Villa Rica was stuffed inside her parents' house. The faces she saw every Sunday at Mountain Baptist Church were mixed with those of other family and friends.

Deborah Anne passed from uncle to aunt, from cousin to co-worker, smiling as questions were thrown to her from every corner.

"So what is Lavelle Roberts really like?"

"Are you really going to be living in Hollywood? Aren't you scared?"

"How much money are you going to be making?"

When her mother and aunts finally began to lay out the food, Deborah Anne tried to find refuge in the kitchen. But Virginia coaxed her back to the party.

"No, baby, go back out there with your guests. This is your day."

"Yeah, Deborah Anne," Aunt Bird added. "Everyone is here to see you. Our little superstar."

Minutes later, Virginia yelled to the crowd, "Let's gather around so that we can bless this food."

There were too many people to fit into the dining room, and the group spilled into the hallway and living room.

Deborah Anne found her father standing next to her mother, and she edged between them, taking their hands.

"Everyone expects me to do this," Elijah began. "But Pastor Duncan is with us, and I'd like to ask him to bless the food."

Pastor Duncan stepped forward. Even though it was Saturday and everyone else was dressed in jeans and other casual clothes, Pastor Duncan wore his Sunday-sermon black suit with his minister's collar. "Before I pray, I'd like to say a few words." He cleared his throat. "Sister Deborah Anne, the time is drawing nigh . . ."

She inhaled a deep breath, willing herself to remain staid. There was no way she wanted to break down now.

"But we all know that you'll do just fine, Sister. Because not only do you have a beautiful gift, but also you know your blessings are from the Lord. He is your light, your stronghold to grasp in the middle of the night. . . ."

Deborah Anne took a quick glance around the room, then bowed her head, hoping to conceal the grin spreading on her face. The shuffling feet and rolling eyes told her everyone had the same question—was Pastor going to start preaching a sermon up in here?

"We are so proud of you, Sister Deborah Anne. We're going to miss that glorious voice that the Lord has blessed us with every Sunday, but now He's spreading that gift for the world to hear. Let's bow our heads."

Deborah Anne wondered if Pastor Duncan heard the sighs of relief and giggles that moved through the group. But seeing the way his eyelids were pressed together so tightly, she doubted it.

"Heavenly Father, we thank You for this day that You have made. We thank You, that You have chosen us to do Your work, to fulfill Your plan. As we gather here today to celebrate the life and future of Sister Deborah Anne, we pray for Your blessings. We pray that You keep her in Your arms and provide the protection and shelter she is going to need so far away from home. . . ."

Why did he have to say that? Deborah Anne thought. Everyone kept reminding her how far away she was going to be, when she needed to believe that everyone was as close as a phone or airplane away.

Virginia squeezed her hand, and Deborah Anne peeked at her mother. Virginia's head was still bowed, but Deborah Anne could see the ends of her mother's lips curled into a smile, and she smiled too. It was like her mother could read her mind. And she could hear every word her mother was sending to her now. "You're going to be okay . . . this will always be your home."

"Amen!" Pastor Duncan finally boomed.

People cheered, and children rushed toward the paper plates stacked on the table.

"Now you kids just wait a minute," Virginia scolded. "Let Pastor get his food, and then the adults."

Moans floated throughout the room.

"Just stop that. You know when you come to this house, there's always more than enough food."

Deborah Anne saw the line of hungry guests forming at the buffet as her chance to take a moment alone. Tiptoeing past the group, she went out onto the porch, closed her eyes, and sighed.

"Too much goings-on in there for you, huh?"

She opened her eyes. "Oh, Mother Dobson, I didn't see you. Don't you want to eat? I can fix you a plate." Before Deborah Anne had finished her sentence, she had already started back inside.

"Not right now. I want you to come over here and sit next to me." Mother patted the space next to her on the wooden bench.

A few moments of silence passed in the breeze, then Mother said, "You're scared, aren't you, child?"

Deborah Anne waited a second before she nodded. "I don't know why. Mother, I've dreamed of this my entire life, and now that my big chance is here, I almost want to run the other way."

Mother covered Deborah Anne's hand with her own wrinkled one. "That's natural. I remember when I left home to marry Martin. I was only fifteen. Chile, 'scared' doesn't even begin to describe how I felt. But I knew two things. One was that God was always with me. And the second was that my parents had raised me right, and prepared me for anything that would come my way."

She let her words settle in before she continued. "You're ready for this, Deborah Anne. Just remember to keep the Lord first."

"Oh, I will, Mother."

"I've already made sure that my grandson is there to protect you. He has special orders from me."

Deborah Anne laughed.

"You know, if that grandson of mine is as smart as I think he is, you might just come back home with a ring on your finger."

"Mother, Triage—I mean, Milton—and I are just friends. Besides, I'm not going to have too much time to think about anything else but singing."

"There's a lot more to life than just a career, my dear. After God, there's family. And you're getting to the age that you should be concerned—"

"Mother!"

Mother Dobson rolled her eyes. "You young folks don't want to listen to me. But"—Mother squeezed Deborah's hand—"I only want the best for you. You're like family to me."

Deborah Anne smiled as she ran her hands over the old woman's silver hair, and she looked at her beautiful face that was creased with the signs of her wisdom. She leaned forward and kissed Mother softly on the cheek.

"Thank you so much."

Mother nodded, then her smile disappeared. "Now stop sitting out here with this old woman," she said sternly. "There are people waiting in there to help you celebrate."

Deborah Anne smiled and went back to the party.

Friends and relatives had returned to their homes hours ago. Each one had passed wishes and wisdom to Deborah Anne, and their kind words still played in her mind as she heard the grandfather clock in the living room chime three times. She climbed out of bed, put on her robe, and stepped around the obstacle course of suitcases and boxes.

She settled herself on the living room couch, crossed her legs beneath her, and gazed through the window. Only the moon's light illuminated the street outside. Peterson Road. Her father and his three brothers had amassed acres over the years, and now they all lived together on the land.

To Deborah Anne it was more than just a home—it was her security blanket, layered like a cozy old quilt, with her parents, aunts, uncles, cousins, and the extended family that she had come to love through the years.

The creaking of the floor behind her made Deborah Anne

turn her head. "Oh, Daddy, I'm sorry if I woke you." In the darkness, she could only see Elijah's silhouette. He was a massive man—over six foot three, and close to three hundred pounds. But he was solid muscle, still in great shape from years of working the fields with his father and brothers. Even now, he still worked as a supervisor in Villa Rica's recycling center.

He stepped toward her and smiled. "You didn't wake me, baby." He sat in the recliner facing her. "I just had a feeling that you'd be out here."

"Just like when I was little, and you'd find me at the piano at four in the morning."

Elijah chuckled, but then his cheer disappeared. "But in those days, I'd just put you back in bed, without a thought, knowing that you were going to be there the next morning."

Deborah Anne let the peaceful silence comfort them.

Finally, Elijah stood. "I have something for you, Deborah Anne."

She watched her father reach for his Bible on top of the piano, then amble toward her. He handed her a white envelope.

She pulled out a money order for two thousand dollars. "Daddy . . ." Teary-eyed, she hugged him. "You didn't have to do this. I have money saved, and I'm going to be making a good living now."

She held the envelope toward him, but he gently pushed her hand away. "I don't ever want you stranded in Los Angeles, wanting for nothing. Just put this in the bank for emergencies. Use it if you have to get home quickly. . . ." His words faded.

This time, when she hugged him, she let her tears fall. "Daddy, I love you so much."

"I love you too, baby." His voice was thick with emotion. "Deborah Anne, I'm so proud of you. I'll be praying every day for God's favor to cover every part of you." He pulled back and looked in her face, lit only by the glow from the moon. With his broad thumbs, he wiped away her tears. "I want you to know your mother and I will always be here. This is your home, and you can come back any time you want or need to."

She nodded, aware that this was more than her father's turn at passing wisdom. Elijah hated public displays of affection. Deborah Anne knew this was his good-bye, even though he would take her and Mama to the airport in the morning. This would be their final private moments together.

He hugged her again, and this time, when he pulled away, he said, "Come on, Deborah Anne, let me put you back to bed."

CHAPTER 10

DEBORAH ANNE LIFTED HER MOTHER'S HEAVY suitcase into the room, then locked the hotel door. "Mama, you have more clothes than I do," Deborah Anne teased, dropping the suitcase on one of the full-sized beds.

Virginia waved her hand as she slid open the balcony door that faced Hollywood Boulevard. "All of *your* things will be here in a few days. I had to make sure that I had everything I needed. You just never know where a mother might have to go with her celebrity daughter."

Deborah Anne laughed and turned on the television. "So what should we do now?" she asked. "Do you want to get something to eat?"

Virginia shook her head. "The first thing I have to do is call your father." She glanced at her wrist. "My watch says it's four—"

"That's because you didn't change your watch back. You have to set it back three hours."

Virginia waved her hands. "My goodness, there's so much to get used to."

While her mother spoke on the phone, Deborah Anne went onto the balcony. It was a small space, much different from the one at the Beverly Hotel. But she was paying for it and chose the Holiday Inn, since she didn't know how long it would take to find an apartment.

She could hear Virginia reassuring Elijah that all was well. "I'm finally here," she whispered into the air.

Last night, even after Elijah had kissed her good night, she couldn't sleep. So she sat up, trying to imagine what this was going to feel like. Twenty-four hours ago she was a country-girl police dispatcher from Villa Rica. Now she was part of one of the most successful musical acts in the country.

"Your father was sitting by the phone waiting for us. He suggested that you get one of those cellular phones, so that we can stay in touch."

"Do you really think that's necessary, Mama?"

Virginia shrugged her shoulders. "It won't hurt to look into it. If it will make your father feel better, then I'm all for it. Your leaving is hard on him, you know."

Deborah Anne nodded. "I know, but you didn't think I'd stay home forever, did you?"

"Of course not, but after you stayed home for college and then all those years afterward"—Virginia paused and laid her hand on her daughter's cheek—"you can't blame us now if we're a little sad."

Deborah Anne took her mother's hand. "I'm sad too, but don't get too comfortable. I plan on making lots of trips home."

"Good!"

"Anyway, now you and Daddy will have that big house to yourself. You won't have me underfoot."

Virginia waved her hand. "Your father will be at one end of the house and I'll be at the other." She smiled. "But seriously, I am so proud of what you're doing."

Deborah Anne bowed her head. "I know you would have preferred that I sing different music."

"Baby, I would never tell a grown woman what to do. You're a woman of God, Deborah Anne. As long as you stay on your knees, He's the only one you should listen to. And He will tell you what to do."

"Hey, let's not get all serious. Let's do something—even if we just walk on Hollywood Boulevard."

Virginia stepped back into the room. "Okay, and let's ask someone at the front desk if they know the best way to search for an apartment. Maybe we should get a Sunday paper and look in the classifieds. I'd love to have you settled before I leave."

Virginia went into the bathroom as Deborah Anne gathered their sweaters and purses. Just then, the phone rang.

"That has got to be your father," Virginia yelled through the bathroom door.

Deborah Anne laughed as she picked up the phone.

"Hey, I hope that laugh is because you're glad to hear from me."

"Triage!" she exclaimed. "How are you? And how did you know I was here? I was going to call you in a few days—"

"Whoa, girl. Give me a chance. First, welcome to LA! I'm fine. I found out you were here from Grandma and Lavelle's people. You didn't think I was going to let you come to LA and not look out for you, did you?"

She smiled. "Well, I am glad you're here. Mama was just talking about when she had to leave, and the thought of being here alone . . ." She sank onto the bed.

"Well, I have my orders from Grandma. If she had her way, you'd be moving in with me."

Deborah Anne felt the heat rise to her face.

"Of course, she'd make us get married first," Triage continued.

"Is that your father?" Virginia asked as she came back into the room.

Deborah Anne shook her head. "It's Triage."

"So, what are you ladies doing?" he asked.

"Mama and I were just going out to get something to eat."

"Then I called just in time. Give me about thirty minutes, and I'll be there."

While they waited in the lobby for Triage, Virginia asked at the front desk about searching for an apartment. In less than thirty minutes, Triage pulled up in front of the hotel, this time driving himself in a black Range Rover.

He hugged Virginia first, then kissed Deborah Anne on the cheek.

"I was thinking that we would go back to my place, and I can fix you both dinner," he said, as he helped them into the car.

"That's so nice of you, Milton," Virginia said. "Maybe I can do a little cooking for you."

"Oh, no, ma'am. I would never let you do that. You and Deborah Anne are my guests." He smiled at her in the rearview mirror.

"You don't understand, Triage." Deborah Anne smiled. "Mama loves to cook. That would be a treat for her."

"Well, Grandma says there is only one person on earth who can cook better than her or her daughters, and that's you, Mrs. Peterson. So you don't have to ask me twice." Triage's enthusiasm for a home-cooked meal made Virginia laugh.

They chatted casually as Triage maneuvered the SUV through the winding hills of Hollywood.

When they drove through the white iron gate, neither Deborah Anne nor Virginia was prepared for the mammoth Mediterranean-style home that loomed in front of them.

When Triage opened the front door, Virginia exclaimed, "Milton, this isn't a house. Mansion, maybe."

He chuckled. "Let me give you the grand tour. We'll start on the third floor and then come down. I always like to show the house that way."

They strolled through the ten-thousand-square-foot home in awe. The third floor held Triage's office and a library stocked with books, floor to ceiling across three walls. His studio, complete with sixteen-track digital recording equipment, completed the enormous workspace.

"My goodness, we could have had my audition here." Deborah Anne laughed.

"This is where I hang out when I really want to chill," Triage said, taking them into the second-floor media room, which housed a seventy-two-inch TV screen, and stereo equipment that lined one wall.

From there, they continued through the eight bedrooms, each decorated in a different color. But it was the master bedroom that Deborah Anne loved most. With the octagonal-shaped sitting room and the gold-and-black-enamel furniture and accessories, the room had an elegant, spacious feel.

As they came down the curved staircase, Virginia said, "I feel like I've walked a couple of miles."

"You have, Mama."

"Well, don't get too tired yet, Mrs. Peterson. I still have to show you the kitchen and the pool."

"Now this is the kind of place where I can really get cooking." Virginia laughed.

The gourmet kitchen was totally white, with granite countertops and embossed lacquer cabinets. As Virginia admired the stainless steel appliances, Triage took Deborah Anne into the backyard, where there were an Olympic-size pool and a Jacuzzi.

"Do you swim a lot?"

Triage laughed. "I don't swim at all. But I couldn't buy a house in Los Angeles without a pool."

Deborah Anne shook her head. "Well then, I'll just have to teach you."

"Girl, you won't have any time. Next week at this time, I'll be calling you and you'll be asking, 'Triage who?'"

"I doubt that. You're too good a friend."

They strolled back into the house and joined Virginia in the kitchen, where she was peeking through the cabinets.

"I hope you don't mind, Milton, but I've already checked the refrigerator. I think I can put together something for us."

"Are you sure, Mrs. Peterson? I can fix something, or we can order in."

Virginia waved him away. "This will be my pleasure. You and Deborah Anne just go somewhere and talk. Tell my daughter everything she needs to know about what she's getting into. She needs all the help she can get."

"Okay." He handed Virginia an apron and Deborah Anne a can of Hawaiian Punch. Then they returned to the pool area.

"Triage, your home is really nice. It's the kind of house I've dreamed of owning. I want a place where my parents can live comfortably when they get older."

Triage leaned his head back as he swallowed a swig of Miller Lite. "You're going to have all of this and much more, Deborah Anne."

"I hope so." She sighed. "I feel like I'm floating in the center of a bubble. I'm afraid that it will all burst, and I'll find myself back in Villa Rica."

He put the beer can onto the wrought-iron table. "What's up with the lack of confidence? Don't you know how well you sing?"

"It's not my singing; I know what the Lord has given me." She dropped her eyes. "I just want to make sure I'm going to fit into this life. When I was at the studio for the audition, I felt so different from Vianca and Emerald. The way they dressed, the way their hair and makeup was done—they *looked* like professional singers. But me . . ." Deborah Anne glanced at the jogging suit she'd worn on the plane.

Triage chuckled. "Do you think Vianca and Emerald came to Lavelle looking like that? Believe me, they've had a lot of help, and you will too." He reached across the table and took her hand. "But, Deborah *Anne*, don't go changing too much. The best people are the ones who stay themselves. You'll find your own style."

She wondered if she should mention the way Lavelle had made her feel when he hugged her, but decided against it. No need to stir the waters for no reason.

"I thank God for you every day, Triage."

He leaned back and smiled. "I keep telling you I have to take care of the daughter of the woman who took care of my mama."

They laughed and waited for Virginia to call them in for dinner.

CHAPTER 11

THE NEXT WEEK PASSED AT THE SPEED OF LIGHT. Triage took time from his recording schedule to help Deborah Anne and Virginia accomplish all the tasks on Virginia's list.

"There's so much to do before I leave," Virginia kept saying.

"Mama, it's fine if we don't get everything done. I can handle it, and remember, I have Triage to help me."

But Virginia could not be diverted. By the time Triage and Deborah Anne drove Virginia to LAX the following Saturday, they had accomplished a long list of to-dos. They purchased a year-old Toyota Camry, leased a studio apartment just ten minutes from the studio, filled the kitchen cabinets with food; had the phone and utilities turned on, bought clothes that Deborah Anne felt more comfortable in, scheduled delivery of Deborah Anne's possessions from the moving company, and cried more tears than either had thought possible.

"You take care of yourself, you hear me," Virginia said, as she pointed her chin forward.

"I will, Mama. And you take care of yourself and Daddy too. I'm going to miss you so much."

They hugged.

"Milton, I can't thank you enough for all that you did for us this week and for everything that you've done for Deborah Anne. But I'm going to ask you one more favor. Keep an eye on her. She means the world to us."

Triage smiled and hugged Virginia. "Yes, ma'am."

They waved and watched until Virginia could no longer be seen in the passenger walkway. Even then, Deborah Anne stood by the window to wait for the plane to take off. Triage stood behind her, signing his name for a few children who asked for autographs. Finally, he took her hand. "Come on," he said gently.

As they walked quickly through the terminal, they were able to avoid any more requests for autographs, though someone called out Triage's name every few steps.

Right before they got to the front door, a paparazzo clicked his camera several times before they were able to get into the car and drive away.

They were on Century Boulevard when Triage finally asked, "Are you okay?"

Deborah Anne had leaned back and closed her eyes. She nodded because she didn't want him to hear how empty she felt inside. Triage placed his hand over hers, and she opened her eyes. The concern on his face made the hole in her heart grow a little smaller.

"No matter how hard I tried to prepare for this," Deborah Anne said softly, "I didn't think I'd feel this sad."

"I know. When I went to college and watched my parents drive away, leaving me standing there on the edge of campus, I knew I'd never be the same. And that was what scared me."

He gave her a sideward glance. "But that's what's so exciting, Deborah Anne. You *will* never be the same. And when you think about it, that's what life's about."

She smiled. "I know I'll be fine. All of my prayers are being answered."

He squeezed her hand.

When they stopped at a red light, Deborah Anne said, "Triage, there is one thing, though."

"What, Deborah Anne?"

"Since I'll never be the same again, why don't you call me *Deborah?*" She grinned, put on her sunglasses, and turned on the CD player, blasting Triage's latest song, "The Truth Be Told," all through the Range Rover.

CHAPTER 12

WHEN THE ALARM BEEPED, DEBORAH RAN from behind the divider that separated the kitchen from the rest of the room and turned off the clock. She'd been up for hours, even though it was just six.

She returned to her kitchen/dining area and picked up her cup of tea, taking it to the two-chair dining table. Her Bible was already opened; she'd been sifting through the pages for almost two hours.

She'd been reading Psalms, and now she turned back to her favorite scripture: "Be still and know that I am God." She read it over and over again, knowing that those words would get her through anything. God had brought her to this point. Surely, He would take her all the way.

When she looked up again, it was only six-thirty, three hours before she had to be at the studio. Yesterday, she had taken several trips from her apartment on Santa Monica over to Sunset. Since she had tested the drive in light Sunday traffic, Deborah knew it wouldn't take her more than fifteen minutes to get to work.

She decided to start getting ready anyway—she would just take her time. But even after showering and dressing in capri-length leggings and a long white man-tailored shirt, she still had hours to wait.

She picked up the phone, then put it back in its cradle. As an ER nurse, Virginia didn't like to take calls at work unless it was an emergency. And Elijah was always out in the yard, even though he was a supervisor.

Deborah sighed, but then a smile crossed her face. She dialed a number quickly. "Hey, Willetta, it's Deborah Anne."

"Oh my gosh, girl. I just spoke your name. I was talking to Steven and told him that I hadn't heard from you. How're you? Are you working yet? I saw Aunt Virginia yesterday in church, and she was so excited. . . ."

Deborah laughed. "Girl, you sound more excited than anyone. I'm glad I caught you. I just remembered that you were off on Mondays."

"Yeah. So how's it going?"

Deborah sank onto the bed that she hadn't turned back yet. "Willetta, I'm so nervous. In a few hours I have to be at the studio."

"So what are you nervous about? They already chose you. You have the job, remember?"

"I know, it's just that I want so much to fit in there."

"What're you talking about?" Willetta said incredulously.

"Willetta, you should see these women I'll be singing with. They are so sharp, so together. When I stand next to them, I feel like a country girl from Villa Rica, Georgia."

Willetta laughed. "Deborah Anne, that's who you are. And that's nothing to be ashamed of."

"I'm not ashamed, not exactly. I'm just so desperate to do well. You don't know how much I want this."

"Girl, that California sun has baked your brain. You sing like Michael Jordan plays basketball. You're at the top of your game. You can't do anything except do well."

"It's not my singing that concerns me. It's that this is a different world. There's a lot I have to learn, and then . . ." She paused. "What if Vianca and Emerald don't like me?"

Willetta moaned. "Oh, brother! I should have moved out there with your crazy behind. When did you start caring about what people think? Honey, you better get right and remember you're a child of God. He's the only one you need to think about. Stop worrying about what people think or else I'm gonna get on a plane, fly out there, and give you a reminder."

After a few moments, Deborah laughed. "That's why I love you so much. If I need to be brought back to reality—"

"Just call me, and I'll slap your behind back where it belongs." They laughed. "Deborah Anne, I really want to chat, but I've got to go—"

"It's okay. Thanks for the pep talk."

"I love you; call me later. I want to know everything about your first day. And don't worry about those heifers liking you."

Deborah laughed, but the moment she hung up the phone, it rang again. "What did you forget to tell me, Willetta?" Deborah was still laughing.

"Nothing."

Deborah chuckled at Triage's high-pitched tone.

"Triage, what are you doing up so early?"

"I wanted to make sure you were up and on time for your first day."

"Are you kidding? I've been up for hours."

"Dang, girl. Did you sleep at all?"

"Not much. I'm so anxious I just want to run over there now."

"Go on; someone will be there."

Deborah looked at the clock. "I'm not supposed to be there for another hour. I don't want to appear too anxious."

"Deborah, in this industry, everyone is anxious. And that's considered a good thing. Go on over there. It'll do you good. You can have some coffee, relax, get to know the people."

She was thoughtful for a moment. "Okay, are you going to be home tonight? I want to tell you all about it."

"Yeah. I have a few meetings today and some friends in town, but I'll give you a call."

Deborah felt her heart drop a bit. Friends? Who were they? But why should I care? she thought. Triage is just my friend.

By the time she hung up and gathered her bag with the clothes she'd rehearse in, Deborah had forgotten about Triage's words and was focused on the day in front of her.

She ran to her parking space and jumped into her car. The sun was still screened behind the clouds, but she was smiling. It could have been snowing in LA and it wouldn't have mattered to Deborah.

Just as she thought, the trip took just about ten minutes. She parked in the back of the building as she'd been told to do and took one last look at herself in the rearview mirror. "This is it, Deborah Anne—*Deborah*. This is what you've been waiting for." Then she closed her eyes and thanked God for every blessing.

Triage was right. The studio was already open. Although she heard voices, the only person in the large room was Emerald, who once again looked like she'd stepped directly from a page in *Cosmopolitan*. She wore cream leather pants with a zebra-print tank.

Deborah looked down at her own outfit. It was an improvement, but still nowhere near Emerald's ensemble.

The sound of Deborah's heels clicking on the parquet floor made Emerald look up from the *LA Times*.

"Deborah, you're here early." She smiled.

Deborah dropped her bag against the wall and took a seat across from Emerald, who returned to reading the paper. She looked up once again and gestured with her chin toward the far wall. "There's coffee and Coke over there."

Deborah frowned—Coke so early in the morning. She nodded slightly and smiled. "Any tea?"

"I don't think we have any tea drinkers, but make the request and it'll be here in the morning." With her last words, Emerald dropped her eyes back to the paper.

Deborah got up and walked over to the floor-to-ceiling windows that covered one wall. There wasn't much to see—the building was surrounded by other concrete masses, hiding the little sun that was trying to break through.

As she waited, she wished that she had stayed at home. It was harder here.

"Good morning, everybody."

Deborah turned around. Vianca bounced into the room, once again in black leggings, but this time wearing a long T-shirt over them and a gold belt around her waist. Deborah smiled, feeling a bit better. "Hey, Vianca," she called out.

Vianca laughed. "Girl, you're in LA now. You can get rid

of that *hey* stuff." As Vianca rushed over to the coffee, she didn't seem to notice that the smile disappeared from Deborah's face.

A moment later, Lavelle walked in with a few of the musicians. He simply waved at Deborah like he'd seen her yesterday, then sat in the corner with Charles.

Vianca slumped into the chair next to Emerald and picked up the part of the paper that Emerald had tossed aside.

Deborah sighed. She'd expected a different reception. What was she supposed to do? A moment later, another woman, dressed in a yellow unitard, came into the room; both Emerald and Vianca looked up and gave the woman a single wave.

The woman looked around the room and moved toward Deborah, her blond waist-length locks swaying as she walked.

"Hi, I'm Tisha, the choreographer. It's just going to be you and me this morning."

Deborah recognized Tisha as the woman who arranged the dance routines for *The Color of Black,* a popular variety show. She smiled. This was the first good news since she'd arrived. Deborah eagerly followed Tisha into an adjacent room.

"You're not going to try to work out in that?"

Tisha's voice was filled with such amazement that Deborah had to look down to see if she'd worn something terrible.

"No, I brought clothes to change into—"

"Well, tomorrow just *wear* them, or get here early and change. This show goes on the road in two months, and there's no time to waste."

Deborah nodded, lifted her bag, and asked for the bathroom.

Tisha looked at her with raised eyebrows. "Girl, please. Just drop your pants and change. No one is looking at you. And anyway, you'd better get used to it. There are no private changing rooms for backup singers. No rooms for prima donnas."

Deborah opened her mouth to explain, then changed her mind. As she quickly removed her top and leggings, tears burned her eyes. She took a deep breath and tried to calm her feelings. It would just take some getting used to—Villa Rica, this wasn't.

"Okay," Tisha said once Deborah had changed. She had wrapped her locks into a large bun. "Let me show you some of the basic steps that we do for all the songs. Then, the rest of the week, we'll work on specific songs and things that you'll have to do." She paused, tilted her head, and looked Deborah up and down. "Lavelle said that you move well. Have you had any dance training?"

Deborah nodded. "I took dance classes until I was sixteen, and then I've watched all of Lavelle's videos."

Tisha looked doubtful. "Uh-huh," she grunted, then sighed. "Well, let's see what you got."

Tisha's locks bounced as she demonstrated steps, then moved aside for Deborah to follow. They worked that way for an hour before Tisha smiled.

"Well all right, girl. It looks like Lavelle gave me something to work with." She clapped. "Okay, let's take five."

Deborah, breathless, nodded and slid against the wall.

"Oh, tomorrow, bring a water bottle with you, but for now, there's a fountain in the hall."

Deborah tried not to stumble as she went for a drink. She leaned against the fountain, taking small sips every few seconds.

Tisha peeked into the hallway. "Come on. I said you were okay, but we still have a lot of work to do."

They worked for another hour without stopping until, finally, Vianca came into the room. "Lunch is here," she announced.

Tisha wiped her face with the towel hanging from her belt around her waist. "Don't you heifers eat too much; you know how you are."

Deborah's eyes opened wide. She opened her mouth to tell Tisha that there was no need for her to speak that way, but before she could say a word, Tisha added, "Deborah, I suggest that you just have some fruit. It'll be easier to keep working after lunch. I'll see you back here in an hour."

Deborah only nodded.

"And one more thing, Deborah. Do you work out?" Tisha asked.

Deborah frowned slightly. "A little."

"Well, I suggest you work out a lot. You need to build your stamina, and it wouldn't hurt to get some of those jiggles toned, if you know what I mean."

Deborah glanced down at her size-eight frame.

Vianca laughed. "Don't worry, Tisha. I'll take her to Bally's with me tonight."

Tisha waved, and left the room through the other door.

"Come on, let's eat," Vianca said to a dazed Deborah. "It looks like you've had quite a workout."

"Yeah. I should've prepared for this."

"There's nothing you could have done. Tisha's tough, but she's so good, she'll have you in shape in weeks."

When they came back to the main part of the studio, only Emerald and Tyrone were there, practicing a song. Taking

Tisha's advice, Deborah took only an orange from the food table that was covered with sandwiches, chips, and cookies. Then she slouched into one of the chairs. She wasn't hungry anyway; she was too tired to eat.

Vianca sat next to Deborah. "Don't worry, it won't be so bad this afternoon. Emerald and I will be joining you."

Deborah peeled the orange and slowly let the juice squirt inside her mouth. "Is it like this every day?"

Vianca nodded. "Especially as we get ready to tour. The heat is on, and everyone has to work hard. Lavelle is great to work with, but he's a perfectionist and only hires people who are the same way."

"How long have you been with him?"

Vianca looked up as if she were searching for the answer in the ceiling. "Just a bit over a year."

"You like it?"

"It's hard work, but you can't beat it—especially if you love to sing. And you can *sang*, girl."

Deborah looked over to where Emerald sat next to Tyrone. They were singing one measure of a song over and over again. "Will we be practicing with Lavelle this afternoon?"

Vianca shook her head. "No, I think this week is going to be devoted to you, Emerald, and me getting our steps and moves in the groove. Once we're a package, then Lavelle will step in."

Deborah nodded but remained silent. Behind the scenes wasn't exciting at all.

When Tisha came into the room to get them, Vianca bounced and Emerald sauntered, while Deborah wanted to crawl behind them. The hour wasn't long enough to refresh her.

The afternoon went much like the morning, only now there were two others for Tisha to pick on, and Deborah was glad to have some of the attention diverted from her. They worked continuously until Tisha clapped her hands. "That's it for today."

Emerald and Vianca were winded and moved as if they had just completed a long aerobics class. Deborah, on the other hand, ached, and her calves throbbed with each step she took.

"Deborah, do you have any plans for tonight?" Vianca asked as she put her bag over her shoulder.

She shook her head. "No, I just want to go home and go to bed."

Vianca nodded knowingly. "Okay. I was going to invite you to go shopping with me, but I understand. But you can't go home yet; you have to join the gym."

"When do you have time to work out?"

"Either we get up early in the morning or work out after the session here. Whatever, we have to get the time in. There's an image we have to protect."

Deborah shook her head. It didn't seem fair that the women had to look a certain way while Lavelle could remain as large and out of shape as he wanted. But it was his group, she guessed, and he called the shots.

"Come on, I'll take you to the gym. It's not far from here. Maybe we can hang out tomorrow night."

Deborah followed Vianca's red Acura to Bally's and was pleased to see that it was only a few blocks from her apartment.

Her muscles seemed to pulse even more after the saleswoman asked if she wanted a tour of the gym.

"No, thank you," she said as politely as she could. "I already know that I want to join."

Vianca nodded her approval. In twenty minutes, the papers were signed, the check had been passed, and Vianca and Deborah were chatting in the full parking lot.

"I'll be here at six in the morning if you want to join me. There's a hip-hop aerobics class that I love."

Deborah knew that she'd sleep tonight and, with any luck, wouldn't wake up until noon. "Probably not tomorrow. When I get up, I'll have to figure out what to do with my hair. But I'll try for Wednesday."

Vianca cocked her head to the side. "Is that your hair?"

Deborah frowned. "What do you mean?"

"You know, is that a weave?"

Her frown deepened. *"No."*

"Girl, you get offended easily, don't you? I was only asking because it looked like it was your hair, and I was going to suggest that you get a weave."

"Why would I do that?"

Vianca sighed like she couldn't believe Deborah's question. "Because you've only been working for one day and already you're a prisoner to your hair. This business is hard on our locks, so people either cut their hair short like mine"—she paused as she ran her fingers through her curls—"or they get braids or a weave. I didn't think you'd want to cut your hair, and Emerald wears braids. So I suggest a weave."

Deborah shook her head. "I don't think so. I'll be able to handle it."

Vianca shrugged. "Suit yourself." She tossed her bag into her car. "Anyway, I'll see you tomorrow. Have a good night."

By the time Deborah got to her apartment, it was almost

eight-thirty. She flopped onto the daybed. It was too late to call her parents, which was fine, because she didn't want them to hear the distress in her voice. Five minutes later, the phone rang.

"Hey, girl, how was the first day?"

She tried to force a smile into her voice when she heard Triage. "Okay. I just got in."

"I figured that. Most people think this business is all glamour, but I don't know many people who work harder, especially when you're preparing for a tour."

"I knew it would be work, but I didn't know it would hurt." She told him about Tisha, and how she'd danced for four hours. "I didn't even get a chance to sing."

"Oh, don't worry about that. You'll be doing plenty of singing."

"I hope so."

"Anyway, do you want to grab something to eat?"

"No, I just want to fall into bed. It'll be better for me tomorrow if I have some rest."

"Okay, but call me tomorrow when you get in. You know my grandmother will want a full report on how you're doing."

When she hung up the phone, Deborah looked around the small apartment. She had wondered how it would be the first night after work, and it wasn't this.

Deborah stripped off her clothes and dropped them in a corner of the room. She didn't even bother to take her shower. After pulling out the sofa bed, she reached for her Bible, but she was too tired to do her nightly reading. Instead, she simply turned off the light and fell into a deep sleep.

CHAPTER 13

I T WAS DAY THREE AND DEBORAH WAS WORKING AS
hard as she had the first day. But it was getting easier,
and last night, when she'd spoken to her parents, she'd
even felt encouraged about the future.

It was after seven when Tisha clapped her hands to end
their session. Deborah leaned against the wall and sank to
the floor to take off the pumps she'd been practicing in.
After the first day, Tisha insisted that they wear shoes similar to the ones they'd wear onstage.

"You need to get used to moving in heels. I'd hate to see
you fall on your face on the first night."

Deborah had groaned at Tisha's words as that vision played
in her head. But then, she'd said a quick prayer, making sure
that would never happen.

Vianca walked over to where Deborah sat and put one of
her legs on the dance barre against the wall. "It's still tough,
huh?" Vianca asked as she stretched.

Deborah nodded. "But it's much better. The first day it

was my calves, yesterday my quads, and today my butt. At this rate, by next Monday I'll have a headache, and then this will all be over."

Vianca laughed. "Well, it might be tough, but you're looking good, girl. Anyone watching would never be able to tell that you're the new one in the group."

"Thanks." Deborah grinned.

"Hey, I'm going shopping. Do you want to come along?"

Deborah shook her head. "No, I was thinking about going over to the gym. I haven't gone since I joined."

Vianca shrugged her shoulders. "Okay."

Deborah chewed on her lip. Vianca had asked her to go somewhere every night, but she always turned her down.

"You know what, Vianca, I changed my mind. I'd love to go with you. Where are you going?"

Vianca smiled brightly. "To the Beverly Center. I'm going to a party this weekend and want a knockout dress."

"Okay."

They decided to leave Deborah's car and take Vianca's.

"Is this your first singing job?" Deborah asked.

Vianca nodded as she turned onto LaCienega Boulevard. "The only singing I'd done before was in church. My uncle knows Lavelle, and that's how I got the audition."

Deborah smiled and turned in her seat, facing Vianca. "I sang in my church also," she said excitedly. "What church do you go to? I want to join one as soon as possible."

"Girl, I don't go to church anymore. Sundays are the only days I get to sleep in."

Deborah turned back in her seat.

"So you found out about Lavelle through Triage Blue, right?"

Deborah nodded. "He heard me singing in church and recommended that I send in a tape."

"So, tell me the real deal. Are you and Triage an item?"

Deborah frowned. "Not at all. We're just good friends."

"That's not what the papers are saying. Look on the back-seat."

Deborah turned around and underneath Vianca's gym bag was the *National Intruder*. She grabbed the paper and read the front-page headline: "Triage Blue Brawls and Makes His Girlfriend Bawl." Underneath the words was a picture of her and Triage—the one taken at the airport after her mother had gotten on the plane.

"This isn't true! They can't make something like this up, can they?"

"Well, if you say it's not true, then obviously they can make it up." Vianca paused. "Are you sure there's absolutely nothing going on between the two of you?"

"No. He's like my brother."

"Uh-huh. Well, I'm sure he wanted *something* for hooking you up with this gig."

Deborah questioned Vianca with her eyes.

"You know . . . did you sleep with him?"

"No!"

"Ooh! I think the lady protests too much."

Deborah wished she had gone to the gym. "Vianca, I didn't sleep with Triage. I'm not like that, and neither is he."

Vianca's laugh startled Deborah. "Yeah, right. You probably haven't heard the truth about Mr. Blue. He gets around."

Deborah crossed her arms in front of her and was relieved when Vianca turned into the mall.

"This is my favorite place to shop," Vianca said, as she led Deborah up the long escalator.

The distress Deborah felt at Vianca's words faded as she strolled along the high-glossed floors, past the upscale shops.

"This is where I want to go," Vianca said, pointing to a store. Gold letters spelling out "Imaginations" were stretched above the store.

Deborah found the unusual window display interesting because the mannequins were dressed in plastic bags. The reason became evident once she stepped inside the store. The dresses, suits, pants, and jumpsuits that lined the walls were risqué and racy. Most of the outfits looked like lingerie.

"Oh, look at this one!" Vianca was standing in front of a mirror, holding a short black dress in front of her. "Do you like it?"

Deborah tried to hold back her shock. "Vianca, there are *holes* in that dress."

"That's what makes it so sexy. Not to worry; it covers what it's supposed to."

"You won't be able to wear any underwear with that," Deborah whispered.

Vianca laughed softly. "Girl, please! I don't wear underwear half the time anyway. I don't think Lavelle would mind, do you?" She laughed again at the look on Deborah's face. "Honey, you've got to get with it. You're a pro-fessional singer now. There's a certain image we have to uphold for Lavelle. We can't look like country bumpkins when we're offstage."

Deborah pressed her lips together. "Nobody's going to dictate to me how to dress when I'm not working."

"Whatever. I'm going to try this on."

Deborah shuffled through the clothes on the rack as Vianca went into the dressing room. She had nightgowns that covered more than some of these dresses. She picked up a tag.

"Three hundred dollars? There's no material!"

When Vianca came out of the dressing room she looked just as Deborah imagined she would. The dress didn't cover much of her petite figure.

"You look fabulous!" one of the sales associates exclaimed. "That dress was made for you."

Vianca grinned. "I think so. Deborah, can't you find anything?"

The saleswoman turned toward her. "I can help."

She held up her hands. "No, thank you. I'm on a bit of a budget right now."

"Girl, you sing for Lavelle. You don't have money problems anymore."

As Vianca sauntered back to the dressing room, the saleswoman, wide-eyed, rushed to Deborah's side. "You sing with Lavelle?"

Deborah smiled. "Look at me." She motioned with her hands. "Do I *look* like I sing with Lavelle?"

The woman was thoughtful, then shook her head and smiled. "If you need any help, just let me know. My name is Marie."

Deborah waited while Vianca paid for the dress, then remained silent as Vianca chatted all the way to the car.

"Deborah, the one thing you need to remember is that in this business, it's not just about you. It's who you represent," Vianca was saying. "So you have to forget all that stuff that you learned in Georgia and get with what people do in Los Angeles. We're stars now. . . ."

She wished there were a way to close her ears, and was grateful when Vianca dropped her at her car. One thing was sure—if this was how the business was going to be, then she had to find a church home quickly.

CHAPTER 14

I T WASN'T UNTIL DEBORAH DROPPED HER BAG AND SANK into the couch that she realized she hadn't spoken to Triage in several days.

It had been a week filled with firsts—first dance lessons, first vocal rehearsals, first fitting. She never realized how many dresses and special shoes were needed for one act. And then today, Lavelle spoke to her for the first time since she'd arrived.

"So, how's it going?" he asked as she stood at the lunch table.

She nodded, surprised by his attention. "It's good. I'm getting used to it."

"Tisha said you're doing great."

"I hope so. I'm working hard. I want to do a good job for you."

A smile crossed his face that Deborah couldn't interpret. "I'm sure you'll do a good job."

When he walked away, Deborah pushed him from her

mind. There was much more to worry about than Lavelle. What she was finding out was that most of the work was done without him.

Now, as she sat on her couch massaging her feet, she tried to put the day's work out of her mind. She sighed when the phone rang and thought about not answering it. Every night Vianca called wanting to chat.

But she couldn't take the chance of missing her parents. "Tomorrow," she said aloud, "I'll get an answering machine." She picked up the phone.

"Hey, how're you doing?"

She smiled, and it wasn't until that moment that she realized how much she'd missed Triage. "I'm great. I survived five days."

He laughed. "I told you. So how were the rehearsals?"

"Fine. I don't want to bore you with things you already know about. What've you been doing?"

"I had some friends in town, and we're also preparing for a new music video."

"Sounds like you've been as busy as I have."

"That's what this business is about. But there's also time to play. I was calling to see what you're doing this weekend. I'm sure there're still some things you need for the apartment."

"What I need is a larger apartment," she said, as she looked around at the four walls. "But that'll have to wait."

"Well, I'll run errands with you. And then on Sunday we can go out on my boat."

"I didn't know you have a boat."

"Yeah, it's not a yacht or anything, but I think you'll have fun. Sounds like a plan?"

She hesitated. "Triage, that sounds great, but actually, I was hoping to go to church on Sunday. I really want to find a church home before I get all into work. Do you know of one?"

Now the pause was on his end. "Actually, I do. I used to go sometimes. I haven't been recently." He stopped for a moment. "Why don't we go on Sunday?"

She smiled widely. "Now *that* I would love."

They made plans to meet the next afternoon, after Deborah's workout. When she hung up the phone, she was still smiling. She'd been feeling like something was missing, but she knew church would help that. And with Triage going with her, that made it all the better.

It was just after nine when she opened out the couch and lay down on the bed. She couldn't find a comfortable place on her pillow, and she turned until her head felt better.

She brought her hands to her scalp and massaged it. Yesterday, she'd done what she still couldn't believe—after constant hounding from Vianca, she'd gone to her stylist and gotten a weave.

As much as Deborah wanted to put this on Vianca, she had made the decision herself. It took her just a week to discover that Vianca was right. All of the dancing and working out had thinned her thick hair, making it limp and lifeless.

"That's why Emerald wears braids and I have this short cut," Vianca had reminded her as she drove Deborah to Flyy Curls in Beverly Hills. "You're doing the right thing."

But even as Deborah sat in front of the mirror with Blair, the stylist, standing behind her, she still had her doubts.

"Girl, look at all this beautiful hair," Blair gushed as he

lifted her hair from her shoulders. "I can just style it for you—"

"No," Vianca had jumped in. "She needs a weave, Blair. I already told you."

Deborah stared at her reflection as Blair and Vianca went back and forth, debating what was best for her.

"I think a nice cut—"

It was Deborah who stopped him this time. "No, Blair. I don't want to cut my hair." Her eyes dropped from her reflection. "A weave will be better. That way I can take it out when I'm ready."

Vianca had crossed her arms in front of her and smiled triumphantly. Deborah spent the next six hours sitting in the chair as Blair transformed her.

It was after eleven when she finally looked into the mirror. Deborah was surprised to see how natural she looked— the long layers fell just a bit beyond her shoulders.

"You can do anything with this, darling," Blair declared. "You can wear it straight, curled, or with or without bangs. I must admit, Vianca girl, you were right."

As Deborah wrote the check to Blair, her only hope was that Vianca really was right.

Blair had told her that she'd be fine in a day or two. She hoped so. Finally, she dropped her hands and sighed.

"I'm still blessed," she said to herself. "I cannot forget that." A few seconds later, she said aloud, "Father, all I can do is thank You and give You praise, honor, and glory. This has been tough and is not what I expected. But I still love it, Lord, because I'm going to be able to use the gift that You blessed me with. Thank You for Your keeping grace, the way You protect me and guide me. And I pray that I continue to do Your will, Lord. Help me to stay on the right path, even in the midst of all of these things that I don't understand. Thank You, Father. Amen." Then she added, "And thank You for gracing my life with Triage Blue."

CHAPTER 15

THE MOMENT SHE STEPPED THROUGH THE DOOR, Deborah felt like she was at home. Macedonia Baptist Church wasn't much bigger than Mountain. Deborah and Triage had waited until exactly eleven o'clock to go inside. The wide-smiling usher tried to escort them to the front, but Triage asked to sit in the last row.

Deborah had never sat so far back in church. Being with Triage was showing her just how different life could become with celebrity. But even fifteen rows back, it felt good to be in the House of the Lord.

As the choir sang, Deborah was surprised that only a few in the congregation stood and sang along. But as others beside her began to rise, so did she. She raised her hands and voice to God, thanking Him for all He had done.

After two songs, Deborah finally sat down. Her foot was still tapping as one of the assistant pastors read from the Bible. And the beat continued to reverberate through her when the pastor stood for the sermon.

"This morning I want to talk to you about 'staying in the course.' The Lord has given each of us a path to pound, a race to run. But it is up to *us* to stay the course and run it well. Turn to Deuteronomy 13:4."

Whispers of turning pages filled the church, and Deborah handed her Bible to Triage. But as she watched him search for Deuteronomy, she leaned over and turned to the chapter herself.

He smiled. "It's been a while."

Her smile told him that she understood.

"'Ye shall walk after the Lord your God, and fear Him, and keep His commandments, and obey His voice, and ye shall serve Him, and cleave unto Him.' The Lord makes it very clear. While you are running the race and moving along this path that He has set for you, you must follow Him."

Deborah smiled. That was why she was so glad to be back in church. The messages were designed just for her. She knew it was going to be a difficult walk—to run after this dream and stay focused on God. But it wasn't a choice. She would give it all up if this business interfered with her relationship with the Lord.

"Now I want you to turn to Matthew 6:24. 'No man can serve two masters; for either he will hate the one, and love the other; or else he will hold to the one, and despise the other. You cannot serve God and mammon.' You see, while God has laid out this path for you, don't think that Satan isn't going to be there, on the sidelines, just waiting. Waiting for the chance to tempt you with something that will pull you from the road. Waiting for the chance to get you to serve him instead of the Lord. Because the path has been *set* by God, but your walk is up to you."

Deborah nodded in agreement and glanced at Triage. He had leaned forward slightly, focused on the pastor, his gaze intent as if the words were meant for him. Deborah smiled.

"Galatians 5:7 says, 'You did run well; who did hinder you.' Run the race, children of God. Run it well. But let it not be said that you *did* run well. Because that will mean that you have not stayed the course. Run for the Lord. In all that you do, serve Him."

As "Amen"s and "Hallelujah"s rose through the congregation, Deborah raised her hands in praise.

"Thank You, Father, for this message that You've given me," she whispered. "I hear Your Word and I receive it. Thank You, Father."

The pastor was still walking across the altar, waving his hands in the air. "We have to stay the course, but there are some of you who may not even know what your course is. For anyone who has not made a decision to know God for themselves or for those who know the Lord but have found themselves straying away from Him, it's time for you to come back into the fold. Please come up now so that I can pray for you." The pastor reached toward the congregation.

Triage took Deborah's hand and squeezed it. He motioned for her to stand, and she smiled. He was going up for prayer, and that pleased her.

She picked up her purse and stood with him, but blinked in surprise when Triage turned away from the altar and led her out the front door.

They walked in silence until they were in the car.

"I hope you don't mind leaving early. I wanted to get out of there before it ended and people started bombarding me."

She nodded as if she understood. "Next time, maybe we

should make arrangements so that we can stay for the whole service."

When he shrugged, Deborah crossed her arms across her chest. They drove in silence with his new CD blasting through the car. Triage had already made arrangements for brunch at the Vine, and once they arrived, they were escorted to a private room. Deborah ordered a clam-and-scallop omelet, while Triage had smoked salmon on a bagel.

"Did you enjoy the service?" Triage asked as soon as the waitress had taken their orders. He smiled.

"I did, but I was a little disappointed that we had to leave so early."

Triage frowned. "The service was almost over, wasn't it?"

She dropped her eyes. "Triage, I understand about the fans bothering you, but you can't let that get in the way of your relationship with God."

He stared at her, then gave her a slight smile. "You're right, but it's not like I have the relationship with God that I used to."

"Don't you want to have that relationship again?"

His smile widened a bit more, and he nodded. "I would, especially after watching you these past weeks."

"What do you mean?"

"Well, I know you think you got this job because of me, but I've gotta tell you, it happened even quicker than I ever thought it would." He paused. "Grandma said it was God."

"I know it was Him," she said quickly.

He raised his eyebrows. "And all this time you've been thanking me."

She laughed. "It was you, because God used you to help me. But it was His plan, and His will that I be here."

He paused thoughtfully. "It's so hard for me to get back to where I was with God. My career is so demanding."

"What does that have to do with serving the Lord?"

"You know, I can't go to church all the time, I don't read the Bible—I don't even have a Bible; I haven't prayed in I don't know how long—"

"Triage, all of that can be fixed *like that*." She snapped her fingers. "What's really holding you back?"

He shook his head. "I don't know."

"I think this is what the pastor was talking about today when he said you can't serve two Gods. We all have to make a decision who our God is going to be."

They had been sitting in silence for several minutes by the time the waitress brought their food.

When the plates were placed in front of them, Triage said, "Would you mind if I gave this a try again?"

She smiled and reached across the table, taking his hands.

"Dear God, we thank You for this food that we are about to receive. We thank You for everything that You've given us in this life and we thank You for caring for us." He paused, but Deborah kept her head bowed, and squeezed his hand. "We thank You because you are God. Amen." He looked up sheepishly. "How did I do?"

She smiled. "That was a great beginning."

❧

As Triage handed his ticket to the valet, a man approached them from the side of the building.

"Triage," he yelled.

They turned toward the voice, and the flash made them blink. Then the photographer disappeared around the corner.

"Don't these guys have a life? How do they know where you are every moment of the day?"

He shrugged. "They pay people at restaurants and hotels to call them."

"Don't you get sick of it?"

He opened the door for her to get into the car. "There's nothing I can do."

She smiled as he got into the car. "But won't your girl-friends mind? Seeing you in a picture with another woman?"

He chuckled. "Haven't you read about it? I just broke up with my longtime girlfriend."

"No, I didn't read that. But I did read about how you made me cry."

He laughed. "I saw that one too. I guess I should have warned you."

"It's fine for me; it's you that I worry about."

"Don't worry about me; I'm in between women right now, so I can hang out with you."

Deborah looked at Triage, but he was looking at the road.

"Speaking of hanging out, I wanted to know if you would go to the premiere of *One of Those Days* with me. It's Wednesday night."

She smiled widely. "Triage, that would be so awesome. I've never been to a premiere." She paused. "Let's make a deal. I'll go with you if you go with me to church next Sunday."

He laughed. "Oh, I see. I do something for you and you do something for me."

"Do we have a deal?"

"Honey, that's one deal that I'm glad to make."

CHAPTER 16

ONDAY'S REHEARSAL SEEMED TO FLY BY, AND even Tisha was pleased with Deborah's performance.

"I don't know what happened to you over the weekend," Tisha said, "but whatever it was, make sure it happens again tonight. I want to see that same energy tomorrow."

Deborah laughed, now used to Tisha's brazen tone. As soon as Tisha and Emerald left the room, Deborah pulled Vianca aside.

"What are you doing tonight?"

Vianca shrugged. "Probably the same old stuff. You don't want to work out?"

"Well, I have something else for us to do." She paused for effect. "How would you like to go with me to pick out a dress for Triage's premiere?"

Vianca's mouth opened as wide as her eyes. "Girl, you told me there was nothing going on with you and Triage."

"We're just friends."

"Uh-huh. Then why is he inviting *you* to the premiere? That is something that these men save for only the *special* women in their lives."

"Well, I'm a *special* friend. So do you want to come with me or not?"

"Of course, girl," Vianca said, backing into the hallway. "You need me. I bet you don't even know where to go."

Deborah laughed. "Well, I was going to ask you for a few ideas."

They giggled as they walked through the lobby and into the parking lot. Deborah decided to drive.

"So where do we begin?"

Vianca looked at her watch. "It's a good thing Tisha let us off early. We still have an hour before the shops on Rodeo close."

"Oh, no. I'm not shopping on Rodeo Drive."

"Why not? I keep telling you about this image we have to have."

"And that image costs too much money."

"You could always have Triage pay for your dress. That's what most women would do."

"Then I'm glad my parents didn't raise me to be 'most women.'"

Vianca sighed. "Well, before you say no altogether, let's go to Gianfranco Ferre. Sometimes you can get some great buys at that boutique." Before Deborah could protest, Vianca added, "And if that doesn't work out, the malls will still be open and we can go somewhere like Robinson's-May."

"Sounds like a plan to me."

"You're kidding, right? You wouldn't really wear a dress from Robinson's-May to Triage's premiere?"

Deborah's glance told Vianca that she would.

Vianca raised her eyes to the sky. "Lord, please help this child."

"Oh, so you've found God now!"

They laughed, and within minutes they pulled up to the boutique. It didn't take many minutes for Deborah to decide they needed to go elsewhere. A few glances at the price tags had her running for the front door.

"I don't know why you're being such a boob about this. You can afford these kinds of clothes now."

"Vianca, I don't know how much money you're making, but I can't afford to spend nine hundred and fifty dollars on a dress that I'll wear once. Even if I could wear it every day, it still wouldn't be worth it."

Deborah held her hand up in front of Vianca's face and marched out of the store. The valet had not even had the chance to move her car, but the five-dollar service charge still applied.

"If you're going to buy something off the rack, at least go to Nordstrom," Vianca pleaded.

It took them almost forty minutes to get to the Westside Pavilion.

Each time Vianca picked out a dress, Deborah vetoed it. The first dress Deborah chose made Vianca gag.

"As one of Lavelle's girls, you cannot wear that matronly bag!"

"Just because I choose not to show every part of my body doesn't make me matronly." But by the time Deborah put on the dress, she agreed with Vianca.

When she came out of the dressing room, Vianca was holding a salmon-colored gown with a high neck. "Now, girl, this is the bomb!" She held the dress above her head. "How do you like this one?"

Deborah smiled as she took the hanger from Vianca's hand. "This is nice." The scoop-necked, long-sleeved dress was trimmed with sequins. Deborah took a quick glance at the price tag—$375 was more than she had ever spent, but this was a special event.

She was surprised that Vianca had chosen this, until Deborah twisted the hanger around. "What happened to the back?"

"That's the style, girl. Come on, you've got to live a little."

Deborah squinted her eyes in doubt.

"Deborah, you've got to think about Triage." Vianca continued to plead her case. "He's a star, and people will be looking at his date." She held up her hand before Deborah could say anything. "I know you're not his date, but everyone else will *think* that you are. So if you don't care about yourself, do this for Triage. Especially after all he's done for you."

Deborah looked at the dress again. Maybe it wasn't that bad.

"Come on, I'll help you get into this," Vianca urged.

A few minutes later, Vianca had zipped the dress and tied it at the waist. She stepped back as Deborah turned from side to side, looking at herself in the mirror.

"Girl, you are drop-dead gorgeous."

"I don't know." Deborah chewed her lip. The low-cut back stopped barely above her waist. "This is a little more risqué than anything I've ever worn."

"That's why you have to do this. It's time for you to live a little. Your life is different now."

Deborah twisted in front of the mirror. I don't know, she thought.

"Go on," Vianca prodded.

"What kind of bra would I wear with this?"

Vianca rolled her eyes. "You don't have to wear a bra at all!"

Deborah raised her eyebrows.

"Okay, okay. There's a Victoria's Secret here in the mall. There are all kinds of things you can wear." She paused. "Triage, just remember Triage."

After a few moments, Deborah said, "All right, but only if I can find a bra to wear with this. If not, we're going to come right back here, and I'll get that grandmother dress!"

Vianca clapped. "Girl, you are finally on your way."

CHAPTER 17

A BOMBARDMENT OF FLASHING LIGHTS BLINDED her as Triage took her hand and helped her from the limousine. The Granville Theater in Westwood was mobbed with fans and reporters, and their screams of "Triage, Triage" overwhelmed Deborah even more than the size of the crowd itself.

Deborah wobbled a bit as they promenaded down the red carpet. The four-inch heels that Vianca had talked her into were at least an inch higher than anything she'd ever worn. She was grateful when Triage stopped to talk to one of the reporters.

"I know you're excited tonight. From just the little bit I've seen, I think *One of Those Days* is your best film yet," said Della Robinson, the only African American reporter on the carpet.

Triage smiled. "Thanks, Della. I'm pretty excited about it too. We'll see how everyone feels about it tonight."

"So . . ." Della smiled. "Introduce me to your date."

Triage squeezed Deborah's hand. "This is Deborah Peterson."

Deborah and Della shook hands.

"Are you two an item?"

"No," Deborah said quickly, not wanting Triage to be put on the spot. "We're hometown friends, in a way."

"Uh-huh."

Deborah noticed that Della's tone was similar to Vianca's whenever they talked about Triage.

"Well, enjoy your night."

Triage paused a few more times to talk politely to reporters; then they posed for the photographers.

"At least they're not chasing us down today," Triage whispered as they grinned for the cameras. It took almost thirty minutes to walk to their front-row seats.

Deborah wondered what was going to happen. Was anyone going to speak? Would they introduce Triage? She was surprised when the lights dimmed and the film began. For the first time she relaxed, and for the next two hours and twenty minutes, she forgot that she was sitting in the midst of some of the country's most famous people.

When the final credits began to roll, Deborah joined in the audience's cheers and kissed Triage on the cheek. "You were fabulous. You didn't tell me the movie was this good."

His smile was proud. "Thank you, baby." He hugged her and then waved as many in the crowd called to him. They were still standing and clapping.

Triage led Deborah from the theater into the lobby where Ted Davis, the producer, immediately approached him. Deborah backed away a bit, giving Triage room. As more people came into the lobby, she was pushed farther back, until she could only see Triage's head.

She sighed. Her eyes roamed the lobby as people rushed by. Now that she wasn't at Triage's side, no one seemed to notice her. She wished she had someone—even Vianca—here with her.

She wasn't sure how much time had passed—it could have been an hour—when Triage took her hand.

"I'm really sorry about that. But you know this business. Are you ready to go to the party?"

She smiled and nodded.

The limousine took them to the Ambassador's Hotel in Century City, where they were then whisked by Triage's bodyguards to the penthouse suite.

The suite was already packed with people, though Deborah was surprised that there weren't many she recognized. The room was sprinkled with a few celebrities, but the rest were unknown faces. It took only a few minutes for Deborah to realize that most were just hangers-on.

Triage tried to keep Deborah by his side, but only minutes later, she found herself sitting in the corner on the couch, holding a plate of three hot wings and assorted vegetables.

She crossed her legs and chewed on a celery stick. The man sitting next to her took a vial from his jacket. Deborah had never seen cocaine before, but she didn't have to; she knew what he was doing as he spread the white powder on the table.

Her eyes were wide as she watched men and women take turns filling their noses. She looked around, but no one else seemed to notice—or care. Laying her plate on the table, she stood, and another woman immediately took her place, eager to join the group.

She had to find Triage. The adjacent room was filled with as many people, and, to her horror, the same thing was going on.

"Hey, I've been looking for you."

She turned around. "Triage, there are people here doing drugs," she whispered.

He took her hand and led her into the hall. "Don't worry. No one is going to get into trouble."

"That's not what I'm worried about." She stopped and looked at him. "You don't—"

"Oh, no." He waved his hand. "I've never done drugs and don't want any part of it."

"Triage, I'm sorry, but I feel—"

He nodded. "I understand."

"Would you mind if I went home?"

"I can have the car take you, but I have to stay. There are people—"

She squeezed his hand. "You don't have to explain."

With his bodyguards at his side, he took her downstairs and gave instructions to his driver. When she was inside the car, Triage leaned through the open window.

"Thank you for inviting me, Triage. I really did have a wonderful time."

"Thank you for coming. I hope I didn't forget to mention that you looked beautiful tonight." He reached into the car and took her hand. "I have to go out of town for a few days."

"Oh." Deborah felt her heart skip a beat.

"I should be back Monday or Tuesday. I'll call you then." Suddenly, he leaned forward and gently brushed his lips against hers. She held her breath, taking in the gentle kiss until, long seconds later, he pulled away.

"Now why couldn't a photographer be here to get a picture of *that*?" He smiled. Then he turned and walked away.

As the car pulled away from the curb, Deborah lifted her hands to her mouth where the kiss lingered. "Don't let this get out of hand," she whispered. "Triage is only a good friend."

❧

Vianca attacked Deborah the moment she walked into the studio.

"I want every detail, girlfriend."

"There's no time for chat." Tisha clapped her hands. "It's already noon, and we have a lot of work to do. Remember, on Monday our time will be cut in half when you start vocal rehearsals with Lavelle."

"You remembered that I was coming in late this morning, right?" Deborah asked.

"Yeah, but you're here now, so let's get to work."

It wasn't until four that Vianca and Deborah had a chance to talk.

"Are you going to the gym?" Vianca asked. "We can talk in the car."

"I'm too tired." Deborah yawned. "I'm going to get up early and go in the morning."

"How late did you get in?"

Deborah shook her head. "Not late at all. I left early." She held up her hands. "Long story."

As they walked to the car, Deborah told Vianca about the

evening. "It wasn't all that exciting, you know. I didn't get to really talk or meet anyone new, and it turned out to be all business for Triage."

"But girl, I know he loved your dress."

Deborah lifted her fingers to her lips. "He said I looked nice."

"Nice? You looked better than nice, so either he's a blind man or you're not telling me the whole story."

Deborah got into her car. "Go to the gym, Vianca. I'll see you tomorrow."

She smiled as she pulled away and looked into her rearview mirror. Vianca was still standing in the parking lot, shaking her head, with her hands on her hips.

The phone was ringing when she put her key in the door. "Wait," Deborah yelled and ran to the phone without closing the front door.

"Deborah Anne?"

"Hi, Mama." She smiled. "I was just getting in."

"We didn't really expect to find you home. We were just hoping. Hold on a second."

Deborah heard her mother call to her father to get on the extension, and her smile widened when her father's voice boomed through the phone. Even though she had spoken to them a few days before, her body warmed to the sound of their voices.

"We couldn't wait to find out about the premiere. How was it?"

Deborah smiled. "Oh, Daddy, it was so glamorous. All the celebrities and the cameras and the red carpet—"

"Oh!" Virginia exclaimed. "Did you get to meet anyone?"

"Not really, though we sat next to Nia Long. She's in the movie too."

Deborah could hear her mother's excitement. "So, tell me what you wore."

The ends of her smile turned down just a bit. "It was . . . nice. But, I can't wait for you and Daddy to see the movie. You'll really enjoy this one."

"Didn't you tell us that there was a party afterwards?"

Deborah sighed. "Yes, but I didn't stay long. You know, I had to be at work this morning—"

"Well, baby, I hope you had a nice time," Virginia said.

"Oh yes, Mama."

They chatted for a few minutes more before Deborah was able to escape from their questions.

"Call us on Sunday and let us know about church," Elijah said before they hung up.

She sighed. "Talk about Hollywood meeting Villa Rica."

She leaned back, put her feet on the table, and turned on the television. She surfed the channels, finally deciding to watch the news.

When the phone rang again, she didn't answer, knowing it was Vianca. Her friend would just have to wait to hear any more details.

CHAPTER 18

THE MORNING LIGHT WAS SHINING THROUGH THE studio window as Deborah paced the floor with the sheet music in her hand.

"You're here early."

She looked up and smiled at Emerald. Today her braids hung past her shoulders, and Deborah admired the teal kimono-style, knee-length top that she wore over teal leggings.

"Hi. I'm just trying to get a little extra practice in."

"You're going to be fine. You've done well so far." Emerald dropped her leather backpack on the floor.

Deborah slumped into one of the chairs. "I'm nervous about working with Lavelle today."

Emerald shook her head as she walked over to Deborah's chair. She sat on the side and put her arm around Deborah's shoulders. "He needs us, darling. Lavelle is nothing without his backup."

Deborah nodded, lowered her head, and covered her nose with her hand. What was that smell? she wondered.

"Good morning, y'all!" Vianca strolled into the studio, two steps in front of Lavelle.

Emerald rolled her eyes, picked up her purse, and rushed into the bathroom.

"Are you ready for this session?" Vianca said, as she sat next to Deborah.

Deborah nodded, then looked up at Lavelle, who had stopped by them. Silently, he handed Vianca her bag and smiled at Deborah. She could count the number of words he had uttered to her since she'd been here.

Lavelle strolled to the breakfast table and sat with the musicians and Brent Holman, the show's director.

"I'm a little nervous," Deborah confided to Vianca. "I've studied the words over and over."

Vianca laughed. "I was like that last year. But think about it, Deborah, the words to the songs are imbedded in your brain permanently. We've been dancing to them for weeks. You probably knew them all before you got here anyway."

Emerald joined them, and Deborah waited for Emerald and Vianca to exchange greetings, but neither said a word to the other. This wasn't the first time that Deborah noticed that they barely spoke.

"Anyway, Deborah," Vianca continued, "I know you'll be just fine. You can sing your butt off, girl."

"That's what I was just telling her," Emerald joined in.

"I'm not concerned about my singing." She paused. "I don't think Lavelle likes me much. He hasn't said much to me since I got to Los Angeles."

"Just give him a minute," Emerald grunted. "Soon, he'll be all over your bones."

Vianca rolled her eyes but spoke to Deborah. "Lavelle likes you. He's just like that. He has to get to know you—"

"And she means in the biblical sense." Emerald smirked.

Again, Vianca spoke pointedly to Deborah, ignoring Emerald. "After today, you'll see. Lavelle's cool people."

Emerald stood. "And Vianca should know." She strolled away from where they sat, leaving Deborah with her mouth dropped open.

"What was that about?"

Vianca sucked her teeth. "Girl, don't pay any attention to Emerald. She's jealous and she's *always* negative."

Deborah shook her head. "I don't think that's it." She stared at Emerald, standing at the window sipping her coffee.

"Okay, everyone," Brent yelled out. "Let's get started."

Deborah stood. She tugged at the short knit skirt she wore under a sleeveless tunic and took a deep breath.

"You look great, by the way." Vianca smiled. "I see you're finally getting some taste in clothes."

Deborah looked down. Suddenly her skirt seemed shorter.

Brent lined them up the way they would be standing onstage. "Okay, let's start with 'Love's Game.' No steps; only sound today."

When Brent signaled to Tyrone to put on the track, Deborah inhaled, hoping to still the tremors that had begun at the bottoms of her feet and filled her now.

"No matter what, let's go all the way through," Brent said. "Lavelle and I want to feel the general sound."

Music filled the room, and the moment Deborah opened

her mouth her tremors were replaced with the knowledge that she was where she belonged.

They sang for over two minutes, blending as if they'd sung together forever. Deborah closed her eyes and swayed. The beat burrowed itself inside her, and when the last note was released, it took her a few moments to open her eyes.

The room was silent until Lavelle said, "I guess we have a lot of work to do." He shook his head. "That sounded awful!"

Deborah wondered what he'd been listening to, but when she glanced at the other faces, everyone was nodding.

"Brent, have the guys check Deborah's mike. I can't hear her. And do something about Emerald's too. She's all in my ears."

Deborah glanced at Emerald. She had crossed her arms in front of her and was glaring at Lavelle.

"What about me, Lavelle?" Vianca asked. "How do I sound?"

He waved his hands. "You're fine." Turning to Brent, he said, "I want to do this again until it sounds right. I don't care how many times. We only have six weeks and all these songs." He flipped through the papers on top of the piano. "We don't have time for mistakes."

As Lavelle's voice got louder, Deborah's muscles tightened.

"Deborah, I need more sound from you," Brent directed.

She nodded.

"Okay, gang," Brent said. "Let's try this again."

They sang for almost three hours, stopping and starting at different points, until Lavelle, without saying anything, left the room.

"Ladies, take a break, but don't go too far." Brent sighed.

Emerald rushed into the hallway and Vianca wandered over to the coffee table. Deborah followed her.

"Is there something wrong or something I should know about?"

Vianca stirred her coffee and frowned at Deborah as if she didn't know what she was talking about.

"Lavelle seems mad about something."

"Oh, that. He's always like that. I told you he's a perfectionist. We're fine, but he wants each note flawless. In a day or two, he'll be laughing with us."

Deborah dropped a tea bag in a cup and casually asked, "What's going on with Emerald?"

At that moment, the door opened and Emerald came back into the room. The smile that Deborah was used to seeing on Emerald had returned, and her eyes had brightened.

"Well, I'm ready to get back to work." Emerald smiled.

"Oh, brother." Vianca sighed under her breath.

"Ladies, can you get to your mikes?" Brent asked. "I want to check them before Lavelle gets back."

For a few minutes, each one sang, and once Lavelle returned, they sang "Love's Game" a few times before Lavelle called a fifteen-minute lunch break.

Afterward, they sang until Emerald and Vianca complained of strained vocal cords. Deborah held her hand to her throat, grateful the others had spoken the words she would never say.

"Okay, let's wrap it tonight. You have tomorrow's schedule?" Brent continued to talk, but all eyes followed Lavelle as he stomped from the room.

Vianca and Deborah barely spoke as they strolled into the parking lot. It wasn't until Deborah was in her car that she realized Vianca hadn't even asked if she wanted to go to the gym or shopping or any of the things she was always suggesting they do together.

As soon as she got home, Deborah swallowed two teaspoons of honey and brewed a cup of lemon tea. She lay on the couch and sighed. Her apartment began to darken as the sun set. Deborah allowed the day to play through her mind. First Emerald's strange behavior, then Lavelle. This was very different from what she'd imagined.

One thing was for sure—what people saw onstage had very little to do with what happened behind the scenes. Deborah sighed. Whatever was going on with them, she knew she could never become a part of it.

She put her teacup on the coffee table and reached for the Bible. Not sure of what she wanted to study, she just opened the book, and it fell to a scripture that she'd been studying for a week now: "No man can serve two masters: for either he will hate one, and love the other . . . ye cannot serve God and mammon."

She closed the book. There was nothing else she needed to read. That scripture alone would keep her focus on God and away from the mess that seemed to be going on around her.

CHAPTER 19

IN THE WEEKS THAT FOLLOWED, REHEARSALS MOVED from five days a week to six. The long hours they'd been working became longer. Between dance and singing sessions, daily fittings, and appointments with stylists, Deborah had little time for anything besides workouts and church. Even homesickness didn't seem to find room in her life, and she felt a longing for Villa Rica only during short conversations with her parents or Willetta.

Although many nights Deborah went home with a sore throat or aching feet, she loved her life. Just as Vianca predicted, Lavelle was much more personable as the days went on. He even took the time to chat with her during lunch breaks, and the band was treating her like a longtime member. Her only concern was Emerald, whose mood swings increased along with their rehearsal time.

She'd been in Los Angeles for two months, and she hadn't had time to make friends outside the group. Deborah didn't miss that as much as she thought she would—she spent much of her free time with Triage.

They'd never discussed that kiss. When he returned from his trip, they returned to their brother-and-sister roles. From attending church to sharing casual lunches to taking strolls on the beach, they spent much of their free time together. But it was clear to Deborah that she had read more into the kiss than was there. And as the day came closer for her to leave on tour, she was able to push her feelings into a far corner of her mind.

Triage came over to help Deborah the night before she was to leave on tour. As she sorted through the last of her mail, Triage struggled with a large suitcase, finally dropping it at the front door. "Are you sure you have everything you need?" he asked breathlessly.

Deborah was turned away from him, checking the carry-on bag still open on the couch. "Uh-huh; why?"

"'Cause I don't think this is heavy enough."

She began to laugh before she even turned around. "Sorry. Do you think I overpacked?"

"No," he said, holding his chest as if his heart were hurting. He slumped into the chair. "I'm not dead yet."

She tossed a pillow at him.

"Do you want any more of this pizza?" Deborah lifted the large box that held one lone slice.

"Nah," he responded, clicking on the television.

Deborah glanced at him, slouched in the chair. "So it's my last night in Los Angeles with you, and all you're entertaining me with is pizza and *Jeopardy*?"

He clicked off the television and frowned seriously. "I'm

sorry. I didn't think you'd want to do anything since your plane leaves so early."

She burst into laughter at the sight of his drawn face. "I'm teasing."

"We can still do something. You wanna go to the movies?"

"No, I really don't want to do anything. I'm too nervous." She sat on the couch and held her head in her hands.

Triage grinned. "You've been waiting for this grand tour!" He moved the suitcase next to her onto the floor and sat down.

"I know," she moaned. "But I have more butterflies now than I had the day I auditioned. Suppose I forget the words to a song? What if I trip onstage and my gown falls off?"

He laughed. "Now, *that* would be funny."

She lifted her head. "It might not be so funny. I might get a standing ovation."

His smile disappeared. "I know I'd clap," he said seriously.

She turned away. "You know, I got you a going-away gift." She took a wrapped box off the corner table.

"I thought you were the one going away, so I brought you something." Triage reached into the gym bag he'd brought with him.

"I guess this is why we're friends." Deborah laughed.

"Open yours first."

She slowly unfolded the pink paper and gasped. She lifted a brown leather book from the box. It had been engraved in gold: "Deborah Anne Peterson, First Tour." She covered her mouth with her fingers. "Triage, this is beautiful."

He took her hand. "Deborah, I know how long you've been looking forward to this, and I want you to remember every moment." Gently, he took the book from her, and flipped through the gilded pages. "What I like best about this book is that not only does it have plenty of room to write, but back here"—he stopped and showed her the pages—"are places for photos. Make sure you take lots of pictures."

She was still shaking her head when he gave her back the book. "I don't know what to say—"

"Thank you will be fine."

She smiled and hugged him. "This is incredible. I'll try to write in it every day. And when I get back, I'll read it all to you," she kidded.

"I don't know if I'm going to want to hear all about your antics on the road. It can get pretty wild out there."

"Well, you should know me by now." She pointed to the box in his lap. "It's your turn. I wanted you to have something to remember me by."

A few moments later, Triage was turning the Bible over in his hand. "You know, the last real Bible I had like this, Grandma gave to me. I don't even know where it is now—probably home with my parents in Chicago." He smiled at her. "So you got tired of me looking over your shoulder, huh?"

"No, I just wanted to make sure that you would keep going to church, even without me."

He laughed. "I'm going to try. Thanks, Deborah. This means a lot." He browsed through the pages. "Hey, what happened to all those different-color markings and notes that are in your Bible?" He laughed.

"You're going to have to make your own. And that means you're going to have to study."

He faked a loud sigh. "Okay." Then he became serious. "I would like to study more. You know, Deborah, hanging with you has taught me a lot more about God, or at least is bringing me back to where I used to be." He glanced at her. "Do you really read your Bible every day?"

She shook her head. "I don't always make the time the way I should. I wish I did, though, because whenever I spend time with God, I feel better. Like there's nothing that can happen to me that I can't handle."

He nodded. "That's the kind of relationship I'd like to have, and going to church with you has helped a lot." He turned the Bible over in his hand. "And this will help. Should I just start at the beginning?" He opened to the first book. "Just begin with Genesis?"

She shrugged. "There are lots of ways to read the Bible; you don't have to read it through like a book." She took the Bible from him and turned to the New Testament. "When I was a teenager, I asked my father where should I start, and he suggested the book of John. He told me that book would give me a good overview of Jesus and His life. It was true. It was so easy to understand, it made me want to read everything."

"Then that's where I'll start."

Deborah smiled. "I'll read it too, and if you have any questions, I'll try to help." She laughed.

"I thought you already read it."

"That doesn't mean anything. Every time I read the Bible, I see it a new way."

He shook his head. "One day . . ." When he looked at his watch, his smile disappeared. "You have to get up early. I'd better get out of here." She followed him to the door.

"I'm going to miss you, kiddo," he said, pulling her ponytail.

"Sure, for a day or two. And then you'll go running back

to all those women you were hanging out with before I got here."

His eyes darkened, and he lifted her chin with his finger. "I don't think so." He kissed her on the cheek. "Have a great trip."

She hugged him.

"The next time I see you, your name will be up in lights." He tapped her nose with his finger, then walked away.

She watched Triage bound down the stairs, then closed the door when she could no longer see him. Triage had been such a great friend, she thought, but if that's all he was, why did her heart ache so?

CHAPTER 20

D EBORAH'S EYES WERE GLUED TO THE WINDOW, and had been that way ever since the Town Car had crossed through the Midtown Tunnel. She'd never seen anything like New York City. The tall gray buildings were squeezed together like Leggos. But the people really amazed her. Deborah had never seen so many in one place before.

As their car crept down Madison Avenue, Vianca exclaimed, "I love New York! I hope we have time for sightseeing tomorrow, after rehearsal."

"Me too," Deborah said, her voice full of excitement. "I'd love to take some pictures of the Statue of Liberty and the Empire State Building and the World Trade Center—"

"Are you kidding?" Emerald's voice was sharp. "You're not going to have time for that. Even if you did, the best thing for you to do is use it for rest. If you think rehearsals make you tired, wait until you find out how performing on the road makes you feel!"

"Oh, Emerald, don't try to scare her. It's not that bad."

"Well, maybe not for you since *you* get *special* treatment." Emerald leaned across Vianca, who was sitting between them. "Listen to me. I've been at this longer than Miss Know-It-All here. There are going to be days when you wish you'd never heard the word 'concert.'"

Deborah couldn't imagine ever feeling that way, but she was relieved when the car stopped and the conversation ended. She jumped from the car and let her eyes rise up the front of the building, which never seemed to stop.

She couldn't hide her awe as she followed Emerald and Vianca into the elegant lobby. She'd been impressed with the Beverly Hotel, but the Madison Palms made it look like a Ramada Inn. The enormous foyer was decorated with richly veined marble floors, glittering crystal chandeliers, and ornate gilt-framed mirrors. After checking in, they took the elevator to the thirty-second floor. Their rooms were side by side, and Deborah couldn't wait to get inside.

"Ladies," Emerald said, "we have to be back in the lobby in forty minutes."

"We know," Vianca snapped, then disappeared into her room.

Deborah quickly stepped into her room before Emerald could say anything. But her thoughts of being between Vianca and Emerald faded quickly as she took in the opulence around her. The chamber was bigger than her apartment. A beautifully made-up king-size bed sat in the middle of the far wall, and to its right, a large sitting area with a couch and two chairs was placed to take advantage of the view through the picture window.

She was admiring the antique desk and matching chair

when there was a knock on the door. Only then did she remember her luggage. She rushed to her purse, then tipped the bellboy as he laid her bags on the luggage rack.

The moment the man left, she changed into jeans and a tank top. She wanted to call her parents, but there wasn't time. In a few minutes, she had to be in the lobby, where they would meet the vans that would take them to Madison Square Garden.

She picked up her purse, tied a sweater around her waist, and pulled her new journal from her carry-on bag, then ran out the door.

❧

The crew was unloading instruments from the tour bus, which had just arrived in New York. Charles screamed out instructions while Brent talked with Madison Square Garden officials. It sounded like controlled chaos. But Deborah hardly noticed.

She slowly moved across the edge of the stage, looking out into the massive darkness of the Garden. The seats were empty, but it didn't take much for her to imagine the auditorium filled with cheering fans, waiting to hear her sing. What a debut!

"This is pretty awesome, huh?" Vianca asked, sitting down and letting her legs swing over the edge of the stage.

Deborah joined her. "In all my dreams, I couldn't have imagined this. I wish they would turn on the lights, so that I can see the entire place."

"No need for that. You won't be able to see anything once we're doing the show."

"Really?"

Vianca shook her head. "Except for maybe a few people in the first few rows, it'll look just like it looks now. It makes it easier for me to perform."

Deborah shook her head. She wasn't sure. What she loved about singing was the pleasure it brought people—the look of joy on their faces.

She opened her mouth to question Vianca more about that when she noticed her friend's frown. Deborah looked in the direction of Vianca's gaze.

A slender woman with long reddish-brown hair past her shoulders was leaning against the wall, and Lavelle stood close to her. "Who's that woman with Lavelle?" Deborah asked.

Vianca waved her hand in dismissal. "That's Phoebe Garland."

Deborah turned toward the stylish woman. She was wearing what looked to be an expensive sweater set over a short python-print leather skirt and matching narrow-heeled pumps. "That's Phoebe?"

Vianca stood and put her hands on her hips. "Yeah, she used to sing backup for Lavelle before she went solo, you know."

"I know that."

"Well, you should also know that *I* replaced her."

Deborah didn't seem to notice Vianca's tone. "She's really attractive—"

"In an obvious sort of way," Vianca snapped.

Emerald sauntered across the stage toward them. "Vianca,

did you see Phoebe? You know, Deborah, Phoebe's joining us on the tour as an opening act," she said sweetly.

Vianca rolled her eyes and stomped away.

"What's going on?" Deborah asked.

Emerald took a sip of the Coke in her hand, smiled, then walked away.

Deborah watched Emerald brush past Lavelle and Phoebe, touching them just slightly.

Vianca stood on the other side of the stage with her arms folded in front of her, tapping her foot.

Deborah shook her head. The show hadn't even started, and the stage was already full of drama. Deborah raised her eyes and looked back into the dark arena, returning to her fantasy. It was much safer there.

CHAPTER 21

D EBORAH CLOSED HER EYES TIGHTLY AS KIM
sprayed the last of the oil sheen over her hair.
"That's it!" Kim said, waving her hands in an
attempt to clear the air of lingering hairspray.

When Deborah opened her eyes, she had to hold back her
gasp. It was hard to believe that it was her own face staring
back.

She stood and looked at her dress in the full-length mirror. The sleeveless, purple silk sheath stopped right above her
knees. It was trimmed with long fringes that fell to the floor.

"You look great, girl," Vianca said.

Deborah turned around and smiled. Vianca was in a two-
piece with a bare midriff. The skirt was trimmed in fringe,
as was the top, but it left her midriff bare.

"So do you."

Tracy, the stylist, held Deborah's three-inch slingback
pumps in her hand. "You can't wait any longer. Let's get these
on." She helped Deborah slide into the purple pumps.

Emerald opened the door to their dressing room and looked them up and down. A slight smile crossed her face. "You girls do clean up nice."

Emerald's micro-braids had been pulled back into a waterfall of curls that sat on top of her head. Her halter dress was edged in fringe like the others.

Brent knocked on the open door. "You ladies ready?"

They nodded and followed him into the hall. Several of the crew members whistled as they passed.

The closer they got to the stage, the faster Deborah's heart raced, and she whispered a prayer. "Thank You, Father, for this abundant blessing. Help me, Lord, to use this gift tonight, in the way You intended—"

"Okay, ladies," Brent said. "Take your places, and have a great show."

The loud murmur of the crowd filled Deborah's ears as she took her place on the stage, at the bottom of the gold-painted stairway. Closing her eyes, she replayed the moves in her mind.

"One minute," Brent yelled from the side.

With her eyes still closed, she went through the order of the songs.

"Ten seconds, nine, eight . . ."

She opened her eyes and took a deep breath.

"Here we go."

As the curtain began to open, the crowd roared, and Deborah pasted a smile on her face. Her body tingled when she raised her hand, stretching it toward the sky. When the music started, smoke filtered through the air, swirling in small circles around the stage. The smoke began to clear, and the audience applauded in frenzy as Lavelle suddenly appeared at the top of the staircase.

He was dressed in a gold sequin-studded jacket and black tuxedo pants. He glided down the stairs singing "Born for You." As they had practiced for more than sixty days, when Lavelle got to the bottom, Deborah, Vianca, and Emerald sang the chorus. Swaying, they joined him at the center of the stage and began their second song.

Deborah looked into the audience for a moment, but it was a sea of black. The heat of the lights warmed the stage quickly, making Deborah drip with sweat. She was relieved when Lavelle paused to talk to the crowd between the fifth and sixth songs.

The screams were deafening, and several times Lavelle had to stop so that he could be heard. After a few minutes, Lavelle walked off the stage, leaving Deborah, Vianca, and Emerald to sing the one song they performed alone.

Deborah had been excited when she found out she'd be singing without Lavelle. It wasn't exactly a solo, but it wasn't backup either. Now she realized the reason. It gave Lavelle a break—while they continued working.

By the time Lavelle returned to the stage and introduced his singers, Deborah was beginning the countdown to the final song. It was only the continuous surge of adrenaline that moved her through to their final bows.

Backstage, they kissed and hugged, but Deborah's feet screamed for relief. She dragged herself to the dressing room she shared with Vianca.

"So how did you like your first show?" Kim asked as she helped Deborah out of her dress.

"It was awesome," Deborah panted. "But I didn't expect to be this tired."

"What did you think?" Vianca asked. "We were singing and dancing for two hours."

Suddenly, the door swung open as they heard a quick knock. "Ladies, are you decent?" Lavelle asked, stepping into the room. Deborah glanced at Vianca, who stood only in her underwear as Lavelle closed the door behind him.

"I just wanted to give my compliments on a great first show, and to tell you, if you didn't already know, it was a sold-out performance."

Vianca, still standing almost naked, clapped her hands. "Congratulations to us."

He smiled. "I'd like to take everyone out for a celebratory dinner and drinks. You up to it?"

Vianca beamed. "You know I am."

Deborah looked at her watch. "It's almost midnight."

Both Lavelle and Vianca looked at her with "So what?" on their faces.

She shrugged. "Okay."

"We'll meet you guys by the door in the back. The same way we came in," Lavelle said as he left the room.

After Kim left, Deborah glanced at Vianca as she zipped on her jeans. "I really didn't plan on doing anything tonight. It's late, and I'm kind of tired."

"Welcome to life on the road."

Deborah looked at her watch again. "It'll be after two by the time we get to our rooms."

"That's about right." Vianca was staring at herself in the mirror, running her hands through her short curls.

"What about rehearsal tomorrow?"

Finally, Vianca turned toward Deborah. "Look, girl, if you don't want to go, don't go. But what's the big deal? This is how we do things. We work late, we eat late, we go to bed late, and we wake up late to start the whole thing over again," she snapped.

Deborah stood and snatched her bag from the floor.

"Hey, I'm sorry if I hurt your feelings, but you were going on and on about nothing—"

"I'll meet you in the back," Deborah said, and closed the door behind her.

Deborah didn't know why she was annoyed. This was her first night on the stage. She had expected to feel elated, and while she'd been excited, the exhilaration was missing.

Emerald was already standing by the door with Tyrone, Charles, and some of the band members. She smiled when Deborah walked up. "So how did you enjoy the first one?"

She returned Emerald's smile. "It was great."

"You did good, Deborah," several of the crew piped in.

Deborah kept her smile pasted in place.

Within minutes, the rest of the group had joined them and they were taken by vans to the Swan Club.

As they sat around the large table with plates of assorted appetizers spread in front of them, Deborah tried her best to enjoy the company. Everyone seemed to be boiling over with energy and excitement. Deborah pushed herself to feel the same, but all she really felt was the ache in her tired bones.

The laughter around her was boisterous, the conversation was bold, and some of the actions were shocking. Deborah dropped her eyes as Lavelle and Vianca kissed deeply, though no one else seemed to notice. She shifted in her seat as the waitresses, dressed in scanty skirts and halter tops, continued to flood the group with a variety of cocktails that they eagerly consumed, with Emerald leading the way.

As the first hour turned into the second, Deborah continued to pick at the calamari and smoked salmon, praying that the night would come to an end.

"You don't have any panties on, do you?"

Deborah's head snapped up at Lavelle's question. At first she didn't know whom he was talking to, but Vianca's giggles filled her in.

What am I doing here? Deborah screamed inside as everyone around her laughed.

"Who wears panties anymore, anyway?" Lavelle continued the game.

"Maybe we should take a survey," Tyrone jumped in.

Oh, God. Oh, God, Deborah chanted in her head. What am I going to do? How can I get out of here? She knew she should just get up and leave, but instead she sat, wanting to fit in.

"You guys are out of control." Charles chuckled. "I'm going to head out of here."

"Party pooper."

"I'll go with you, Charles," Deborah said quickly.

He nodded as he stood, and took her hand, helping Deborah step over a chair that blocked her way.

"Hey, Charles," Lavelle called out. "Maybe you can hit that tonight."

The laughter followed them to the front door, but neither Charles nor Deborah turned around.

"Sorry about that," Charles said, as he helped Deborah into a cab.

She waved her hand in the air. "I know it's just fun." She tried to smile, but inside, her screams had not subsided.

They rode to the hotel in silence, and Charles escorted Deborah to her room. She held her breath; with what she'd seen tonight, she didn't know what to expect. But she gratefully exhaled when Charles said good night at her door.

Even though it was almost two and she was bone tired, she paced the floor. "This is just how it is," she said aloud. "This is just how they do things in this business. You cannot be such a prude. There's no room for a goody-goody in this place," she continued to lecture herself. This was another moment she'd always tried to imagine in her dreams: her first night after her first show. The reality was far from her fantasy. Exhaustion didn't allow her to think any more about it, though. She undressed and crawled into bed. It took only moments for her body to reward her with the relief of a sound sleep, but not before one last thought: "Welcome to the road, Deborah. Welcome to your dreams."

CHAPTER 22

DEBORAH SLEPT LATE AND WAS AWAKENED BY A call from her parents, anxious to hear the details of the first show. She filled her story with the good parts and left out most of the disturbing details.

Deborah crawled through rehearsal, then returned to her room to rest before leaving for the Garden.

By showtime she had blocked out most of the previous day, and her euphoria returned. She moved with the smoothness of an expert, but once she left the stage, exhaustion returned with a vengeance, and she chose to return to her room instead of repeating the previous night's escapades.

"I'm just too tired, and if I start off this way, I'm afraid it's going to get worse," Deborah explained to Vianca.

Vianca was sitting in front of her mirror, fluffing her hair. She pulled up her tube top and stood. "Do whatever you want, Deborah. You don't have to explain anything to me. But I'm going to hang out with Lavelle."

As she rode in a cab to the hotel, Deborah wondered if she'd made the right decision. She knew it was important to be part of the group. But last night had made her so uncomfortable—she knew that with rest she'd be able to handle it all better.

By the time Deborah was covered with bubbles as she soaked in the full-sized tub, she thought she'd made the right decision. Thirty minutes later, when she was lying on the chaise with her Bible in her hand, she knew she'd been right.

When the phone rang at midnight, Deborah frowned. She hoped it wasn't Vianca, demanding that she join them. But her doubts shifted to smiles when she answered the phone.

"Triage!"

"How's it going, Miss Superstar?"

She laughed. "Is that what I am?"

"From what I heard—"

She lay on the bed. "Who told you that?"

"Girl, you know I have my sources. How're things going? What are you doing in your room?"

"Things are going great, and I'm in my room because you never told me how tired I'd be."

"I thought you guys would be hanging out."

"They are. I'm the only one who returned to the hotel. But before you say anything, I know I should hang out and get to know everyone, and I will—in time. So how is Los Angeles without me?"

"Not the same. I miss my best friend, but I've been busy. I'm leaving tomorrow for a promotional tour for the movie, but I'll be back in a week to begin recording again."

"You're making me tired all over again."

They laughed.

"Have you had a chance to write in your journal?"

She brushed her fingers against the leather book that she had sitting on the nightstand. "No. I've wanted to, but haven't had time. But I'll write something before I go to bed. Have you read your Bible?"

"Okay, you got me. But I promise that the next time I call, we'll be able to chat about that guy John." He laughed. "Well, I just wanted to check on you, Deborah. I'll call you again when I get back to LA."

It took a few minutes for them to say their final good-byes, and by the time she hung up the phone, it was almost one.

She sighed. So much for getting to bed early. But it was still earlier than it would have been if she'd gone out. She pulled back the covers and slid between the smooth sheets. Before she turned out the light, she picked up her journal, dated the first page, and made her first entry: "In New York . . . Triage called." Then she closed the book and went to sleep.

CHAPTER 23

FROM NEW YORK THEY TRAVELED TO ATLANTIC City, Philadelphia, and then Richmond. Deborah's system had adjusted to the performer's schedule, but it was the road antics that she could not get used to.

In Atlantic City, they'd gone to the Trump Hotel, after their performance, for "dinner." Deborah watched the drama unfold while sitting at the long table with eleven others.

"Where's Lavelle?" Vianca said suddenly.

"He went to get something from the bar," Tyrone responded, then asked, "Does anyone want to go gambling with me?" He nudged Deborah. "Come on, Deborah."

"I don't gamble."

"That's why you should come with me. You'll be my good luck charm." He put his arm around her shoulders, and though Deborah felt uncomfortable, she only smiled.

"I don't see Phoebe, either." Vianca's eyes had narrowed as she looked around the large room.

Deborah saw Emerald exchange an amused glance with Tyrone.

"I'm going to look for him," Vianca said.

When Vianca stood, Deborah followed her, as much to get away from Tyrone as anything. "I'll go with you," she called after her friend. When they were away from the table, she asked, "What do you need Lavelle for?"

Vianca looked up at her. "I *need* him to be with *me*."

Deborah wanted to tell Vianca to be careful, but before she could say anything, they saw Lavelle with Phoebe, pushed against the wall next to an elevator.

"Oh, no," Vianca said, pulling off her earrings. "She's about to go down!"

Deborah pulled her back. "Vianca, come on. You can't handle it this way."

Tears filled her eyes. "Lavelle said that he loved me. That is was different with me than the others."

Deborah put her arm around Vianca's shoulders and led her in the other direction.

"Things would be better if Phoebe didn't have to be here. She's a slut!"

Deborah nodded, not knowing what to say.

"She doesn't care about Lavelle; tomorrow she'll be with someone else."

It took Deborah thirty minutes to convince Vianca to return to the hotel. Once there, Deborah sat in Vianca's room listening to her talk about Lavelle until her friend fell asleep. Only then did Deborah drag herself to her own room, where she slept until almost noon.

The next night, just as Vianca had predicted, Phoebe was

wrapped around the drummer while Lavelle was kissing a smiling Vianca.

In Philadelphia, Deborah declined Vianca's request to spend the few free hours they had before the first show touring the city. Deborah hoped for some time alone and went to the hotel's restaurant, seeking refuge from the theatrics that followed the others.

But as soon as she entered the hotel's restaurant, she saw Emerald sitting at one of the front tables, studying the menu. Deborah hesitated, then turned away. But before she had taken two steps, Emerald called her name.

Deborah smiled as she approached the table. "Hi. I didn't see you."

"Sure." Emerald smirked and motioned for Deborah to sit down.

"I don't want to disturb you—"

"No, I could use the company, honey."

Deborah nodded and took a menu from the waitress. She'd never spent any time alone with Emerald and didn't feel particularly comfortable now. So much for her peace.

"I'll just have a Caesar salad," Emerald said.

Deborah nodded. "I'll have the same, with a grilled turkey breast."

"Would you like anything to drink?" the waitress asked Deborah.

She glanced at the teacup that Emerald had. "I'll just have some tea."

"Are you enjoying yourself?" Emerald asked.

Deborah nodded stiffly. "It's not what I expected, though."

"Tell me about it. I've been doing this for three years, and I'm still surprised at some of the stuff that goes on."

Deborah was grateful for the waitress's interruption, and she stirred Sweet 'n Low into her tea, trying to stall.

She took a sip. "So how long have you been singing with Lavelle?" She couldn't think of anything else to say.

"I just told you—three years."

"Oh, I didn't know if you'd toured with anyone else."

Emerald shook her head and sipped her tea. As she put down the cup, she said, "Lavelle Roberts is the only man for me." She pushed her chair back from the table. "Excuse me." She picked up her purse. "I'm going to the rest room." She stumbled slightly and grasped the side of the table.

"Are you all right?" Deborah asked.

She nodded. "Yeah, my heel just got caught in the carpet."

Deborah's shoulders slumped as Emerald walked away from the table. She had tried to befriend the woman several times but had always been pushed away. Now, three months into their relationship, Deborah still couldn't have a regular conversation with her.

"Here're your salads."

Deborah helped the young woman rearrange the small table so she could set the plates down. She waited for a few minutes, but when Emerald didn't return, Deborah bowed her head and blessed the food. She took a bite of the salad and looked toward the rest room. Maybe she should make sure that Emerald was all right.

She picked up her cup of tea, sipped, and almost spat out the drink. Her eyes narrowed in confusion. Just as she raised her hand to tell the waitress that something was wrong with the tea, Emerald stumbled back to the table.

Deborah stared at the woman she worked with, and when Emerald felt her eyes, she shrugged her shoulders. "What?"

"Are you all right? You were in the bathroom for a long time."

Emerald waved her hand in the air. "I'm fine. I needed to redo my makeup and take care of a few other things."

Deborah reached across the table and laid her hand on top of Emerald's. "If there is anything I can do for you, Emerald, please just let me know," she said softly.

Emerald gently pulled her hand away and grimaced. "I don't know what you're talking about."

Deborah pointed to the cup. "I took a sip of your tea by accident, and . . ."

It took Emerald a moment to understand. "Oh, don't go making any assumptions about that. I just need something to help me relax before the show. That's why I mix it with tea, so it won't be so strong."

Deborah nodded as if she understood, but she didn't believe a word of it. She'd smelled liquor on Emerald's breath too many times.

"I'm not an alcoholic or anything," Emerald continued.

"Emerald, if you ever need anyone to talk to, or"—Deborah paused—"to pray with, I'm here."

Emerald chuckled. "That's right, you're the little church girl." Emerald leaned across the table, and Deborah could smell the alcohol on her breath. "What are you going to do, Deborah? Pray my demons away?"

Without hesitation, Deborah responded, "Yes."

Emerald sat back, startled, then lifted her bag. She pulled out a twenty-dollar bill and tossed it on the table. "I've lost my appetite." She stood and marched out of the restaurant.

As Deborah watched Emerald stomp away, she said a silent prayer.

This was one of their early nights. They were retiring early to their Richmond hotel room—it was only one A.M.

"Deborah, do you want any company?" Tyrone asked as he held the elevator door for her, Emerald, and Kim. Lavelle and the other men laughed.

"No thank you, Tyrone," she replied. "Good night, everyone."

She said good night to Emerald and Kim at their doors. Before Deborah got to her room, she put her ear to Vianca's door. Vianca had caught a cold in Philadelphia and had stayed in tonight, filling herself with antibiotics and other pills that worried Deborah. There weren't any sounds from Vianca's room, and she knew it was too late to call her. She'd check on her first thing in the morning.

Deborah took off her clothes and wrapped the luxurious hotel bathrobe around herself. She had just gone into the bathroom to wash her face when she heard a knock on the door.

She peeked through the door's peephole and frowned. She opened the door and stepped aside.

"Lavelle, is something wrong? Did something happen to Vianca?"

"Vianca? No." He shook his head and closed the door. "I just wanted to talk to you about something."

Without an invitation, he sat in the chair closest to the bed. Deborah tied her bathrobe tighter.

"I'm waiting," Deborah said impatiently. "Is it something about the show?"

"No, I just wanted to spend some time and get to know you better."

Deborah looked at him incredulously, and let her eyes rest on the clock. "Lavelle, maybe you didn't notice the time, but I think we can do this in the morning," she said firmly.

Lavelle leaned back in the chair as if he had no intention of leaving. Deborah took a deep breath. She had fought off suggestive remarks and come-ons throughout the tour, but no one had been so bold as to come to her room. Why didn't she see this coming? Maybe because she thought Lavelle was involved with Vianca.

She cleared her throat. "I'd really like to go to bed."

His smile widened. "Now you're talking. We can do that together." He stood and moved toward her.

Deborah backed away.

"What's wrong, baby? Is it Triage? He won't mind; we don't even have to tell him."

She held up her hands and tried to remember the words of the counselor in the self-defense class that she and Willetta had taken one weekend.

"Lavelle, I just want you to leave," she demanded, her tone leaving no doubt.

He pointed to his chest. "Me? Lavelle? You're telling me to get out of your room? Baby, do you know how many women would give anything to be in your position right now?"

She wanted to scream at him to go and find one of them, but she remembered her training—talk to him evenly, and keep the strength in her voice. She wanted to shrink in fear, but she showed her fury.

"Lavelle, you need to go with someone who wants to be with you so that you won't have any problems in the morning. Because if you stay here, there is definitely going to be a problem."

His eyes blinked rapidly. "You *really* want me to leave?"

"Yes!"

He looked as if her statement didn't register, but when he shrugged and started toward the door, Deborah sighed with relief. A moment later, he turned back to her.

"I'll give you a second to reconsider."

She pointed toward the door.

The moment he stepped into the hall, she bolted the door and leaned against it. This was too much. How could she continue with this tour when all of these things were going on around her? She sank onto the bed. She probably wouldn't have to worry about this anymore anyway. By morning, she knew, she wouldn't have a job.

CHAPTER 24

WHEN SHE FINALLY CRAWLED OUT OF BED, Deborah had only thirty minutes to get ready for rehearsal. She hadn't heard anything from Lavelle—though she didn't expect to. If she were fired, Charles would be the one to call her. Since he hadn't, she continued to get ready for the walk-through.

She thought about calling Vianca, but didn't want to answer her questions about last night. Deborah knew that once she began talking, she'd be tempted to tell Vianca everything.

When she opened her door to meet the group in the lobby, Lavelle was standing in the hall.

Deborah sighed loudly.

"May I come in . . . please?" Lavelle said softly.

"Lavelle, I don't want to go through this again. If you've come to tell me that I'm fired—"

"Fired? No way. I want to talk to you. Really." He looked around the hallway. "Please, I don't want to do this with the world watching."

Deborah hesitated, but then thought about Vianca in the next room, and she stepped back so that Lavelle could enter. She closed the door but stood right there, folding her arms in front of her.

"What is it, Lavelle?" she asked, fully expecting him to fire her.

"I came to apologize. I'm really sorry about last night. I'd been drinking, and I just expected that you . . ."

She kept her arms folded. "I'm not like that. I don't sleep around. I'm only here to do one thing, and that's to sing."

"I understand."

"I don't want to have to quit the group, Lavelle."

He held up his hands. "I don't want you to do that either. That's why I'm apologizing. I'm hoping that some way we can erase last night, and take our relationship back to where it was."

She stood still, not saying anything.

"Please?" He forced a smile. "Forgive me?"

Deborah sighed. He had said the word that she'd been taught since she was two years old: "forgive." She dropped her arms, though she didn't smile when she said, "I accept your apology."

He exhaled. "There's another favor I have to ask. Could you keep what happened between us?"

"That's no problem. It's not something I'm anxious to share."

Lavelle smiled weakly and opened the door. Just as he did, the door across the hall opened, and Emerald stepped out.

Lavelle mumbled something to Emerald that Deborah didn't understand; then he rushed away.

Emerald put her hands on her hips. "And all I did was

have a little drink." She walked away before Deborah could say anything.

Deborah closed her eyes. It was time to start counting down the days to her return home.

⁓

Everyone was in the lobby waiting for the vans. When Emerald looked at Deborah and laughed, Deborah went into the gift shop. As she wandered through the small store, she felt a hand on her shoulder.

"You're Deborah, right?"

She smiled. "Yes, and I know who you are. Nice to meet you, Phoebe." Deborah held out her hand. Outside of a few hello nods, Phoebe had never spoken to her.

"How are you enjoying the tour? Lavelle's wonderful to work with, isn't he?"

Deborah thought back to last night and forced herself to remember the way he was this morning.

"Yes, he is," Deborah said. "I'm grateful for this chance."

"From hearing you sing, I know this group is lucky to have you. You have a terrific voice."

"Thank you." Deborah smiled. "You have a great voice too. Congratulations on your solo album."

"Thanks. Look, when we get to Orlando, let's get together for lunch."

"Okay." Deborah watched Phoebe saunter out of the shop and kiss one of her band members. Phoebe's sexual escapades were the talk of the tour, but it didn't seem to bother her at all—she seemed to flaunt her frolics.

Her mother had always told Deborah that people judged you by the company you kept. Yet there was something about Phoebe that made Deborah want to know her better, some hurt or sadness deep inside that drove Phoebe. That could be the only reason a woman would behave the way Phoebe did. What Phoebe needed was a friend, someone to talk to. A friend who could pray for her and with her. That's what Deborah would be. She looked forward to Orlando.

They were given a break the first day they were in Orlando, and Deborah had lunch with Vianca. They sat next to each other on the plane, but Deborah remained silent through Vianca's chatter and gossip.

Vianca's prattle continued as they sat in the hotel's restaurant.

"He would probably sell his mother for a rock of cocaine," she muttered as one of Phoebe's band members strolled by. "And Phoebe's bad too."

Deborah wiped her mouth with her napkin. "I never heard that Phoebe was taking drugs."

Vianca smirked. "I don't know if she is or not, but she doesn't need to. She's sleeping with *everybody*." Vianca leaned across the table and whispered, "And from what I heard, she'll do anything with anybody."

Deborah shook her head. "This tour has showed me things that I never thought I'd see."

"Well, you know what they say, the freaks come out at night." Vianca chuckled. "Everyone's talking about Phoebe."

Deborah wanted to tell Vianca that everyone was talking about her and Lavelle too. But instead, she said, "I think Phoebe needs a friend. Actually"—she paused and popped a French fry into her mouth—"she asked me to have lunch with her while we're here."

Vianca raised her eyebrows. "Really? I wouldn't do that if I were you. Her reputation isn't the best."

Deborah looked directly at Vianca. "From what I've seen, no one here is a Girl Scout." She softened her tone when Vianca dropped her eyes. "Between the drugs and the sex, doesn't anyone worry about AIDS?"

Vianca shrugged. "That's what condoms are for."

"Everyone knows that condoms are not one hundred percent safe. Abstinence is the only safe method."

Vianca laughed. "Well, thank you, Mother Teresa." She took a sip of her water, and Deborah watched Vianca's eyes widen. "Deborah, don't tell me that you're still a virgin!"

Deborah lowered her eyes. "Why would you ask me that?"

"Because of what you just said. Well, girlfriend, if you are, then more power to you. But you need to grow up. As the world turns, people do drugs, people have sex and lots of it. There's nothing wrong with it as long as it's between consenting adults."

Deborah bit into her hamburger. She wasn't going to argue. It wouldn't do any good anyway. It was like the world had evolved backward, heading toward Sodom and Gomorrah, and no one seemed to care.

CHAPTER 25

T HE LIMOUSINE TRIED TO EDGE FORWARD AS
women screamed and pounded on the window.
Lavelle leaned back in his seat, eating his fifth
piece of Kentucky Fried Chicken. "This craziness
still amazes me."

Vianca gave a short laugh. "Remember the woman we almost ran over in Canada? She came close to being road pizza."

Vianca and Lavelle chuckled.

Deborah didn't find that funny, and she glanced at Emerald,
who was pouring a drink from the limousine's well-stocked
bar.

"Hand me that bottle of champagne," Lavelle said, laying
aside the box that had been on his lap. He filled two flutes
and handed one to Vianca. Then he slipped his hand into
hers.

Deborah rolled her eyes and then noticed Emerald looking straight at her, a half smile on her face.

Deborah turned away to stare out the window. She was

tired of the late nights and all the drama. This certainly wasn't the dream she had imagined.

When they got to the hotel, Deborah got out first and walked quickly to the elevator. No one seemed to notice that she ran into the hotel without saying a word. All she wanted to do was get away.

But as she opened her hotel room door, the phone was ringing.

"Hey, it's Phoebe. I saw you run upstairs by yourself, and I wanted to know if you wanted to join our group and grab something to eat."

Deborah could hear chatter and laughter in the background, but her entire body was engulfed in tides of weariness. "No thanks, I'm kind of tired."

"Suit yourself. What about lunch tomorrow? I'll meet you in the lobby around one."

"That sounds good. I'll see you then."

Deborah lay on the bed and covered her eyes with her hands. Tonight, as she watched Lavelle with Vianca, she knew she could never tell her about what had happened. Deborah knew Vianca would never believe her, or worse, that she'd accuse her of coming on to Lavelle.

No, she would stay away from that. She would just continue to pray for her friend. She sat up in bed. "Vianca, I sure hope you know what you're doing."

With heavy steps, Deborah labored into the bathroom, where she stared at herself in the mirror. Her face was drawn, and she'd lost weight. The lines around her eyes told her that this tour was weighing heavily on her. But she promised herself that she'd find a way to make it through.

It was too late to call her parents, but not Los Angeles.

She dialed Triage's number, and it rang six times before the answering machine came on, so she hung up without leaving a message. He had his own life; he didn't need her burdens. But as she lay on the bed, she wished with all her heart that she could talk to him.

Deborah and Phoebe had taken a taxi to the Palm Court. The restaurant was elegant and expensive.

"Wow, this is quite a place."

Phoebe smiled at the maître d' and whispered to Deborah as they were led to a window table. "Don't worry, I'm paying."

"That's not what I meant."

"I know, but it's good to go out with a girlfriend once in a while." Phoebe's eyes wandered around the room. "Actually, it's even less frequent than once in a while. I don't have a lot of women friends."

Deborah tilted her head. "I'm surprised. I'd think that lots of people would want to be your friend."

Phoebe smirked and replied, "Not women; they don't like me."

"You seem to have a lot of friends on the tour."

"What you see are the men. Men look at me with longing, while women look at me with loathing."

Deborah took a sip of her water and was grateful when the waiter brought the menus, allowing them to change the subject. Phoebe suggested the Indian salads. "And of course, two Mountain Dews."

Deborah waited until the waitress had left the table. "You must love Mountain Dew." She laughed.

"Yeah, girl, don't you?"

"It's okay. I grew up on Coke."

"But there's more caffeine in Mountain Dew."

Deborah cocked her head to the side. "Caffeine?"

"Yeah, I drink Mountain Dew to keep me up on the road. I don't like coffee, and tea's okay, but nothing can do you like Mountain Dew."

When the waitress brought their sodas, Deborah watched as Phoebe drank half the tall glass in what seemed like one swallow, then motioned for the waitress to bring her some more.

Deborah took a sip of her drink, then asked, "So how long have you known Lavelle?"

Phoebe laughed. "Almost my entire life. We played in the sandbox together in the Detroit projects."

Deborah raised her eyebrows. "I didn't know that."

She nodded. "With just a little twist of fate, Lavelle could have been singing backup for me." She laughed. "But he's good people, and I'm happy for him."

"And now it's your turn."

The waitress brought their plates, and after they were settled, Deborah bowed her head and prayed. When she looked up, Phoebe was smiling at her.

"I haven't done that in a long time."

Deborah merely smiled and laid her napkin on her lap.

"In fact, I haven't seen anyone do that in a long time. Boy, that brings back memories, though—of going to church with my grandmother."

"In Detroit?"

She nodded. "Every Sunday and many days in between. Sunday school, Bible study, prayer meetings, youth groups. Whatever was going on, Lavelle and I had to be there. His daddy was the preacher."

Deborah couldn't hide her surprise. Judging from Phoebe's description of her childhood with Lavelle, it seemed there wasn't much difference from the way she herself had grown up. But she and Lavelle both seemed so different from her now. They did things that made her blush even when she thought about them.

"Lavelle and I used to sing in the choir, and we would have those seats rocking," Phoebe continued.

Deborah laughed. "It seems we all got started that way. I sang the solo almost every week."

"Girl, you just had one solo a week? Lavelle and I sang a solo or duet on every song. People came to church just to hear the concert."

"Do you still go to church?"

Phoebe shook her head. "It's hard on the road. And when I get home, all I want to do is rest. Plus"—she paused and dropped her eyes—"the last time I went to church, one of the deacons told me that he didn't like the last video I made. He said it dishonored God." She took a sip of water. "I haven't been back since."

"Sometimes, people can be judgmental, but you shouldn't let anyone keep you from your relationship with God."

Phoebe nodded as if she agreed. "But you can't go to church on the road, either. What do you do?"

"It's hard. I try to read my Bible every day, and I pray a lot."

Phoebe looked thoughtful. "Next time you're praying, would you say a little prayer for me?"

Deborah smiled. "I'd be glad to, but maybe tomorrow morning we could have Bible study together."

Phoebe shook her head. "I don't think so; just the next time you're talking to Him, remember my name. Anyway," she said quickly, wanting to change the subject, "have you ever thought about going solo?"

The question surprised Deborah. "No. When I used to dream about singing, I saw myself as a solo singer, but I think it'll be a while before I think about that."

"Why? You're really good."

Deborah shrugged. "I don't know. I haven't thought of anything much since I began singing with Lavelle. I've just been working."

Phoebe leaned across the table. "Let me give you a little piece of advice. Always think about your career. Always be looking for the next gig."

"Really? I would think that you'd want to get settled with a group first and learn the ropes."

Phoebe shook her head emphatically. "Oh no, honey. No one is settled in this business. Everyone is looking for the next best thing. You never know what's going to happen, so you have to look out for yourself."

The look on Deborah's face told Phoebe that she was confused. "Don't worry, honey. It's always good to have someone on your side, and I'll look out for you." Deborah smiled, and Phoebe patted her hand. "You'll be all right with me."

Deborah sighed. There was so much to learn in this business.

They chatted and laughed through the rest of lunch and continued all the way back to the hotel. It was the first really enjoyable time she'd had on the road. When they returned to the hotel, Phoebe gave Deborah a hug.

"I can't remember the last time I enjoyed myself so much."

"Me too, Phoebe. I guess I'll see you in Ohio."

"Yeah, and we'll have to do this again. I have to check something with the front desk, so I'll see you later."

As Phoebe walked away, Vianca came off the elevator. Her eyes narrowed, and she stomped over to Deborah. "So I see you really are hanging out with Ms. Phoebe," she said.

"We had a nice lunch," Deborah said, walking into the gift shop.

"Well, don't say I didn't warn you." Vianca rolled her eyes as she followed Deborah into the store. "I guess now you'll be spending all your time with her."

Deborah stared at Vianca. "What's this about? I had one lunch with her, and you sound like you're jealous."

"I don't have anything to be jealous about," Vianca protested. With her lips pursed, she walked over to the magazine stand and picked up one of the tabloids. "Well, looky here."

Vianca's lips spread into a smile as Deborah looked down at the magazine in her hand. The cover of *The Grapevine* was filled with a photograph of Triage and Tia, the hottest African American model on the European runways. They were embracing in what looked like an elevator.

"So I guess your man decided to hang with Tia while you were away." Vianca smiled and glanced at Deborah.

Deborah stared at the picture, then looked up and smiled. "I keep telling you Triage and I are just friends."

"Um-hmm, then why do you have tears in your eyes?"

Deborah couldn't believe Vianca's hurtful words, and she was tempted to fight back. But instead she turned to the cashier and purchased a copy of *Essence* magazine.

"So you're not upset?" Vianca asked. When Deborah remained silent, Vianca said, "I know I would be if he were my man."

As Deborah took her magazine she said, "Vianca, instead of being all in my business, maybe you should spend more time trying to keep Lavelle in your bed instead of having him wandering the halls when you're asleep!"

Deborah stomped out of the store, but not before she saw the pain that spread over Vianca's face. She was relieved that an elevator was already waiting, and when she was inside, she pressed the Close Door button as quickly as she could. She leaned against the mirrored panel and closed her eyes. She wished she hadn't said those words. Deborah knew that Vianca had to know what was going on with Lavelle. But for her own reasons, Vianca chose to ignore it.

There was no reason for her to affront her friend that way—except for one. Vianca had gotten under her skin with that talk about Triage. She had been hurt, and she wanted to hurt back. But what Deborah couldn't figure out was why. If she and Triage were just friends, why did she react to his picture that way? And why did she feel like crying?

CHAPTER 26

DEBORAH LOOKED OUT THE WINDOW AS THE VAN turned into the circular driveway of the hotel.

"Girl, we should talk more often," she heard Vianca saying to Kim.

Deborah rolled her eyes. Vianca had avoided her during the ride over to the Mecca and throughout the rehearsal. On the way back, Vianca plopped down next to Kim before Deborah had a chance to say anything.

But as Vianca passed Deborah to get off the van, Deborah tapped her arm gently. "Vianca, can I speak to you for a moment?"

Vianca glared at her, then shrugged her shoulders. "Sure."

Deborah followed Vianca from the van, then took her hand and led her to the far side of the lobby.

"Vianca, I've been trying to talk to you since last night. I am really sorry about what I said yesterday."

Vianca stared at her with hard eyes and then broke into a smile. "Girl, I know you were kidding."

Deborah nodded. "I'm sorry if I hurt you."

Vianca's smile disappeared. "I *said* you were just kidding, right? So why are you going on about this?"

"I'm not . . . I just—"

"Don't worry about it." Vianca held up her hand. Her smile returned. "Listen, I have to talk to Kim about something. Let's get together later, okay?"

Deborah watched Vianca saunter away from her. She knew things were not okay, but there was nothing more that she could do, and she took the elevator to her room.

There were still a few hours of daylight left, and Deborah stared into the sapphire sky. The clouds that rolled past looked soft to the touch.

Deborah sighed and basked in the beauty of God's creation. With all that was going on, this scene reminded her of what was important. When she lived in Villa Rica she always took a few minutes each day to appreciate her surroundings, but she hadn't done it recently. The view outside her window inspired her, and she reached for her journal to write the words to another song.

When she finished, she stared at the words and smiled. There was nothing better than being inspired by the Lord.

CHAPTER 27

THE CITIES WERE PASSING BY, AND A FEW WEEKS later they were in Chicago. The city reminded Deborah of New York—a jungle of concrete occupied by cars and cabs.

They had arrived early, so their calendars were free until the next day. Deborah was looking forward to some time alone, and as she began to unpack the bag on her bed, she heard a knock on the door.

Her mouth dropped with surprise when she peeked through the peephole.

"Triage!"

"Hey, girl," he said, hugging her.

"What are you doing here? I thought you were wrapped up in some big project. How did you get to Chicago?"

"Whoa, girl." He closed the door behind him. "Give me a chance." His eyes roamed up and down her body. "Look at you. You looking good, girl."

She beamed. "So what *are* you doing in Chicago?"

"Well . . ." He plopped on the bed. "I had to come see my homegirl, in my hometown. My parents live here in Chicago, remember?"

"I forgot!"

"So I came to see you onstage and to take you to meet my folks. They have a big dinner planned. Tonight!"

"I can't believe this."

"So are you ready?"

Deborah glanced at her reflection in the mirror and ran her hand through her hair. "Look at me. I can't meet your parents like this."

"Deborah, you look great. It's just a backyard barbecue."

She looked in the mirror again. Her black-and-white-striped blouse and white capri pants would just have to do. "Will you at least let me freshen my makeup?"

In the bathroom, Deborah touched up her foundation, then smoothed her lips with gloss. As she puckered her lips, she smiled and then jumped when she heard the knock on the bathroom door.

"Deborah Anne! Get out of that bathroom. You have been summoned. My parents are anxious to meet you!"

The moment they drove up in front of the two-story brick house and Erlene Waters opened the door, Deborah felt at home.

"It's so good to meet you." Erlene pulled Deborah into her arms. She was a smaller, younger version of Mother Dobson.

"Milton talks about you all the time. His *homegirl*," she said, mimicking her son.

"Hey, hey, hey!" Walter Waters rushed into the hallway. "You must be Deborah Anne Peterson. You look just like your mother."

When he lifted her in a bear hug, Deborah laughed.

"Pops, put her down before you hurt her." Triage joined in the laughter.

They led her into the large living room, and Deborah took in her surroundings, surprised at how similar the room looked to her parents' house. The centerpiece in the room was a grand piano that eclipsed the other furniture.

Triage pulled Deborah onto the couch next to him, and even as they chatted with his parents, Deborah was acutely aware of his arm around her shoulders.

"How are your parents, Deborah?" Erlene smiled at her. "I haven't seen them in years."

"They're fine, ma'am. I know they're going to be excited that I had a chance to meet you."

"Are you kidding, Deborah? They already know you're here," Triage said.

Deborah frowned questioningly.

"My folks may live in the North, but the South still runs through their blood. I'm sure the moment I walked out of here to pick you up, Mama was on the phone to Grandma."

Walter's laughter filled the entire room. "Erlene, your son certainly knows his mother. Milton," he said, turning to Triage, "your mother was on the phone before you put the key in the ignition."

Erlene pouted playfully. "I'm not paying any attention to either of you. And, Deborah, don't you pay them any mind."

She stood, straightening her five-foot-two frame. "I'm going to finish dinner. Walter, you need to tend to that barbecue."

"Is there anything I can help with, Mrs. Waters?"

"Absolutely not. You're a guest, and I know how busy you are on the road." She patted Deborah's hand. "You just relax." She started toward the kitchen. "Walter, turn on the TV for the kids."

Walter chuckled, then tossed the remote toward Triage. "I think you *kids* can turn on the television for yourself."

They laughed as Walter headed to the backyard.

"Your parents are great," Deborah said, opening a photo album that sat on the coffee table.

Deborah laughed as Triage grimaced at the pictures that his parents had collected of him and his sisters over the years. When Erlene heard them laughing, she brought out stacks of other albums. They spent an hour going through the pictures until Walter called them into the backyard.

Deborah and Triage helped Erlene carry the food outside, and Deborah was pleased when Walter told them to hold hands and bow their heads, to bless the food.

As they sat down with their plates filled with barbecue chicken and ribs, Walter said, "Milton, you sure are blessed today. Your mother listened to you this time and didn't tell the whole neighborhood you were coming home." He turned to Deborah. "Usually, Erlene has everyone on this block stuffed in this house to see her baby."

Erlene pushed her chin forward. "You think I'm the only one? Deborah, when you get back to Villa Rica, I'm sure it will be the same way. We're just proud of our children."

They sat in the backyard until the warm afternoon began to fade into the cool of evening. Inside, they ate pieces of peach cobbler and coconut cake, until Deborah screamed, "No mas!"

It was almost nine when Triage announced that he had to get Deborah back to the hotel.

"Mrs. Waters, I can't tell you how much fun I've had." Deborah reached for her hands. "And thank you so much for the food. After weeks of restaurants and hotels, this was wonderful."

"We were glad to have you. You've grown up to be such a beautiful young lady." She touched Deborah's cheek.

"Now, we'll see you tomorrow," Walter said. "Thanks to Milton, we have backstage passes."

"I'm so excited. I just love Lavelle," Erlene gushed.

"Geez." Walter laughed.

"What about your own son?" Triage asked.

They were still laughing as Erlene and Walter walked Triage and Deborah to the car.

By the time Triage walked her to her room, Deborah thought that she couldn't remember when she'd had a better time.

"Thank you, Triage. I can't tell you how much today meant to me."

He took her hand and smiled. "That's what I wanted. I know how tough road life can be, so I wanted you to have a good time."

Deborah put her key in the lock, and when she turned around to say good-bye, Triage leaned forward and kissed her on the lips. A gentle kiss, just like the one they shared the night of the premiere.

He pulled away and said, "I'll see you tomorrow." He walked

away, leaving Deborah with a smile wider than the one she'd been wearing all day.

❧

The next day, Deborah waltzed through rehearsals. During the show, knowing that Triage and his parents were watching, she sang each song from the depths of her soul.

After the show, Triage met her backstage with a huge bouquet of roses. Deborah was surprised at the joy she felt at seeing him.

"Where are your parents?"

"I sent them home in the car. Mama was tired, but she said to tell you that you were wonderful. The way she was beaming, you would have thought you were her own daughter."

Deborah buried her nose in the flowers. "So how long are you going to be in Chicago?"

He looked at his watch. "Actually, I have to be at the airport in an hour."

She was glad that her back was to him, so he couldn't see the way her face dropped at this news.

"I have to get back to LA in the morning."

She forced a smile and turned to face him. "I understand."

He took a step toward her. "But we'll see each other in a few weeks, right?"

She lowered her head and nodded. Why did she feel so sad?

"You'll be finished with the first half of the tour, and I should be just about finished with what I'm working on." He lifted her chin with the tips of his fingers. "We'll get to spend some time together."

She swallowed. "I'm glad you came to Chicago. Thank you."

He kissed her again and silently walked out the door.

CHAPTER 28

FTER CHICAGO THEY PLAYED ST. LOUIS, AND
THEN they arrived in the hot, humid air of an
Atlanta August. Deborah was so excited to be
home. She'd spoken to her parents almost every
night for the last week, each time listening to her mother re-
cite the growing list of people who were coming to the show.

"I think all of Villa Rica is going to be there to support
you," Virginia had boasted.

Deborah had been excited, but now that they had checked
into the Atlanta Regency, jittery nerves began to set in. The
ringing phone didn't give her a chance to give in to them,
though.

"Hi, Deborah, it's Phoebe."

"Phoebe, I wasn't sure if you'd be back," Deborah said, re-
ferring to the fact that Phoebe had missed the St. Louis show.
"I was so sorry to hear about your grandmother."

"Thanks," Phoebe said. "I had to get out of town pretty
quickly. But I'm back now." She sighed.

"Are you up to performing tonight?" Deborah asked.

"It's the best thing for me. Anyway, I just wanted to get in touch with you. Since we'll be here for a few days, maybe we can get together."

"Sure . . ." Deborah paused at the knock on her door. "I'll see you tonight." She hung up and rushed to the door, and was surprised to see Brent.

"Deborah, Emerald's sick," he said as he stepped into her room. "You're going to have to perform the duet with Lavelle tonight."

"What's wrong with her?"

Brent shrugged. "I have no idea—exhaustion, too much Jack Daniel's, who knows. We just need you to step in. You'll have to do the song and the dance. You can practice at rehearsal. The vans will be leaving in twenty minutes."

Deborah sighed as she closed the door. Why tonight? With her family in attendance, she'd have to dance onstage as if she and Lavelle were lovers.

Oh well, she thought. If her parents wanted to see what she did for a living, tonight would give them a good idea.

Deborah peeked through the curtains as Phoebe sang her last song. The way Phoebe swayed and swung and exuded sex amazed Deborah. No wonder men often tried to climb onto the stage.

The Georgia Dome was packed to capacity, and Deborah had no doubt that many of the seats were filled with residents of Villa Rica. She held her hands to her face. The last time they saw her, she was sitting primly in the choir singing "Amazing Grace."

Well, everyone knows what I do, she thought. And just because her family was in the audience, that didn't mean she was going to hold back. In fact, she was going to sing her heart out. It was the dance with Lavelle that worried her the most.

Moments later, she and Vianca had taken their places at the bottom of the stairs, and the crowd roared as Lavelle crooned his way to the bottom. It was just like it was in all the other cities, only tonight Deborah was sure that she heard her name yelled from the audience.

They sang the songs, one after another, and Deborah moved across the stage with the ease of a performer who had been on the road for two months.

But when Lavelle put his arms around her for the duet, her shoulders tensed. She leaned against his portly frame and smiled into his eyes as they sang "Loving You."

Deborah's strapless dress felt like it was falling as she shimmied against Lavelle, and she had to resist the urge to pull it up.

At the end, she bowed from the waist and nearly sagged with relief because the show was finally over.

❧

Deborah rushed to her dressing room. As she had requested, Kim was waiting to help her make a quick change into her pants suit. She had just zipped her top when she heard a knock on the door.

Aunt Bird was the first to enter. "Deborah Anne, you were just terrific out there." Deborah hugged her, then Uncle

Moses. "I didn't know you could sing like *that*." Aunt Bird fanned her face playfully. "That Lavelle sure is a looker."

Anxiously, Deborah moved to her parents. "Hi, Mama." She kissed her mother, then turned to her father and kissed him. "Did you enjoy the show?"

Elijah smiled. "My little Deborah Anne on a big stage like that. It really was something." His eyebrows furrowed together. "But that dance you did with Lavelle—that was interesting."

"I usually don't do that," Deborah quickly explained. "Emerald does that duet, but she's sick. That's why there were only two of us on the stage with Lavelle."

"Even before that duet, you girls had some sexy moves," Bubba said, but then lowered his head when Deborah glared at him.

"Well, I know it's late, but do you guys think we can get together tonight?" she asked.

"That's what we were planning, Deborah Anne," said Virginia. "We're staying at the Ramada Inn and thought you'd come over and have a little late dinner with us."

Deborah smiled. "Oh, I'd love it. I'm just sorry I won't have time to come home this time."

"Well, you're busy, dear." Virginia hugged her daughter. "We'll wait for you outside."

"Good. I want to introduce you to Lavelle and the rest of them."

As her relatives flocked from the room, Deborah sighed with relief. It hadn't been as bad as she expected. It looked like her father had accepted what she was doing with the gift that God gave to her.

She grabbed her bag and rushed to meet her family.

CHAPTER 29

HOUSTON AND DALLAS WERE THE LAST CITIES on the first part of the tour. As Deborah went through rehearsals and then the six shows, she marveled at how well she'd become acclimated to life on the road. She wore the three- and four-inch heels as if she'd always worn them; she learned to stay awake until the early morning hours; and she drank Mountain Dew as if she owned stock in the company. She learned to ignore the sexual innuendoes and exploits and all of the other things that happened around her.

The only thing that lessened her joy was that she hadn't heard from Triage, and the few messages she'd left him had gone unanswered.

He's just working, she thought to comfort herself. But she couldn't forget the kiss and wondered what he was thinking.

When they landed in Los Angeles, her eyes wandered around the gate area, then again around the baggage claim area, hoping that Triage would surprise her. But by the time the car service driver had packed the trunk with her bags, she knew he wasn't coming.

Only exhaustion allowed her to sleep through the first night at home. The shrill ring of the phone awakened her. She peeked at the clock with one eye and saw that it was almost noon. She smiled, hoping it was Triage.

"Deborah?"

"Oh, hi, Lavelle." She sat up in the bed.

"I'm sorry, it sounds like you were asleep."

"Uh-huh. I'm surprised you're up. I thought you'd sleep for a week."

He laughed. "I will, when I finally get to bed. I was calling to see if we could get together for lunch."

Deborah frowned. She hadn't had any problems with Lavelle since that one incident, and she didn't want to go back there.

"Lavelle, I don't know. Is it something that we could discuss on the phone?"

"Deborah, I promise you this is business, and it's important to me." He paused, but with her continued silence, he went on: "We don't have to do lunch. We can do a quickie, drinks maybe?"

After a bit more cajoling, Deborah finally agreed to meet at the Sunset Room.

When she arrived, Lavelle was already seated. Charles and a bodyguard Deborah didn't recognize sat at a separate table behind him.

Lavelle held the chair for her as she sat down.

"Thanks for joining me, Deborah. You look rested."

She looked him up and down. "And you look terrible. When are you going to get some rest?"

He chuckled. "There are a few things I have to take care of first, but believe me, tonight I'm going to sleep straight through to next Friday. By the way, I'm having a big birthday party."

"I heard something about it."

He reached into his pocket and slid a card across the table.

She picked up the card and smiled when she saw it was an invitation. She looked up at him. "Thanks for the invite, but is this the reason you wanted to meet today?"

"No, not really. I wanted to ask if you'd join Vianca and Emerald and sing at the party."

She smiled. "I'd be glad to."

"There's another reason I wanted to talk to you, though." He lifted the glass on the table that was half filled with a golden liquid and took a swallow. "I wanted to tell you how much I like having you as part of my team."

She smiled, but remained silent.

"Deborah," he said in a low voice. "I'm really sorry about what happened, and I hope you've forgiven me."

Her eyes narrowed. "I said it was no problem."

"I know what you said, but you still seem distant, not like you were before, and I'm afraid now that we're back in LA you might be thinking of leaving. I really wouldn't want you to do that because of me."

"I'm fine, Lavelle, and I don't have any intention of leaving the group."

"Okay . . ." He sounded doubtful.

"I'm just trying to get used to the road. It's a different life."

He frowned. "I hope we haven't made it hard for you."

"No." She hesitated, thinking of the Vianca-and-Lavelle saga, Emerald's drinking problem, and all of the other things that had jolted her into the real world. "I just have some personal things to work out."

He was visibly relieved. "You have a great future in this business, Deborah, and I want to help you in any way I can. I wanted to clear that up. So you really forgive me?"

"I'm a Christian. I have to do that." She smiled.

He snickered. "You should tell that to my father." When Deborah frowned, Lavelle waved his hand in the air. "Sorry, just some issues I have with my family."

She paused before she said, "Anything you want to talk about?"

He looked down at his drink. "My father is a preacher, you know."

She nodded. "Phoebe told me."

He swallowed what remained in the glass. "Let's just say that he and I disagree about how I should be making my living. He thinks I should be standing in his pulpit singing songs to God."

Her father's face jumped into her mind. "I know how you feel. I think my parents feel the same, but they've been supportive."

"I can't say that about my father. My career has really fractured our relationship."

"I'm sorry to hear that."

He looked into his empty glass. "I haven't really spoken to him in years. Sometimes he'll say hello if he answers the phone when I call home." When he stopped, Deborah remained silent, knowing he had more to say.

Lavelle raised his glass, signaling the waiter. He looked at Deborah and chuckled. "But the one thing about my father is that he sure knows how to accept a gift. He may not speak to me, but he graciously accepted a new Mercedes and a new house that I built for them." He sounded bitter.

"Do you miss him?" Deborah asked softly.

He nodded. "We were best friends."

"You should try talking to him. Maybe enough time has passed. When was the last time you went home?"

"A few weeks ago—when we were in Raleigh. But I didn't go to my parents' house. With the way things are, I didn't want to upset my mother."

"I understand how you feel, but you've got to try to make peace with him before it's too late. Lavelle, we just never know."

He shook his head. "I've thought about trying, but I guess since I don't know what to expect, I just stay away."

"You have to remember that you're talking about your parents. No matter what happens, you have to find a way to bridge this gap."

"I don't know—"

"Of all the commandments, the first one with a promise is to honor our parents. Sometimes that may mean that we have to be bigger than they are. We have to take the first step."

"It's been a long time."

"That may be good. Time may have helped your dad a bit." She took his hands. "At least pray about it."

Lavelle picked up the glass that the waiter placed in front of him, then put it down and smiled. "I think I just might try that. Who knows? If I pray, God just might have a message for me."

Her smile matched his. "I bet He will."

"Well, all I can say is, amen to that."

CHAPTER 30

DEBORAH COULDN'T BELIEVE HOW QUICKLY HER first week at home had passed. Without rehearsals and with no communication from Triage, she had expected the time to drag. Instead, she'd spent full days trying to get settled back into LA life. She spent the first few days cleaning the apartment. No matter what she did, she couldn't shake the feeling of being like a smothered pork chop. It was time for her to look for something bigger, and buy it if it was affordable.

Phoebe agreed when she came by to pick Deborah up for lunch one day.

"Girl, what are you doing living in this box?"

"I was just thinking that I have to do something about this."

Phoebe stood with her hands on her hips. "Well, stop thinking, and let's start doing!"

Deborah ran around town with Phoebe for a solid week looking at condos and townhouses in every area from the

South Bay to Bel Air. Deborah was in awe as she traipsed through some of the beautiful models filled with expensive furniture and designer accessories.

That same week had passed before she got a message from Triage. As she did every day when she returned home and saw the blinking light of her answering machine, she held her breath. But this time, she exhaled when she heard his voice.

"Hi, Deborah. This is Triage. Welcome home. Sorry I haven't been in touch. Been kind of busy, and now I'll be out of town for a few days. I'll be back next Friday, in time for Lavelle's party. I'm sure you'll be there, so I'll see you then. Hope all is well. Peace out."

The words were noncommittal, and his tone revealed even less. But at least she would see him at Lavelle's party. She didn't know how she was going to do it; she certainly didn't want to have one of those "chick conversations" in which she would ask Triage, "Where do we stand?" But she needed an answer, and she just had to find a way to ask the question.

At lunch the next day, Deborah confided in Phoebe.

"We've been friends ever since he introduced me to Lavelle. He thinks of me as his homegirl, but then there are these times when we're together when I feel like we're a couple."

"Here's what you should do," Phoebe began as she stuck a raw vegetable into her mouth. "The next time he kisses you, just stick your tongue down *his* throat."

Phoebe laughed when she saw the look of shock that instantly blanketed Deborah's face. "I'm serious, girl. It's winner take all in today's games."

"I'm not looking for a game. I just want to know if we're going to try to have a relationship."

Phoebe waved her hand, dismissing Deborah's words. "It's the same thing. Listen, I'll tell you what we're going to do." Phoebe pulled out her wallet and placed her credit card on the table.

"I was going to pay for lunch today," Deborah protested. "You always pay."

Phoebe waved her hand. "Look, we don't have any time to argue." She snapped her fingers, signaling the waitress. "We need to get out of here and find you a fabulous dress. Something that will make you look knock-down, drop-dead gorgeous. Something that will have Triage not knowing if he is going or coming."

"I don't know—"

"We need to find a dress where you won't have to say a word. Triage will just fall to his knees."

Deborah laughed at Phoebe's enthusiasm. "Is there a dress out there like that?"

Phoebe smirked. "Girl, if you haven't learned anything else from me, it's that you can bring a man to his knees with your dress. Let's get out of here," she said, grabbing Deborah's hand.

❧

The last time Deborah was on Rodeo Drive, she had quickly pulled Vianca elsewhere. But today she let Phoebe stroll with her through several boutiques.

"You've got to let me pick the dress, Deborah. I know what I'm doing."

Deborah sighed, knowing that there was no way she would

wear anything that Phoebe picked out. So while Phoebe scanned the racks, Deborah kept her eyes open for something that would suit her own taste. But there was nothing that took her fancy. Maybe it's the prices, she thought.

In Escada, Phoebe brought out two dresses. "One of these will do the trick."

Deborah couldn't hold back her look of shock. "Phoebe, neither one of those dresses look like me."

"That's the point, Deborah. You don't want to look like you. That hasn't worked yet, has it?"

Deborah turned away and looked at herself in the mirror. Her hair was pulled back into a ponytail, and while the white sweat suit she wore was fashionable, she looked like a high school student next to Phoebe in her silk georgette two-piece long skirt with matching tank top. Deborah knew she looked good, so why did Phoebe's comment make her feel so bad?

"Come on, Deborah, just try it on."

She took the hangers and marched past, though Phoebe didn't seem to notice her sudden attitude. But the moment that Deborah put on the dress, she changed. The strapless tube dress felt luxurious as the black jersey hugged her body like a glove. The short train that came down the back added drama.

When Deborah stepped from the dressing room, Phoebe clapped.

"I told you. Look at you, you're absolutely gorgeous."

In spite of herself, Deborah smiled. "This dress does look nice."

"Nice? Please. Nice is how you used to look. This is drop-to-your-knees gorgeous."

Deborah swung around, looking at her reflection in the

mirror. "But Phoebe, look at this," she said, pointing to the panty lines. "What can I do?"

"Girl, you don't wear underwear with this kind of dress."

Deborah frowned. "I could never do that." She continued to turn from side to side. The dress made her feel even more glamorous than some of the outfits she'd worn onstage.

"Think about Triage," Phoebe whispered in her ear.

She hesitated. "What about a thong?"

"See, that's the misconception. Even a thong will leave a line on a dress like this. Trust me, I know what I'm talking about. What's the big deal anyway? No one will know, and besides, I can bet you that ninety percent of the women there will be underwear-free."

Deborah took a deep breath. She did want to look nice.

"Triage will be there, you'll be singing onstage," Phoebe continued, "and if you really want to make an impression . . ."

What's the big deal? Deborah asked herself. It's not like I'll be wearing a sign saying I don't have anything on. She looked in the mirror once more, inhaled, and said, "I'm going to do it."

Phoebe smiled widely and pushed her into the dressing room. "Perfect; let's get moving."

Deborah pushed aside her doubts, thinking instead of how she'd look to Triage. After all, she was in Hollywood now, and she needed to start acting that way.

CHAPTER 31

DEBORAH STAYED IN HER APARTMENT ALL DAY. She talked to her parents and Willetta, caught up on the latest novel, wrote in her journal, and watched the clock. Four hours before she was to leave, she filled the tub with warm water and lavender bath salts. Even though the sun tried to force its rays through the tiny bathroom window, she burned candles on the tub's edge, savoring the sweetness of the minutes. With her eyes closed, she tried to imagine what the night would bring, and she smiled as Triage's face came to her mind.

She still wasn't sure what she was going to say to him, but there was one thing she was sure of—she'd take Phoebe's advice. If Triage kissed her again, she would respond. She'd never go as far as Phoebe suggested, but she'd leave no doubt that she was interested.

After the long bath, she took her time fixing her hair and applying makeup, using the tips she'd learned on the road. By the time Deborah slipped into the dress, the churning that she'd felt in her stomach about being naked underneath had disappeared. She knew she looked good, and she knew that Triage would appreciate it. Tonight was going to be her night.

Deborah had declined Phoebe's offer to ride with her. Not only did Deborah want to leave all her options open, but Phoebe was bringing her new man to the party, and Deborah hated being the third wheel. She hadn't heard from Vianca, who was probably staying with Lavelle. So Deborah was more than happy to drive herself to the party.

Her plan had been to arrive early because she was singing. But the valet service that Lavelle had hired was already backed up with lines of waiting Mercedeses and Rolls Royces. Deborah sat for almost fifteen minutes before one of the young men opened her door. She chuckled when he frowned at her Camry. She could almost hear him ask "What is she doing here?"

The staff greeted Deborah by taking her wrap and offering her champagne. Deborah declined the refreshment and walked into the large sunken living room.

She'd never been to Lavelle's house, though she'd seen it featured in *Metropolitan Home* and *Architectural Digest* many times and felt as if she knew where each room was.

She wandered through the living room looking for a familiar face. She saw Lavelle and Vianca laughing with people she didn't know, and she continued her stroll into the next room. She smiled when she saw Triage's back. She moved toward him, but then stopped when he turned. As he moved, Tia came into view. Her arm was folded around his, and Triage kissed her cheek as they laughed.

The knife-sharp pain that pierced her heart kept Deborah's legs bolted to the floor, but only for a few moments. As she turned to walk away, Triage saw her.

"Deborah," he called, dropping Tia's hand.

She turned back to face him and pasted a smile on her face. "Triage, I didn't see you."

He smiled widely. "Welcome home." He hugged her. "It's good to see you."

She nodded, not trusting herself to speak.

"Hey, I want you to meet a friend of mine." He took Tia's hand. "Tia, this is my good friend Deborah."

Tia reached her hand toward her. "*Deborah Anne*, I've heard so much about you."

Her good home training allowed Deborah to keep smiling as she shook Tia's hand.

"Excuse me, I have to find Lavelle."

Triage placed his hand on Deborah's shoulder. "Is everything all right? You seem different."

She nodded and waved her hand, then rushed off to find refuge in another room. She made her way to the bathroom, but when that door was locked, she ran up the curved staircase, knowing she'd find one on the second level.

She locked the door, but didn't bother to turn on the light. Instead, she sat on the padded vanity bench and held her face in her hands.

How could I have been so stupid? she thought.

It was the knocking on the door that made her stand. Still in the dark, she smoothed her dress and opened the door, but then was pushed back inside by Phoebe.

"I saw you come up here," Phoebe said as she closed the door behind her and turned on the light. "Please don't tell me that this has anything to do with Triage being here with Tia."

Deborah shrugged.

"You know why he's here with her, don't you?" When Deborah remained silent, Phoebe continued. "Their agents probably put them together because Triage didn't have a date. They knew that the media would be here, and Triage's people are always very concerned about his image."

Deborah looked at Phoebe's reflection in the mirror. "How do you know that? How do you know that he's not really involved with Tia?"

"Because of the way he looks at *you*. I saw it when you guys were backstage in Chicago, and I saw it just now. There's a chemistry that neither one of you have acknowledged."

"The only chemistry that you see is what's coming from me," Deborah moaned. "I just read too much into the times I've spent with Triage."

"You're reading too much into what you're seeing now. Believe me, this is a fix-up."

"Why would Triage have to be fixed up?" Deborah asked. "That doesn't make any sense."

Phoebe sighed and rolled her eyes. "I love you, Deborah, but sometimes, you are so naïve. Triage's people are always putting him with some model or actress because they want to squelch the rumors."

Deborah frowned in question.

"They don't want anyone to think that Triage is gay."

Deborah turned around to face Phoebe directly. "He's gay?"

"No! I know that for a fact." Phoebe held up her hand when she saw the question on Deborah's face. "Don't ask, but the thing is Triage has never been one to sleep around, or grab the first piece who throws herself at him. Because of that, rumors started, and though Triage doesn't seem to care, the people who manage him do. So, when they have to, they put him with women."

Deborah shook her head.

"But none of that matters. Because if you want Triage, you're going to have to go after him."

Deborah took a deep breath, fixed a smile, then hugged Phoebe. "Thanks, but I'll handle it my way."

Phoebe sighed and shrugged, then turned out the light as Deborah stepped into the hall. They walked down the stairs together. "Where's Thomas? I wanted to introduce you to him," Phoebe said as her eyes wandered the room.

"I see Lavelle. I want to tell him that I'm here. I'll catch up with you later."

She walked over to where Lavelle stood with Vianca and Emerald. "Hey, you *are* here." He kissed her cheek.

"We were getting ready to sing without you." Vianca smiled and took her hand. "Let's go. We've got to sing this for my baby."

A small stage had been set in the middle of the living room, and Vianca began singing the traditional version of "Happy Birthday," while Emerald and Deborah took Lavelle's hand and led him onto the stage.

When Vianca sang "Happy birthday, dear Lavelle," the three women began clapping their hands, and switched to Stevie Wonder's version. As the crowd joined in, Deborah allowed her eyes to search for Triage, and she found him, standing in the back with Tia at his side. Even when she looked away, Deborah could feel Triage's stare and was grateful when the birthday chorus ended and she left the stage.

She chatted as she passed people she knew on her way to the front door. But just as she got to the foyer, Triage grabbed her hand and pulled her into the downstairs bathroom. He locked the door behind them.

She held her hands in the air. "What is it with you LA people and the bathroom?"

Triage frowned. "What are you talking about?"

She shook her head and folded her arms across her chest.

"Deborah, what's going on with you?"

"I'm trying to go home."

"You haven't said one word to me all night."

She dropped her eyes. "I haven't been here that long. And I didn't want to interfere with your date."

He lifted her face with his fingers. "Is that what's bothering you? Why do you have a problem with Tia?"

She didn't answer him, fearing that if she opened her mouth, tears would follow.

"Deborah, is there something going on here that I don't know about?"

She barely shook her head. This was embarrassing, almost humiliating. How did she get here?

With as much strength as she could gather, Deborah forced words through her lips. "Triage, I'm not feeling well, and I want to go home."

There was a knock on the door.

"Give me a minute," he yelled, then turned back to Deborah. "I'm not letting you out of here until you talk to me. I thought we were friends."

She stared at him for a long moment. "Is that what you thought?"

"Deborah, you're going to have to talk to me."

There was another knock on the door; this time Triage didn't answer.

"There are people waiting to get in here, Triage."

"Well, they are going to wait a long time. I'm not letting you go anywhere until you talk to me."

"I can't. Not now and not here."

"Okay." He paused, thoughtful. "What about tomorrow? Let's get together."

The banging was more insistent. "Is anyone in there?"

"One second," Triage yelled back. To Deborah, he said, "What about it? Tomorrow?"

Deborah remained silent, but jumped when the banging continued on the door. "Triage, we have to get out of here."

He leaned against the door and folded his arms.

Deborah looked around the small bathroom. There was no way out—except past the man who blocked the door. "All right," she relented. "Tomorrow."

He continued his stance. "What time?"

She sighed exasperatedly. "Whatever . . ."

He didn't move. "I want a commitment."

She held up her hands. "At noon," she said, giving in.

He smiled, and his eyes moved over her body. "Thank you."

"Hey buddy, other people want to use the bathroom."

As he opened the door, Triage whispered, "You really look fantastic."

Deborah rushed past the line that had formed at the door.

"Hey, I was just taking care of a little business. Sorry," she heard Triage say behind her.

There were laughs in the hallway, but she didn't wait to hear anything else. Deborah rushed through the hall to the foyer, then out the door.

CHAPTER 32

THOUGH SHE HADN'T SLEPT MUCH, SHE FELT AMAZingly alert. She had played through the scene with Triage over and over again all night. How could she have acted that way? How could she have thought there was anything between them? They were just friends—he'd made that abundantly clear, and now she would have to face the humiliation of another meeting.

What was she going to say? How would she get out of it?

"I'll just feign illness," she said aloud, pacing the small room. "I'll tell him I was sick last night and I don't feel well now." She fell onto the couch, but within a few seconds, Triage rang her doorbell.

She looked at the clock. Five to twelve. With a deep breath, she opened the door and smiled.

"Hi."

He smiled and stepped into her apartment. "As I was driving over here, I was thinking you probably wouldn't be living here much longer."

"What do you mean?"

"I know this studio has to be getting to you."

"I have been looking for a condo or something. I could use the space and the investment."

"Really? You should let me help you. I know a lot of people in the real estate business."

She nodded and folded her arms in front of her. He had already sat on the couch, and with just the one other chair in the room, she had to sit across from him.

His stare made her uncomfortable, but she refused to speak first. He was the one who had called this meeting.

"Deborah, are you mad at me?"

"Why would you think that?"

"Maybe because you're having a hard time looking at me. Or maybe because last night the only way I got you to talk to me was to hold you hostage. Or maybe—"

She held up her hands. "You don't have to go on. I'm not mad. I just wasn't feeling well last night. And I still don't feel up to par." Her fake cough sounded hollow.

"Sounds like you're getting better." He smirked.

"What did you want to talk about, Triage?" She sighed. "I have things to do."

He leaned forward. "Which is it, Deborah? Are you sick or are you busy?"

She folded her arms but remained silent.

He sighed. "Okay, I'll say it first." He stood, then knelt on the floor in front of her. "Deborah, is there something going on here?" he asked softly.

Her heart began to beat faster, but she remained silent.

"I mean, between us. I'm feeling that maybe there's a little more . . ."

When she still didn't respond, he leaned toward her, lifted her chin and kissed her gently on the lips.

Her heart pounded, but she didn't move, frozen in place, waiting.

He leaned back. "That's what I thought."

For the first time, she smiled.

"Deborah, I can't have this conversation by myself."

She sighed. "I know," she whispered. "It's just that I got so hurt last night, I don't know what to say now."

"Oh . . . so that's what last night was about." She stood, but in the small room, there was nowhere for her to go. So she sat on the couch, in the place where Triage had just been sitting.

"I'm so embarrassed. There was no reason for the way I acted last night. I felt like a jealous girlfriend."

"I like the sound of that."

She rolled her eyes.

"Seriously, we're past that, but where do we go from here?"

"I don't know. I haven't had a conversation like this since high school, when Philip Harper asked me to go steady."

He laughed. "Okay, so maybe we don't have to go there just now. Maybe we should just try taking our relationship up a notch and see what happens."

"Is that what you want to do? You're not doing this because of what happened last night?"

"No . . . this is all on me. I wondered if there was anything between us since I first kissed you. But when you didn't say or do anything—"

"It wasn't because I didn't want to. I just didn't want to mess up our friendship."

He laughed and sat on the edge of the couch. "You can't do that. I hope, no matter what, we'll always be friends." He lifted her chin. "You're my homegirl, remember?" His voice was husky.

She nodded as he moved closer to her, and this time when he kissed her, she responded, putting her arms around his neck and allowing her tongue to finally meet his. They were both breathing heavily by the time Deborah pulled away.

"As the preacher says, amen!"

Deborah laughed. "You're so crazy!"

"I think we should consummate this agreement with a date. Let me take you out to lunch."

"Okay," she said as she reached for her purse and sweater.

He held her hand as they walked to his car, and as he helped her into the Ranger Rover he asked, "Deborah, whatever happened to your cold?"

She pursed her lips and slammed the door. But as he walked around to his side of the car, she tingled with excitement. They hadn't even had their first real date, and Deborah already felt like she was in love.

After lunch, they walked silently hand in hand on the hard sand where the ocean met the coast. The Santa Monica beach was still sprinkled with people wanting to get their last feel of the summer, even though it was the middle of September. Deborah was pleased that none of them had recognized Triage; she guessed those large dark glasses and cap really did work.

Suddenly, Triage grabbed a small stick from the sand and ran a few feet ahead. "What are you doing?" Deborah asked as he leaned over and began writing in the sand.

When he finished, Triage stood and kissed her. "Well," he said.

She looked down at the words he'd written in the sand: *Deborah, would you go with me?*

She nodded, and they sealed their agreement with a kiss.

CHAPTER 33

OVER THE NEXT WEEKS, DEBORAH AND TRIAGE tried to spend time together, but their schedules made it difficult. Deborah was in the studio working on the new album, as well as new steps for the second half of the tour.

Triage was recording a music video that took him up and down the California coast, leaving Deborah to wonder what kind of life they would have if their relationship did progress.

She missed having Triage around all the time—especially after stress-filled days with the emotional divas—Emerald, Vianca, and Lavelle. Even though they'd finished almost half of the album, Lavelle decided to add a duet with Deborah to both the album and the tour, which brought concern from Emerald.

"What does this mean for *my* song?" Emerald demanded.

"Absolutely nothing," Lavelle snapped. "You'll still sing. I'll just be singing more."

"How come I'm not being given a chance for a duet?" Vianca cried.

Deborah stepped into the hall, not wanting to be part of the ensuing scene. When it was over, she was still singing with Lavelle. Emerald's duet would come first on the album and would be last in the show.

When Triage was in town, they spent their time together—even going to church—and she was proud when Triage was able to find most scriptures on his own.

"See, I'm studying," he whispered one Sunday when the pastor told them to turn to Haggai, and he found the scripture in his Bible before Deborah got to hers.

One Sunday after church, Triage announced that they weren't going out to brunch as they normally did.

"So what am I supposed to eat?" she cried playfully.

"Be quiet, woman!" he teased. "Just follow your man."

But she frowned when Triage stopped at a gated condominium community in Marina del Rey.

"Where are we going?"

"Sshh," he whispered, taking her hand and helping her from the car. They walked to one of the buildings right on the beach. Triage took a key from his pocket, opened the door, and led Deborah into the impressive foyer. Its rich marble floor and cathedral ceiling created a feeling of grandeur. Large picture windows in the living room faced the ocean, and a dramatic black-slate fireplace went from floor to ceiling. They walked from the living room into a kitchen the size of her apartment. Upstairs there were two large bedrooms and a massive master suite that seemed as long as a football field.

"This is beautiful," gasped Deborah as they finished touring the twenty-five-hundred-square-foot space. "Is this going to be your beach house?"

He grinned. "Nope." He handed her the key. "I bought this for you."

Her jaw dropped, and then she began shaking her head. "Triage . . . this is wonderful. I can't believe you did this for me, but I can't accept it."

The smile slowly disappeared from his face. "Why not?"

She took his hand, and they sat on the carpeted staircase. "I can't accept a gift like this from a man."

"I'm not just a man, Deborah. I'm *your* man."

"But you're not my husband. A gift like this can only come from the man I'm going to marry."

He stood. "I don't understand."

"Look at it this way. Suppose things don't work out for us, and I'm living in this house. How would I explain it to the man God has chosen for me?"

"Just tell him that your ex-boyfriend bought it for you."

"And how would that sound?"

He was thoughtful. "Okay, but how do you know that I'm not that man?"

She smiled. "The way I feel about you right now, I pray that you are." Her smile faded just a bit. "But we don't know yet, do we?"

He shook his head, but after a few minutes, he pulled her from the stairs. He held her. "I don't know too many women who would turn this down."

She looked around the room. "Believe me, I would love to live here, but not this way. And not at this time."

"I've gotta tell you, I'm blown away."

"I hope that's a good thing."

He kissed her forehead. "Deborah Anne, that is a very good thing."

She brought her lips to his, then, after a few seconds, pulled back. "Now let me take you to the place that *I'm* going to buy."

❧

Triage carried the last box into Deborah's new condo in Manhattan Beach and dropped it in the middle of the kitchen floor. "This should be the last of it." He put his arms around Deborah as she placed silverware in one of the kitchen drawers. "Are you sure about this place?"

"I know you're not still talking about that."

He laughed. "I can always try."

Vianca took a stack of towels from a box. "I'm going to put these in the linen closet, okay?"

"Thanks." Deborah nodded.

"I'm going to take this entire box into your bedroom," Phoebe said.

The moment they were alone, Triage pulled Deborah into his arms and kissed her deeply. After a while, she gently pushed him away.

"What's wrong?"

"Phoebe and Vianca could come in here any moment."

"So? They know how I feel about you." He leaned forward to kiss her again, but she slipped from his arms. "Fine." He smiled. "We'll just save it for later. I've been thinking about a way to christen this place, and I know just how we'll do it."

When Vianca and Phoebe came back into the room, Deborah sighed with relief. She and Triage had been going out for a month now, but they hadn't gone far enough for her to announce that she was a virgin. But the time was coming, she could feel it, and she hoped she hadn't made a mistake by not saying anything before.

The knock on the door interrupted them all, and Triage took out his wallet to pay for the pizza.

"Okay, let's eat," Deborah announced.

They devoured the pepperoni pizza, washing it down with plenty of Mountain Dew as they chatted about the upcoming holidays.

"Are you gong to fix your first Thanksgiving dinner here in your new home?" Vianca asked.

Deborah took her time wiping her mouth. She hadn't had the chance to tell Triage. "No, I think I'm going home," she said slowly. She could tell by his raised eyebrows that he was surprised. "It's my first time away from home, and I know my parents expect me."

"I would've thought you guys would spend the holidays together," Phoebe said.

Deborah took Triage's hand and kissed it. "We'll probably be together for Christmas."

They had almost finished the pizza when there was another knock on the door.

"Visitors already?" Triage smiled. "Who's coming over here that I don't know about?" When he opened the door, the smile fell from Triage's face. A large, angry-looking figure loomed in the doorway.

"Is Phoebe here?" the man asked as he looked past Triage, avoiding eye contact with him.

Inside, Phoebe groaned and whispered, "It's Thomas." She

pushed her chair back and rushed to the door. "Hi, baby." Phoebe took Thomas's hand and brought him inside. "Everybody, this is my friend Thomas." She introduced him to the group, but Thomas just gave a perfunctory nod and continued staring straight ahead.

"Thomas, we just finished the pizza, and I don't have any other food yet," Deborah said.

"I don't want anything," he replied flatly. He turned to Phoebe and asked, "Are you ready to go?"

"I haven't finished with everything here—"

"Oh, that's all right," Deborah jumped in. "I can put away the rest of the stuff." She hugged Phoebe. "Thanks so much for your help."

They watched in silence as Phoebe gathered her belongings and left with Thomas, who made no secret of his impatience.

"Who *is* that guy?" Triage asked.

"That's her new man," Vianca said. "I told her I didn't like him."

Deborah shook her head. "This is the first time I've met him. I don't even know what he does. Maybe he's just having a bad day."

"No, I met him when she brought him over to Lavelle's, and he acted the same way. He's big bad news."

Deborah shrugged and began putting their plates into the dishwasher.

"Well, I'm going to get out of your hair too," Vianca said, "but I've got to call Lavelle first."

In a few minutes, Deborah knew, she'd be alone with Triage, and she dreaded it. They'd been alone plenty of times, but tonight he was looking at her with lust. She knew this would be different.

They were clearing the rest of the table in silence when Vianca walked back into the room.

"Deborah, I have a big favor to ask you. I can't find Lavelle, and I don't have a place to stay."

Deborah frowned. "What happened to your place?" She knew Vianca spent most of her time with Lavelle, but she did have her own apartment.

"I got rid of it and moved in with Lavelle. But it's an interesting situation. He won't give me a key."

Triage moaned.

"I've asked him for a key plenty of times," she explained. "But—"

"And you don't know where he is now?"

She shook her head sadly. "He's not answering his pager."

It was Deborah's turn to shake her head. Vianca was taking her relationship with Lavelle too seriously. Vianca had to see how Lavelle was around other women, and Deborah was convinced that it wasn't friendship with Phoebe and Lavelle. Vianca had to know it too.

"If he doesn't answer his page, I won't have a place to stay tonight."

Deborah wanted to ask Vianca why had she stupidly given up her place. She wanted to know how you could live someplace where you didn't have a key. But all Deborah said was, "You can stay here."

Triage sighed aloud, and Deborah shot him a "What can I do" look.

"Thank you so much. I'll help you unpack everything tonight."

Deborah smiled. This could turn out to be a good thing, in more ways than one.

"Honey, you don't have to stay," she said to Triage. "Since Vianca will be here, I'll get a lot done. Besides, you did all of the heavy lifting, so go home and get some rest."

Vianca had gone into the bathroom, and Triage pulled Deborah into his arms. "I didn't want to leave," he whispered. "I was hoping we'd spend your first night here together."

Yes, she thought, it's time for the talk. Tomorrow.

"Are you busy in the morning?" Deborah asked.

"Oh, a woman after my own heart. A morning lady. I'll be here bright and early."

"I'll call you when Vianca goes home."

He kissed her like he never planned to leave, and by the time Vianca came back, Deborah had to push Triage out the door.

"Thanks again, Deborah—"

Before she could finish, Deborah threw a towel at Vianca. "Let's see if you're still thanking me in the morning."

CHAPTER 34

DEBORAH YAWNED AS SHE ROLLED OUT OF HER bed and went into the hallway to answer the intercom. "Who is it?"

"It's me," Triage boomed through the small speaker on the wall.

She buzzed him in, then tapped her fingers against the wall. What was he doing here so early, and why had he come without calling first? He had never done that before. Obviously, to Triage her move had signaled a change in their relationship. She tightened her bathrobe around her waist and smoothed her hair. It was time for the talk.

She held the door open for him as he stood grinning with a Starbucks bag in his hands.

"Surprise!"

"I told you that I would call you when I was ready for you to come over," she said gruffly.

He kissed her cheek. "Is that any way to greet your Tazo tea and your man?" His eyes roamed the living room. There were no boxes in sight. "Wow, you and Vianca must have been up all night!"

"We were up pretty late—that's why I said I would call *you*."

He frowned and dropped the bag on the dining room table. "What's the big deal? Is Vianca still here?"

"No." Deborah crossed her arms in front of her. "Lavelle paged her at four A.M., and she went running out of here."

Triage shook his head. "That's one strange relationship."

Deborah nodded. "I know, and I don't think it's going to work out for Vianca."

Triage shrugged. "But that has nothing to do with you and me." He edged toward her and grinned, wrapping his arms around her waist. "So that means that we're alone in your new place."

"Yes."

He pulled back to look directly at her. "You sound like you're mad. Or are you just tired?"

"I'm not mad, I'm just surprised that you came over here without calling first. Especially since it's so early."

"Oh, well, I'm sorry if I woke you." He nuzzled her neck. "But if you're tired, that's no problem. What I had in mind will take you back to bed anyway."

With her palms out, she pushed him away gently. "Triage, we have to talk."

"Talking is not what I had in mind," he said, pulling her back to him.

She turned away and sighed.

"Deborah, what's wrong? I thought you were as ready for this as I am."

She turned to face him. Deborah loved the way he looked.

It was only seven in the morning, but he was pulled together with jeans and a tailored shirt, looking more like a preppie from Harvard than a rapper.

All she wanted to do was fall into his arms and never have this conversation. But it had to be done, and she realized there was only one way to do it.

"Triage, I know we should have talked about this before, but what happened between us happened so fast—"

"Deborah, what is it?"

"I'm still a virgin."

His eyes widened, and he grinned. "Wow! Oh, baby, that's wonderful." He pulled her to him again and hugged her tightly. "I'm glad I'm going to be your first."

Deborah held up her hand. "I don't think you understand. I'm a virgin because I'm waiting for my wedding night."

He drew back, confusion written on his face.

"My virginity is going to be a gift to my husband," she explained.

"You're kidding, right?"

She shook her head.

If he hadn't looked so sad, Deborah would have laughed, but she remained silent.

He ran his hand over his head. "Man, I didn't know there were people who still felt that way."

"I know, but this is something that I've wanted to do since I was a very young girl. And I only have one chance to do it right."

"But who says this isn't right? I'm falling in love with you, Deborah, and I know there's nothing wrong with two people expressing how they feel about each other."

"I can quote you scripture after scripture that says *this* is right, Triage. God says that fornication is not for our body and that we should flee from it. But I don't want to lecture you, and I'm not trying to judge you. I'm just telling you what's right for me."

"Wow." This time when he said the word, the excitement was gone.

"Triage, I hope that you'll respect my decision," she began with her head lowered. "But I also understand if this changes things. I should have told you before, so I will understand if—"

He held up his hand, interrupting her. "I can't say that I'm not disappointed. I couldn't sleep last night just thinking about what I thought we'd do this morning." He took a step toward her. "But I do respect you and what you want to do." He lifted her face toward his. "You really are a beautiful woman, but I already know that there is so much more to you than that. So if this is how you want to do it, I'll try."

She smiled weakly. "That's all I can ask."

"You know, I never thought I'd be in this position. Being around you and getting to know the kind of person you are makes me want to be a better man."

He kissed her and turned toward the door.

"What's wrong?" she asked.

"I've got to go home. I might be better, but I'm still a man. I just hope there's a cold shower waiting for me at my house!"

Before she could say anything, he was gone.

CHAPTER 35

THE FIRST THING DEBORAH SAW WHEN SHE STEPPED off the plane was Willetta and Maxine waving their hands wildly in the air.

They hugged, and laughed so loudly that others in the gate area turned and stared.

"I can't believe my famous cousin is home," Willetta screamed. "You even *look* like you're important now."

They walked straight to the car, since she'd brought only a carry-on bag. Even so, it took almost thirty minutes to maneuver from the gate to the car and out of the airport. Deborah could see why the day before Thanksgiving was considered the most traveled day of the year.

During the hour-long ride home, Deborah tried to answer the questions her cousins bombarded her with. By the time they pulled into the town of Villa Rica, Willetta and Maxine were satisfied that they knew all about their cousin's new life.

"Well, I can't wait to come and visit you now that you have

your new place," Willetta said. "Maybe right after the New Year."

"You know you're always welcome," Deborah responded, though her eyes were on the streets of the hometown she loved. She was so glad to be back in the cocoon of her hometown—less than seven thousand people, who still had to be reminded to lock their front doors.

The streets looked the same, but she felt so different. When they turned onto Peterson Road, Deborah could barely wait to jump from the car. Both her mother and father ran onto the porch when they heard Willetta's Chevy pull into the driveway.

It took several minutes for the hugging and the kissing to pass, as aunts and uncles and cousins came running from all directions.

Elijah had ordered pizza, since the kitchen was bustling with preparations for tomorrow's dinner. Relatives continuously flocked to the house until after ten, when Elijah put everyone out.

"My daughter needs her rest," he said kiddingly, then pushed everyone out the door.

Deborah was glad when it was just her and her parents.

"So how are things really going, Deborah Anne?" Elijah asked.

Deborah curled up on the couch and smiled. "It's really good, Daddy. It's a lot harder than I thought it was going to be, with the long hours and constant rehearsals."

He nodded, and Deborah could tell by the look in her father's face that he was proud, even if it wasn't what he would have chosen for her.

"I'm even taking on a new role with Lavelle. I'll be singing a duet regularly with him now, and it will be on the new album. I'll sing it the first time at our Christmas show on December twenty-seventh."

Elijah's smile turned down just a bit. "Is it that duet you sang when you were in Atlanta?" His voice was low.

"No," she said quickly. "That's Emerald's song. The one I have with Lavelle is much different. In fact, it's Bebe and CeCe Winan's song, 'I'm Lost Without You.' Lavelle let me choose it."

His smile returned, and he nodded. "I like that," he paused. "Have you found a good church home in LA?"

She nodded. "I thought I told you. Triage and I go to Macedonia Baptist Church. I miss Pastor Duncan, but Macedonia is a Word church, and I'm still growing in God."

He smiled. "I'm glad to hear that, baby."

"Now, Elijah, that's your problem. Deborah Anne is not a baby anymore." Virginia smiled as she entered the room.

They all laughed.

As Deborah lay in bed that night, she marveled at how different things seemed to be. Only five months had passed, but her room seemed to have shrunk to the size of a pillbox. It didn't really matter, though, because it felt so good to be home. Deborah sighed with contentment. This was where her dreams had begun. And now those dreams were real. She was singing professionally and traveling to places she'd only read about. Best of all, she was with a man with whom she hoped she'd spend the rest of her life.

In that moment, she did something that she hadn't done since she left home—she got on her knees and prayed, thanking God for all that had been given to her. And she prayed that she would continue to live and stand for the Lord.

Thanksgiving was like it always was at the Petersons'. Mountain Baptist didn't have a Thanksgiving service, so every year, Elijah would hold early-morning prayer at their house.

It was dawn, and Deborah was still dressed in her pajamas and bathrobe when her aunts and uncles started to pour into the living room. Deborah's cousins rarely attended the early-morning service, so she was surprised when Willetta showed up with her parents.

"I never get to see you anymore," Willetta explained. "So I have to take every opportunity." She hugged her cousin.

After prayer, Aunt Bird and Aunt Eleanor joined Virginia in the kitchen. Deborah and Willetta, assured that the other women had everything under control, went in to Deborah's bedroom.

"This reminds me of high school." Deborah giggled. "When you would come over and we would gossip about everyone in class."

"And that's what I want to do now," Willetta said, pulling her legs under her on the bed. "I didn't want to ask you this in front of Maxine yesterday, but what is going on with you and Triage Blue? I've seen all the pictures in the paper."

Deborah waved her hands. "I used to believe those tabloids too, until I got to LA and ended up in half of them. Willetta, they make those things up."

"Well, even Mother Dobson said that you and Triage were together. She said that he took you to meet his parents in Chicago." Willetta searched her cousin's face for answers.

Deborah smiled. "That's true. Triage and I are an item."

Willetta screamed, and Deborah covered her face with a pillow. "Be quiet; I don't want everyone running in here."

Willetta kicked her legs in the air. "I knew it! My cousin Deborah Anne, and Triage Blue! Oh my goodness. I couldn't even imagine being with someone that famous."

"I don't see him that way. He's just a guy, and I'm just a girl."

Willetta waved her hand. "Oh God, that sounds like a line from a movie. Triage is not just a guy!"

"He *is* pretty special," Deborah agreed.

Willetta sat up on the bed, and her smile disappeared. "So," she started, lowering her voice, "have you guys . . ." She paused. "You know."

Deborah shook her head. "No, we haven't."

"You haven't had sex yet?" Willetta asked, surprised.

"We're not going to have sex at all."

"What are you waiting for?"

"Willetta," Deborah exclaimed. "You *know* I'm not having sex until I get married. We agreed."

Willetta dropped her head, and Deborah's mouth dropped open.

"Have you and Steven—"

She nodded. "Lots of times. I've even started taking the Pill."

Deborah dropped back against the headboard. "I thought we were going to wait until we got married."

Willetta waved her hand in the air. "We made that promise when we were fourteen. Times have changed."

Deborah shrugged. "That's what everyone says, but it hasn't changed for me. I'm still a virgin."

"Wow!"

"That's exactly what Triage said." Deborah shook her head. "He said he didn't think there were people like me left in the world."

"He's right about that. Even your teenage cousins have beat you, Deborah Anne."

Deborah shook her head. "It's amazing how cavalier people are about sex. I mean, what about what we learned in church?"

Willetta shrugged. "I don't know. I pray about it all the time. I know I'll have to answer to God. I just hope He understands."

"I don't want to get in front of the Lord and just 'hope.'"

Willetta nodded. "I know. But it's hard today, and I don't think you can really have a good relationship without sex."

Deborah stood up and pointed at Willetta, but before she could open her mouth, there was a knock on the door.

"Deborah Anne, Willetta, can you help us with something out here?"

"Saved by the knock. I felt a big lecture coming on."

Deborah laughed. "I wasn't going to lecture you."

"Yeah, but just in case, I'm glad Aunt Virginia called. Come on!"

Deborah shook her head as she followed Willetta into the hallway. She thought the world had gone crazy, but the biggest surprise was that all of this craziness was going on right in Villa Rica, and right in her own family.

Thanksgiving weekend passed like a ride on the Concorde, and before she knew it, Deborah was tipping the driver who had brought her luggage into her condo. After closing the door behind him, she stepped over her bags and headed straight to her answering machine.

She'd spoken to Triage only once, on Thanksgiving, and it surprised her how anxious she was to see him. She smiled as she heard her first message.

"Where are you, woman? I thought you'd be back and we could spend the entire day together. Call me the moment you get in. I missed you terribly."

Deborah almost stopped the machine to call him immediately, but instead she decided to listen to the rest of the messages. The next one made her forget about Triage.

"Deborah, this is Emerald. I don't know if you're in town or not, but Vianca was rushed to the hospital this morning. It's Sunday, so if you're checking your messages, please check on Vianca. She's in Cedars Sinai."

Deborah picked up her purse and rushed from her apartment. In less than thirty minutes, she was standing in Vianca's room. She held her breath as she looked at her friend, who was curled into a ball in the middle of the bed.

"Vianca, it's me, Deborah."

Vianca slowly opened her eyes. "Hey, girl," she said weakly.

Deborah ran her fingers through the curls that were matted to Vianca's head. "What happened? Are you going to be all right?"

Vianca nodded weakly. "I just feel so bad." She paused. "I was pregnant, but I lost the baby." Her eyes filled with unshed tears.

Deborah's mouth dropped open. "I'm so sorry. I wish I'd known—"

"I didn't tell anyone, not even Lavelle. He still doesn't know—only Emerald, and she told me she called you."

Deborah sat on the edge of the bed. "Don't you think you should tell Lavelle?"

Vianca shook her head. "I don't want him to think that I'm trying to trap him."

"He couldn't think that now."

Vianca began to sob softly. "I just lost the baby. I can't lose Lavelle too."

Deborah squeezed her hand. "Vianca, you're putting all of your faith in Lavelle. He's just a man. Put your faith in God."

"Please don't lecture me about God right now. Not with what just happened."

Their heads turned as the door opened and Lavelle walked in. In the hallway, Deborah could see Charles and one of Lavelle's bodyguards.

"What's going on in here?" Lavelle's face was taut.

"How did you find out?" Deborah asked.

"Emerald called me, drunk. She said I put Vianca in the hospital." He took a step forward. "What's going on?" he repeated.

Deborah began to move away, but Vianca took her hand. With her eyes on Lavelle, Vianca said, "I was pregnant, but I lost the baby."

Deborah didn't miss the look of shock, then relief, that swept through Lavelle's eyes. But when she looked down at Vianca, Deborah could tell that the only thing Vianca saw was that Lavelle had come to her.

"You two need to be alone," Deborah said. "I'll be back,

Vianca." She paced the hall until Lavelle came out of the room twenty minutes later.

"Deborah, would you make sure that Vianca gets back to my place? I have to make a run."

Deborah pursed her lips. "Does she have the *key*, Lavelle?"

"Yeah," he said defiantly, then turned and walked toward the elevator.

When she returned to the room, Vianca was sitting up. "Did you see Lavelle?"

"Yeah, how did it go?"

Vianca forced a faint smile. "He said that he would have wanted the baby, and that he still wants to be with me."

Deborah wanted to scream and shake Vianca until her brain turned to mush. But instead, she simply held her friend's hand.

Vianca continued. "Of course, he's not saying that he's in love with me or anything. He enjoys my company."

"How do you feel about that?" Deborah asked. "Don't you think you deserve more?"

Vianca shrugged. "Maybe, but I think Lavelle will eventually change his mind. Look at what happened today. He came to the hospital, he said he cared about me, and he wanted to make sure that I got back to his place safely. . . ."

Deborah had a hard time believing that they had seen and heard the same thing, but she still said nothing as the nurse came in and helped Vianca dress.

By the time an aide wheeled Vianca to the lobby and Deborah helped her into her car, Vianca was smiling like she was just coming from an amusement park.

As Vianca chatted about the future that she and Lavelle were sure to have, Deborah prayed silently—for Vianca, for Lavelle, and finally for herself.

CHAPTER 36

THE CHRISTMAS LIGHTS WERE ALREADY SHINING along Wilshire Boulevard. This had always been Deborah's favorite time of the year, but now it was bittersweet—her first Christmas away from home. Triage made a quick turn into the circular driveway, and before he could stop the car, the valet was standing at the door to help Deborah out. They ran into La Mirage almost thirty minutes late for their dinner with Phoebe and Thomas.

This was Deborah's favorite restaurant. Since it catered almost exclusively to celebrities, Deborah and Triage could enjoy a meal without constant interruptions from autograph seekers or people with tapes of themselves or a family member who "could really sing."

The maître d' walked them to the table where Phoebe and Thomas were waiting, and the four exchanged greetings.

"I'm so sorry we're late," Deborah said as Triage held the chair for her to sit. "This time it's my fault."

As the waiter handed them menus, Triage asked, "What do you do, Thomas?"

"What do you mean by that?" Thomas growled.

"Thomas is in security, but he's looking to break into the movies," chirped Phoebe, trying to sound cheerful.

"It's not like I'm sitting around waiting. I'm working," Thomas added, admonishing Phoebe with a wave of his hand.

Deborah buried her face behind the menu and tried to change the subject. "I just love the tortilla soup. Have you guys been here before?"

"I have," Phoebe said. "And I love the soup too."

"Well, *I* haven't. What's the big deal?" Thomas snapped.

Deborah could feel Triage tap her gently under the table, but she refused to look at him, knowing that he had a "Who is this guy?" expression on his face.

After they placed their orders, Deborah and Phoebe fought to find a topic that would make Thomas feel comfortable, but to no avail. When Triage became as quiet as Thomas, Phoebe excused herself to go to the rest room, and Deborah followed.

"I'm sorry," Phoebe apologized as soon as the bathroom door closed behind them. "Thomas is being a complete jerk tonight."

"What's wrong with him?" Deborah asked as she pulled out her lipstick.

Phoebe sighed. "He accused me of flirting with the valet. Can you believe it? I think I'm going to have to get rid of this one. Anyway, tell me about you and Triage." Phoebe smiled. "Looks like things are moving along."

"Let's talk about it tomorrow," Deborah said. "I don't want to leave my man out there with yours for too long."

"I know what you mean." Phoebe laughed. "I don't want to go out there myself."

They struggled through dinner, though by the time they drove home, Triage and Deborah were laughing about Thomas.

"Just make sure you never embarrass me like that." Deborah chuckled.

"Are you kidding? Moi? I'm a lover, baby, not a fighter."

"Oh," she moaned. "I thought you were a writer. Couldn't you come up with a better line than that?"

Triage kissed her at the door and waited until she went inside. It didn't matter where they were or whom they were with. Their time together was just getting better and better.

CHAPTER 37

DEBORAH AND TRIAGE CUDDLED IN FRONT OF THE fireplace. The living room windows were open, and a warm late-morning breeze waltzed through the room.

Deborah tucked her legs underneath her and picked up the box she'd wrapped for Triage. As he reached for it, she suddenly pulled it back.

"Do you know how hard it is to buy something for you?"

"Just give me my gift." He laughed.

She brought it behind her back. "First, listen to me, Triage. I'm trying to be serious."

Triage laid his hands in his lap and sat stoically. "Okay, go ahead."

"It's so hard to find something for you. I wanted to get you something special that would tell you just how I feel about you."

He smiled and ran his hand along her cheek. "Can I please have my present?"

She handed it to him, then held her breath. While he opened the box, she squeezed her eyes shut.

"This is beautiful."

She opened her eyes and watched as he turned the leather book over in his hand. "This is just like the journal I got you," he said, looking up at her.

She nodded. "I wanted to find something that was similar, but there is one difference." She reached over and opened the pages. "For the last few months, I've been writing in this. Some are songs I've written, some are poems, some are just my thoughts about you."

He was silent as he flipped through the pages. The long moments of quiet unnerved Deborah.

"If you don't like it . . ."

He finally looked at her. "Deborah, this is so special. Thank you."

She finally breathed.

"Now I don't know if I should give you this." Triage held a small box in his hand.

She playfully snatched it from him and shook the box. "It's too small for a house or a car. Hmmmm . . . maybe it's a boat!"

Triage laughed. "Very funny."

Deborah tore into the gold paper and opened the container that held a scarlet velvet music box. She pulled up the lid and listened to the melody. "I've heard this before," she said, squinting and trying to remember.

"It's a song I've been working on. You heard me playing it, but you didn't know that I was writing it for you. It's called 'Our Love Is Perfect.'"

Her eyes filled with tears, and she wrapped her arms around his neck. "I love you."

"I've been waiting to hear you say that." He gently ran his fingers along her face. "Because I love you too."

Deborah had no idea how long they sat on the floor, holding each other and kissing, but when she looked up at the clock, she suddenly stood up, sending Triage tumbling.

"We're going to be late."

Looking at the clock, Triage jumped up and straightened his pants.

"Give me five minutes and I'll be ready." Deborah ran into her bedroom.

They walked hand in hand into Macedonia and joined the other volunteers who were serving dinner and passing out gifts to the homeless. As Deborah piled the plates high with food, she watched Triage from the corner of her eye. He played with the children, handed out toys, and signed autographs.

"That is some man you got there," remarked Miriam Kelly, the woman they sat next to in church every week.

"I know." Deborah smiled as she scooped macaroni and cheese and yams onto the plates.

It was after five when they finally drove to Triage's house for a catered dinner of Cornish game hens stuffed with wild rice. They talked softly of past Christmases and their hopes for future ones.

They were late getting to Phoebe's house for dessert, but the moment they walked through the door to her large townhouse, Phoebe pulled Deborah into her bedroom.

"My goodness, you're glowing." Phoebe smiled. She lifted

Deborah's hand and searched her fingers. "'Fess up. Did you guys become engaged or something?"

Deborah laughed. "No, it was something better. He told me that he loved me."

Phoebe hugged her. "You're right. That *is* better."

"How was your Christmas?" Deborah asked as they went into the living room to join the other guests.

"Peaceful! Girl, I gave myself a great gift. I got rid of Thomas."

"Oh," was all Deborah could say.

"Now don't be pretending that you're sad or anything. You're just too nice to tell me the truth. I should have gotten rid of that man a long time ago."

"Well, now that you mention it . . ."

They laughed as they joined Lavelle and Vianca at the piano to sing "Silent Night." As Deborah leaned back with her head on Triage's chest, she couldn't remember a better Christmas Day.

CHAPTER 38

IT SEEMED LIKE WEEKS HAD PASSED SINCE DEBORAH was last onstage, and it wasn't until she sat in her dressing room that she realized how much she'd missed it.

There was a light tap on the door, and Kim came in. "You look great," she said, as Deborah stood and twirled in the purple-sequined dress. Kim took a makeup brush and skimmed over Deborah's face. "Are you ready for your big night?"

She nodded.

"I saw your man out front." Kim smiled. "Why didn't he want to watch you from backstage?"

Deborah laughed. "He said he wanted to see me the way the audience sees me."

"Girl, you're all over the papers now."

"I know." Deborah sighed. "That's the only bad thing. You don't have any privacy, and ninety percent of what they say about you isn't true. But that's the price, right?"

Brent knocked on the door. "Showtime!"

Deborah passed Phoebe in the hall, and they hugged.

"I can't wait to hear you tonight, girl."

Deborah took her place onstage between Emerald and Vianca. It had been Lavelle's idea to move Deborah to the middle, and though she knew Vianca didn't like it, Vianca hadn't said a word.

They ran through the first part of the show as they always did—with Lavelle swooning and women panting. And when Lavelle came back onto the stage after his jacket change, Deborah stepped forward and stood beside him.

The crowd cheered when they heard the orchestra's first notes, and Deborah took a deep breath.

Here she was, standing center stage in the Los Angeles Arena, listening to the orchestra's introduction mix with the roar of the crowd. Deborah felt as if God's abundant blessings were pouring directly on her at that very moment.

It wasn't difficult for the words to flow from her soul. She closed her eyes and sang to the Lord, telling Him with her song that she loved Him, she worshiped Him, she praised Him.

She bent over and held her hand against her waist as the words flowed from her: "I'm lost without you . . . so don't ever go away. . . ."

It was only when Lavelle took her hand for them to take a bow that she remembered where she was. Deborah wasn't sure how long their standing ovation lasted, but when the show was finally over, she was overwhelmed with the backstage reviews.

"I don't know what got into you tonight, girl, but you were fantastic," Lavelle said.

"Where did that come from? You were great," Vianca added.

"My goodness. If I could sing like that, I'd be rich," Kim gushed.

Phoebe had tears in her eyes. "You were wonderful."

Her heart didn't return to its normal beat until she was sitting at her dressing table. There was a knock on her door, and she didn't have to turn around to know it was Triage.

He came behind her and pulled her from the stool. He kissed her. "I know you've heard it all, but I don't know what happened to you onstage tonight. Girl, you belted out that song. I hope you were thinking of me."

I'm lost without you . . .

She smiled and kissed him on the lips.

Two days later, Lavelle and Deborah were in the studio with the musicians to record their duet. They'd been working since nine A.M. As the light was beginning to fade, Deborah begged for mercy.

"How much longer?"

"Not much." The engineer laughed.

Lavelle and Deborah reentered the sound booth and sang their parts. Five more retakes and forty-five minutes later, they called it a wrap.

Lavelle lifted Deborah from the floor and kissed her. "You know, girl, with a voice like that, you should consider a solo project."

Deborah's eyebrows furrowed. "Really? You think I could do it?"

"You're ready."

"I hope you're telling her that she's ready to leave," Triage said as he walked into the studio.

Lavelle laughed. "She's ready for that too."

Deborah grabbed her coat as quickly as she could. She waited until they were in the car before she told Triage what Lavelle had suggested.

"I totally agree. Deborah, honey, you are more than ready. I never had any doubts. And the way you sang the other night . . . you *need* to have an album."

She was thoughtful for a few minutes. "What would I sing? Which label would I go with, and who would I talk to?"

"First of all, you're loaded with material. Think about all the songs you've written."

She nodded.

"We can talk to my manager tomorrow if you want. Or I can make a few calls." He reached over and took her hand.

"If I do this, there is one song I'd like to record." She turned sideways in the seat. "Maybe you'll do it with me. 'Our Love Is Perfect.'"

She could feel the car slow down as Triage put his foot on the brake. "Are you serious?"

"Of course. I love that song. And you did write it for us, right?"

"That would be great."

She sat back in the seat.

"This could be the beginning of a real career for you."

She smiled. "I'll think about it."

CHAPTER 39

THROUGH THE NEW YEAR AND THE WEEKS THAT followed, Deborah had little chance to think about a solo project. Triage's manager referred her to the William Martin Agency, which signed her after one meeting. She'd spoken with Mr. Martin several times since, and he told her that there was a lot of interest in her at Capricorn Records.

While the buzz continued about a possible solo career, Deborah's attention was elsewhere. Rehearsals for the second part of the tour had been pushed into high gear, but it was their upcoming Grammy performance that was getting most of the group's attention.

It was hard for Deborah to believe that not only would she be going to the Grammys, but she'd be performing at them as well. A year ago she and Willetta had ogled over the award show on TV, and now she was a part of it.

Deborah was glad that this time she didn't have to drag Vianca or Phoebe into the stores to buy a dress. The stylists brought sample outfits for both their stage performance and their red-carpet appearance.

The dresses were delivered to Deborah's condo. She examined the garments' plunging necklines, low backs, and waist-high side splits. She couldn't believe how different her eye was nine months into her career. These were the same dresses that made her turn up her nose almost a year ago. But now, she saw them the way she'd been taught—how would they look on the stage? Would they add to the sexiness of the act?

The day of the Grammys, Kim was assigned to meet Deborah at her condo to help her get ready. By the time Triage picked her up in the limousine, she was decked out in a shimmering lavender halter gown covered with hundreds of glinting beads. The jewel neckline made the dress seem conservative, until she turned around to reveal the daringly open back with crisscrossed straps.

"Have I ever told you that you're beautiful?" Triage asked as he nuzzled her neck.

"You've mentioned it once or twice."

He kissed her as the driver held open the door to the limousine.

Since Triage was the opening act, they were among the first to arrive at the Shrine Auditorium. Deborah waited with Lavelle and Vianca, and they all breathed a sigh of relief when Emerald entered just moments before the show began.

Deborah beamed when Triage came onstage and clapped along with the crowd as he rocked the arena. But her smile was even wider when Triage won the Grammy for Best New Single.

After the award for Best R&B Song was given, Deborah

followed Lavelle, Vianca, and Emerald backstage to prepare for their performance.

Deborah shivered with excitement as she changed into her black tuxedo pants and white rhinestone-covered blouse. In just a few moments she'd be center stage, televised across the nation and to Villa Rica specifically.

When the music began, Deborah led the others as they sashayed across the stage, running their hands across the brims of their matching black hats.

Deborah smiled as she rocked her body to the beat and spread her arms wide. The crowd roared when Lavelle began singing as he appeared from behind the curtains. Deborah, Vianca, and Emerald surrounded him, sauntering with him toward center stage.

As they sang the last note, Deborah took off her hat and tossed it in the air with the others. Judging from the crowd's excitement during their final bow, she knew it had gone well.

Excitement charged the air backstage as they were congratulated by other groups standing by.

"I knew I should have gone on before you guys," Whitney Houston said before she rushed onto the stage.

Phoebe hugged Deborah. "Girl, you guys were terrific."

Deborah grinned. "That was so exciting for me. I kept thinking about my parents. They're having a Grammy party to watch me."

Phoebe laughed. "Girl, walk me to the bathroom."

"How does it feel to be nominated?" Deborah asked Phoebe as they sat in front of the mirrors in the rest room. "Are you nervous?"

Phoebe waved her hand in the air. "There's nothing to it." But a moment later, she burst into laughter. "I'm so excited,

I can't even sit in my seat. Do you know what it would be like to win Best New Female Artist?"

Deborah bobbed her head.

"Well, let me get back to my date." Phoebe dropped her lipstick into her purse.

"It's not Thomas, is it?" Deborah moaned.

"I told you, I have a new man. Though Thomas still keeps popping up." She sighed. "I'm going to have to get a restraining order."

Deborah frowned. "You don't think he's dangerous, do you?"

"No, he's just a nuisance. I can handle it." Phoebe kissed Deborah. "I'll see you guys after the show."

The rest of the night continued to unfold like a dream, as Triage won two more Grammys and Phoebe was named Best New Female Artist.

Deborah was still shivering with excitement when the four-hour show finally ended. As they waited for the limousine outside, Triage pulled her close.

"Are you cold, baby?" he asked, covering her bare shoulders with his hands. "We can go back inside and wait."

"No, I'm fine. It's just that this was so incredible for me. Thank you for such a great evening."

"I had nothing to do with that part. But you can thank me later on tonight. 'Cause, girl, we have some partying to do tonight." He wrapped his arm around her waist and led her into the limousine.

CHAPTER 40

THE NEXT AFTERNOON, LAVELLE'S GROUP WAS ON a plane heading to northern California for seven shows. When Charles knocked on her hotel door the first night, Deborah wasn't surprised.

"It looks like it's all you tonight . . . again. Emerald is too sick to go on."

Deborah turned from where she was sitting. "How is she?"

Charles shrugged. "I don't think Lavelle is going to put up with this much longer. It's a good thing you're with us. Lavelle feels comfortable doing the duets with you."

Deborah nodded and half smiled at Charles as he left. It was flattering to know that Lavelle liked singing with her, but she didn't like what Emerald was doing to herself.

Kim put the finishing touches on Deborah's hair and sprayed a bit of oil sheen on top to make it glisten. "You know, you should think about cutting this weave."

"I don't think so."

"Well, at least wear it up sometimes. You have a great face. You'd look good with it pulled back."

"I can't think about that now, Kim. I'm really concerned about Emerald. I wish she and I were closer so that I could help."

Kim pursed her lips. "It wouldn't do any good. People have been trying to help Emerald for a long time, but she's determined to destroy herself."

Deborah sighed. "What could possibly be going on in her life that makes her feel that all she can do is drink?"

"Lavelle."

Deborah turned around slowly. Though no one had ever told her about Emerald and Lavelle, it didn't take a Rhodes Scholar to figure that out. So it wasn't Kim's words that shocked her, it was her tone.

"What do you mean?"

"Well, I'm not one to gossip," Kim said, then paused as she rolled a stool over to Deborah's dressing table. "But Emerald *really* loved Lavelle. Then one day, out of the blue, he dumped her."

"Oh," Deborah said simply.

"I don't know why Emerald didn't see it coming. He was sleeping with Phoebe at the same time—some say that he still is—and everyone could tell that Lavelle was never serious. Now the same thing is happening to Vianca."

Deborah wished that Kim hadn't dumped this on her right before she had to go onstage. But she'd learned to perform through all kinds of adversity and drama. By the time they finished the show, it was clear to Deborah that she had learned the lesson well. The crowd screamed her name as much as they called for Lavelle.

Emerald was back on the stage the next night, talking about how awful her cold had been. But by the time they returned to Los Angeles for a three-day break, Deborah had replaced Emerald in two more shows, and her concern was growing.

"I think I'm going to talk to Emerald," Deborah told Triage her first night back. She lay with her head in his lap as they watched *Titanic* for the tenth time, and she recounted her conversation with Kim.

"I think you should stay out of it, baby," Triage said. "Emerald is an unhappy, bitter woman. I don't know why she stays with the group. Hanging around Lavelle is making her drinking worse."

"Well, if she doesn't want to talk to me, at least I could invite her to come to church with us on Sunday."

Triage sighed, knowing that he wasn't going to talk Deborah out of it.

Deborah called Emerald for two days, leaving numerous messages that were left unanswered. By the time they were ready to leave for three performances in San Diego, Emerald had called Charles and told him that she wouldn't be making the trip at all.

"This thing with Emerald can't go on much longer," Deborah said to Triage when they returned.

"Yeah, but from what I'm hearing, your stock is rising. Have you seen what the papers are saying? They're calling you Lavelle's next jewel. I think you really need to think about going solo now. Why don't you call William Martin while you have this break?"

"I don't think I want to leave Lavelle right now, with everything that is going on."

"You don't have to, baby. All I want you to do is talk to William, see how serious Capricorn is, and move from there. You can release an album and still sing with Lavelle."

"I can?"

"Lots of people do it that way. Phoebe kept singing with Lavelle until her second album." He wrapped his arms around her. "Look, let's just talk to William, okay?"

Deborah sighed, but agreed. "Okay, when I get back from Phoenix."

CHAPTER 41

AFTER FIVE SHOWS IN PHOENIX AND SCOTTSDALE, Deborah was thrilled to have a weekend off. Triage was out of town making a personal appearance at Tower Records in New York. Though she missed him, it gave her time to catch up with Phoebe.

They spent Saturday running through Neiman Marcus and Saks, shopping as much as dodging autograph hounds—although Deborah was secretly thrilled when a fan asked for her autograph.

Back in Deborah's apartment, Deborah and Phoebe shared seaweed soup and almond chicken and laughed over family pictures Deborah had pulled from an album.

"That's my cousin Willetta," Deborah said, pointing to a group picture of Willetta's Sweet Sixteen birthday party.

"Girl, you really were square." Phoebe laughed.

Deborah giggled, but stopped as she caught a glimpse of herself in the reflection from the granite fireplace. Phoebe was right; she looked very different now than she did a year ago. She was wearing a denim miniskirt and handkerchief top—something she never would have considered in Villa Rica. She had changed, and she wasn't sure when it all happened.

"What's wrong?" Phoebe frowned as she sipped her soup.

"Nothing, really. It's just that I'm beginning to realize how different I am."

"There's nothing wrong with that. You've grown."

Deborah nodded. "I guess, but I don't want to get too far from the things that are important to me."

"And what things would that be?"

"My family, Triage, but most important, God."

"Well, from what I see, there's very little chance of that. I wish I had what you have with God."

Deborah smiled. "Phoebe, it's no secret. You can have a relationship with God any time you want it."

"That's what I've always heard, but I tried God, and He didn't seem to listen. I used to pray so hard, begging Him to stop the pain." Phoebe grimaced. "But nothing ever happened. He never heard my prayers."

Deborah sat next to Phoebe. "I don't think that's true; maybe you just didn't recognize God's voice. I've learned that sometimes you have to be still to hear Him."

"Even if I tried to talk to God now, He wouldn't listen, for sure. With all that I've done, from the booze to the drugs, the men . . . I tried everything to put aside all that I was feeling."

"Maybe you've been looking for peace in the wrong place."

Phoebe held up her hands. "I know what you're going to say. But if God can be there for me now, why wasn't He there when I needed Him the most? Why wasn't He there when my stepfather . . . my uncle . . ." Her eyes filled with tears. "Why didn't He stop them?"

Deborah took her hands. "Phoebe, I don't know why those things happened to you, but I do know that God *was* there. He did help you survive."

Phoebe nodded and wiped away her tears. "It was just so horrible. I think that's the reason why I'm like this now. I've tried to be different, but somehow, I always return—"

"Phoebe, if you really want to make a change, there's only one way to do it. The drinking and drugs, the sex and men— none of that will work. Only God can pull you away and deliver you from that."

Phoebe shook her head silently.

"I have an idea," Deborah said suddenly. "Why don't you come to church with me tomorrow? Triage won't be getting back till late, so it'll be just you and me."

For the first time in minutes, Phoebe laughed. "Girl, I haven't been to church in so long that the building just might fall apart when I walk in."

Deborah laughed with her. "That won't be a problem; it's a brick building."

It took Phoebe a few moments before she said, "Okay. Let's go to church and see if God is still there for me."

The next morning, Phoebe called to tell Deborah that she wasn't feeling well. It took Deborah almost twenty minutes to convince Phoebe that it was just the devil trying to keep her away.

By the time they walked into Macedonia, the choir had already begun singing. Phoebe motioned to the last pew, and Deborah agreed, wanting Phoebe to feel comfortable on her first visit. The key was to get her to come back.

Throughout the service, Deborah held Phoebe's hand and guided her through the scriptures. When Pastor Clarke spoke of Jesus being the true vine, and His children the branches, she watched Phoebe from the corner of her eye.

"Any branch which does not bear fruit, will be cut away. If you're not living for God, if you're not bearing fruit for His kingdom, then He has no need for you. The Lord said, 'Every branch in me that beareth not fruit, he taketh away and every branch that beareth fruit, he purgeth it, that it may bring forth more fruit.'"

Deborah saw Phoebe edge in closer and nod her head slowly as if the pastor's words were sinking in.

When the choir stood for the last selection, Phoebe and Deborah joined them, but only Deborah sang and clapped. It wasn't until they were in the car that Deborah asked Phoebe how she enjoyed the service.

"It was fine, good really." Phoebe twisted her hands. "I felt like the pastor was talking to me."

"I feel like that all the time." Deborah chuckled. "So do you think you'll come back?"

Phoebe nodded. "We'll see. I'll be out of town next weekend. My new man, Paul, wants to take me to Palm Springs for a lovers' getaway."

Deborah only smiled, though her disappointment weighed heavily.

"Okay, you can come back the week after that."

When Phoebe remained silent, Deborah said, "Just remember, Phoebe, that God loves you no matter what you're doing or who you're with. You're the one who's going to have to make a commitment to Him, because He's already made a commitment to you."

Deborah stopped the car in front of Phoebe's townhouse, and Phoebe hugged her. "Do you know how much I love you?" Phoebe said. "You're such a good friend." She pulled back. "And that's all you've ever been. You've never wanted anything from me, and I can't tell you how much I appreciate it."

Deborah hugged her back and was surprised how tightly Phoebe held on to her. When they pulled back this time, both had tear-filled eyes.

"I'll call you tomorrow."

The lump in Deborah's throat was too large for her to say anything, so she just smiled. She watched Phoebe walk slowly to her front door and felt a strong urge to pray. And she didn't stop praying—she fell to her knees once she arrived home.

CHAPTER 42

DEBORAH TOOK THE ELEVATOR TO THE SEVEN-
teenth floor of the Capricorn Records building,
wishing Triage were with her.

"Deborah, how will that look?" Triage had said
when she begged him to come with her.

"You think I care about looks? I don't know what I'm doing.
All I did was sign on to sing with Lavelle, and now I'm on
the verge of having my own career," she screamed.

His laugh echoed through his large living room. "That's
what you've wanted, remember?"

"Oh, yeah." She chuckled. "But I'm nervous about this
meeting."

"You'll be fine."

"How do you know?"

"Because I know you. And I know God. You'll pray tonight;
you'll pray tomorrow when you wake up. You'll pray as you
drive over to the meeting, and while they're talking, you'll be
praying. And on top of that, I'll be right here, waiting for

you to call, and I'll be praying too. So there's no way things won't work out right."

Deborah smiled now as she remembered their conversation last night. Triage was right—she hadn't stopped praying.

She had barely stepped off the elevator when William rushed over to her.

"You're right on time." William ran his hand over his beard. "They're waiting for us."

Deborah smoothed her red suit and followed William into the office marked "Patrick Robinson, President."

The moment they entered, two men stood and walked across the large office to greet her.

"Deborah, it's so nice to meet you. I'm Patrick," one man said, shaking her hand. "And this is Drew, our artists' manager."

"It's nice to meet you." She followed them as they returned to the massive desk that sat in front of the glass wall. Behind Patrick, Deborah had a clear view of the Hollywood sign. When she turned her attention to the men, they were all smiling at her.

Finally, William said, "I've told Deborah about your proposal, Patrick, but I knew you wanted to talk to her yourself."

As Patrick went through Capricorn's proposal, she held her face still, hoping it hid the trembling excitement she felt inside. It grew more intense as she listened to the details of their proposal—three-record contract, six-figure advance, ten percent of money earned from records sold.

"We like what you do with Lavelle; your sound has people wanting to hear more of you already. So we want to play on that. Maybe make you a bit sexier, more on the edge. We think you could give Phoebe Garland a run."

She frowned. She had hoped to pull back a bit from the image that was taking her further away from who she wanted to be. But she would discuss that later.

After another twenty minutes, Patrick finally said, "Deborah, as you know, we only sign stars." He motioned to a wall filled with photos of some of the biggest names in the business. "And we plan on making you as big as any of them." He leaned back in his chair. "So what do you say?"

Deborah returned his smile. What should she say? Here she was, a twenty-seven-year-old woman from a small town in Georgia, sitting in an office with three white men dressed in almost identical navy suits. They stared at her as if they expected only one answer—yes! Who would turn this down? the expressions on their faces said.

Deborah took a deep breath and said, "This all sounds good, but I want to review this with my lawyer."

Patrick looked at William as if her response surprised him, and William twisted in his seat.

"Uh, Deborah, I'm an attorney, and I've looked this over. It's one of the best contracts you'll get."

"I understand, but I still want to take this home and look it over." She paused. "And I need to pray about it."

She almost laughed aloud at their confused stares. She stood. "Gentlemen, thank you so much for meeting with me. I'll get back to William in a day or two." She turned to William.

"Uh, I'll call you later, Deborah," he said. "I have some other business here."

She shrugged, then smiled before she left the office.

Through the reception area, into the elevator, then out into the parking lot, she remained calm. It wasn't until she pulled through the guarded gate and drove onto the freeway that she punched Triage's number into her cell phone and screamed when he answered on the first ring.

"Triage, I'm on my way over there! We have a lot of praying to do." She was giddy with excitement.

"So it went well?"

"Let's just put it this way: My tithing envelopes are going to be a whole lot thicker from now on!"

CHAPTER 43

DEBORAH COULDN'T WAIT TO GET TO PHOEBE'S apartment and tell her friend the final news— she had signed the Capricorn contract this morning!

Phoebe had been so happy for her the day before, and Deborah had readily accepted when Phoebe invited her to a celebratory dinner. She was so eager to see Phoebe, she was tempted to ignore the speed limit on the way to her friend's house.

Both Phoebe and Triage thought there were big changes coming for her now. "Just wait," they joked, "you're going to be big-time. Maybe you'll finally break down and trade in that Camry!"

But she wasn't thinking about fancy cars or elaborate homes. She was thinking about how blessed she was to be able to use the gift that the Lord gave her in a way that would bring her the fame and fortune she'd always dreamed of.

"Thank you, Father!" she thought as she turned into the guest parking lot at Phoebe's townhouse.

Sirens were blaring and lights were flashing. Three police cars and an ambulance blocked off the parking lot. Several people stood outside Phoebe's house. Deborah's heart was beating loudly in her chest.

She jumped from her car and ran toward Phoebe's front door, but a uniformed cop stopped her.

"Miss, this is a crime scene. No one can go in there."

"My friend lives there," Deborah cried. "Please, what happened?"

Two policemen came down the steps of her friend's house escorting Thomas, who was in handcuffs. Deborah gasped. A second later, Phoebe was brought out on a stretcher, and Deborah pushed past the cop.

"Phoebe!"

With half-opened eyes, Phoebe reached toward her, but the oxygen mask covering Phoebe's mouth prevented her from saying anything.

Deborah turned to the paramedics. "Please, I'm her . . . sister. I want to ride with her."

They nodded and allowed Deborah to accompany Phoebe in the ambulance. The medics worked on Phoebe all the way to Cedars Sinai, and Deborah kept out of the way. Fifteen minutes passed before a doctor allowed Deborah to see Phoebe.

"She's been asking for you," the doctor said simply as he led Deborah to the cubicle where Phoebe lay on a gurney. "But only for a moment. We have to get her into surgery."

The bandage that surrounded her head was soaked with

blood, but she was awake, her eyes tiny slits. She lifted her hands, reaching for Deborah.

"I'm here, Phoebe." Deborah sniffed. She wanted to know what had happened, but none of that was important now.

"Deborah." Phoebe's voice was low and raspy. "I need you to do me a favor."

Deborah took Phoebe's hand. "Sshh, don't try to talk," Deborah said as tears streaked down her cheeks. "You need your strength. They said you have to have surgery—"

"I'm not . . . going to make it."

"Don't say that," Deborah cried, shaking her head.

"It's all right. I'm tired. . . ." She paused and swallowed. "But . . . I need you to do something for me."

"Anything." Deborah choked the word through her throat.

"I didn't do right by God," Phoebe whispered. "Please ask Him to forgive me."

Deborah's lips trembled with grief, but she took Phoebe's hand in both of hers. "I don't have to do that for you, Phoebe. You can do it."

"I don't know—"

"Phoebe, you can accept Jesus right here, right now, and He'll forgive all your sins. Just say that you accept Jesus Christ as your savior and that He died for your sins."

"That's it?"

Deborah nodded, then swallowed hard before she spoke. "Do you accept Jesus as your savior?" she sobbed.

"Yes, please, Jesus." Deborah could barely hear Phoebe, but that didn't matter. She knew Jesus heard.

Deborah continued through her tears. "Phoebe, once you've asked Jesus into your heart as your savior, you're saved. There's nothing else you have to do. God loves you and has forgiven you."

"I'm sorry, miss," a nurse interrupted them. "You have to leave now."

"I just need—"

"Now!"

Phoebe's fingers slowly slipped out of Deborah's grasp, and Deborah backed away from the bed.

Outside, she asked a passing orderly for directions to the basement chapel, and through tear-heavy eyes, she found her way there. She knelt at the altar.

"Please, God, please save Phoebe. She is just getting to know You. I know that doesn't matter," Deborah cried. "But Phoebe has so much to offer You, Lord. There is so much that she can do here in Your name. Please, Father . . ."

She stayed on her knees for another fifteen minutes, then rushed back to the emergency room.

When she pushed open the door, she gasped as she heard the doctor say, "Record the time of death as nine twenty-seven. . . ."

⤴

She was still trembling when Triage rushed into the emergency room and pulled her into his arms.

"Oh, baby," was all he said, as she finally released her anguish.

"I can't believe she's gone," she sobbed.

"Neither can I," Triage said, squeezing her closer to his chest. "But at least you were with her."

Deborah nodded and lifted her head. "And I got to pray with her right before...."

His thumb gently wiped a tear from her cheek. "Deborah, that's all that matters." He pulled her back into his arms, and they sat in the waiting area, surrounded by women who held small children and men who paced, waiting to hear news of loved ones.

It was after eleven by the time he drove her home. Triage would send one of his friends to pick up her car in the morning.

When Deborah put the key in the door of her condo, she turned to him. "I'm really tired. I'm just going to go to bed."

"That's fine," Triage responded. "But I'm not going to leave you alone. I'm going to stay with you tonight."

When she began to protest, Triage opened the door and gently pushed her inside.

"I know how you feel about this, Deborah, and believe me, I'm not trying to pull anything. I'll sleep on the couch."

"But that won't look right—"

"I don't care how it looks. It's just for one night. I can't leave you alone. Please take a look at this from my point of view and try to understand."

She nodded, too tired to argue, and showed him the closet that held the extra blankets.

"If you're going to stay, you can sleep in the other bedroom—"

"The couch will be fine," he said, kissing her forehead. "I'll see you in the morning."

It didn't take long for her to undress and crawl into bed, ignoring her nightly ritual of a shower, brushing her teeth, and then reading her Bible. She was too weak to do any of those things.

As she reached to turn off the light, she noticed the blinking light on her answering machine, but she wasn't going to check her messages—not right now. It was probably just people who had gotten the news about Phoebe, and she couldn't talk about that right now.

"Oh, Phoebe." Deborah squeezed her pillow and cried softly. "I am going to miss you so much."

While she thought it would take hours to fall asleep, she was blessed with unconsciousness a few seconds after she closed her eyes. But her slumber was filled with memories so real that when the telephone rang, abruptly pulling her from her sleep, she couldn't remember if what had happened last night was real or part of a dream.

When she heard the gentle knock on her door, and Triage softly calling her name, she remembered that Phoebe was really gone.

"Deborah, your father is on the phone."

Quickly, she lifted the receiver. "Hi, Daddy."

"Deborah Anne, are you all right?"

Concern soaked his words, and Deborah knew her parents had somehow found out what had happened. "I'm fine, Daddy."

"I know it's early. Milton said that you were still asleep—"

She wanted to explain why Triage was there, but all she said was, "Daddy, my friend is dead."

"I know, sweetheart," Elijah said. "I just heard it on the news. The reporter said that she was murdered."

"Yes," Deborah said, "it looks that way. When I got to her

apartment last night, her old boyfriend, Thomas, was being led away in handcuffs."

"You were there?"

The way her father asked the question, Deborah was sure that he would take the next plane to Los Angeles and snatch her back to Villa Rica.

"I got there right after the ambulance arrived. But I was able to ride with her to the hospital, and once we got there, I was able to pray with her, Daddy. Phoebe received Jesus before she died." Deborah sobbed softly.

There was a silent moment before Elijah said, "Thank the Lord for that."

"Is Mama there?"

"No, she had to be at the hospital early this morning. I don't think she knows anything about this yet. I'll tell her when she comes home."

"Okay—"

"Deborah Anne, maybe you should come home for a few days."

"I wish I could, Daddy, but I'm going to start recording my album in a few weeks, and we have other shows to do—"

"I don't care about any of that," Elijah said gruffly. Then his voice softened. "I just care about you being all right."

"I'll be fine. I'll call you and Mama tonight."

"Okay. I love you, baby."

"Me, too," she said, then hung up the phone.

She was still sitting up in her bed when Triage knocked again.

"Deborah, I made some tea," he said through the closed door.

"Thank you. I'll be right out."

She grabbed her bathrobe and thought about how blessed she was to have Triage. He would help her get through this time.

The moment she opened her bedroom door, the Tazo tea that Triage had prepared greeted her. He was already sipping a cup, and he stood when he heard her footsteps.

He hugged her. "How are you?"

"I'm doing better than I thought," she said, sinking into the couch.

He handed her a teacup. "I listened for you all night, but I guess you slept pretty soundly. I answered your phone because I didn't want it to wake you." He took a sip from his cup. "Did your dad ask what I was doing here?"

She shook her head. "He heard about Phoebe on the news and wanted to know how I was doing." Deborah leaned back into Triage's arms and rested her head on his chest. "When I first woke up this morning, I thought I had dreamed this whole thing."

"You'll probably feel like that for a few days."

She nodded. After a few silent moments, she said, "You know, when Phoebe first asked me to pray with her, she said something that I just can't get out of my mind. She said that she had disappointed God." Deborah paused. "What a horrible thing to feel when . . ." She didn't finish her sentence. After a while, she asked, "Have you ever felt like that, Triage? Like you've disappointed God?"

He was thoughtful. "Yeah," he said simply. "Even though I've known God since I was a kid, I've just been doing what I want to do as an adult, living life the way I want to live it—all the time knowing better. I blamed a lot of it on this industry, and I was just doing what I had to do, but I knew God wasn't pleased."

"How did you deal with it?"

He shrugged his shoulders. "I just pushed it aside and tried not to think about it. That's why I didn't go to church and why I stopped praying. It was easier if God wasn't in my face all the time." He paused. "But I don't feel like I'm disappointing Him anymore. I think He knows I'm trying. I'm not where I want to be, but I'm better than I was."

She nodded silently.

He continued: "You know, one of the things that's bringing me closer to God is this whole celibacy thing that you have me going through."

She looked up at him. "I'm not trying to make you go through anything."

He pulled her back into his arms. "I know. What I mean is, I've learned so much about myself over these last few months. When you first told me that you were a virgin and planned to stay that way, I was shocked into agreeing with you. But to be honest, I began to think about who I could call when . . . you know . . ."

She didn't know how she should respond, but when his arms tightened around her, she sat still and silent.

"But I've surprised myself. This is different, but I really feel like I'm getting to know you on a level that I've never known a woman before. And the best part is that I'm getting to know some things about myself too."

They sat silently watching the picture on the television screen. Finally, Deborah said, "I wonder if I'm disappointing God."

Triage shook his head. "I don't think so." He chuckled. "You're doing all the things He wants you to do."

"You're talking about going to church and reading my Bible and praying, but I'm talking about something else."

Triage frowned.

"What if I'm not using my voice the way God wants me to? What if I'm not doing the right thing?"

"I don't think God has a problem with what you're doing. You're not like a lot of these other singers—dressing like they don't have any sense, talking like they've lost their minds. Anyone who spends five minutes around you knows how spiritual you are."

But that's not enough, Deborah thought, though she remained silent. Triage doesn't understand. He thinks I'm talking about what others think. But I care about what God thinks.

He got up to refill her cup and then turned up the volume on the television as a news report came on about Phoebe. Tears instantly filled her eyes. It was surreal, the way the reporter stood with the microphone in her hand talking about someone that Deborah knew.

As the woman told what had happened, the camera cut away to shots of Phoebe's apartment and then cuts of Phoebe onstage. The final shot was of Phoebe at the Grammys just a few months earlier.

"Eyewitness News has learned that Thomas Davis, an acquaintance of Phoebe Garland, has been indicted for murder in the slaying. What makes this more tragic," the reporter continued, "is that a restraining order against her killer had been granted to Ms. Garland just two days before the tragic—"

Triage clicked off the television, then ran his hand over his face.

"I think you should go home and get some rest," Deborah said as she stood and hugged him.

"I am tired, but I don't want to leave you alone—"

"I'm fine now. I really should do some things. I need to call Lavelle; he and Phoebe were so close. And then Vianca and Emerald—"

The ringing phone made them smile. "I think they're going to beat you to it," Triage said, and kissed her forehead.

Deborah picked up the phone. "Hi, Lavelle."

Triage kissed her again. "I'll be back in a few hours," he mouthed, and closed the door as Deborah sank into the couch and began to share her grief with Lavelle.

She was crying by the time she hung up. Lavelle was stricken with sorrow, and Deborah had been able to console him only after she told him that she and Triage would come by.

She left a message for Triage at his house, then went into her bedroom. She reached for her Bible, but instead picked up the journal that she kept on her night table.

The words came quickly, and she wrote furiously:

> Oh, Lord, I don't understand . . .
> Is this the way . . . is this Your plan?
> Why is there so much pain and heartache along the way?
> If I remain prayerful, will there be a brighter day?
>
> Oh, Lord, is there any peace for me?
> I need to hide away in You, can't You see?
> I'm seeking refuge on behalf of my family . . .
> Right now, we need You so desperately.

This is my prayer . . .
This is my prayer . . .
I submit myself unto You.

Here are my burdens,
I rest them here with You
'Cause I know this is
The only way we'll make it through . . .

She leaned back, closed her eyes, and prayed for Phoebe
and all those left behind who loved her so.

CHAPTER 44

ᗺ

THE CROWD IN FRONT OF TRINITY CHURCH could have been gathered for a music industry event. Singers, producers, writers, and agents slowly filed into the large sanctuary. Sadness filled the air, reminding everyone that this was the final farewell to Phoebe Garland.

Deborah and Triage were escorted to the second-row pew where Lavelle and Vianca were already sitting. She refused to look at the altar where the white coffin sat. Instead, Deborah glanced around to see if she could find Emerald among the mourners. There was no sign of her, and Deborah sighed. Emerald was going to have to find help, or soon, Deborah feared, they'd be returning to this setting for her.

Soft whispers mixed with the organ music, and Deborah knew that she would have to garner every bit of strength to make it through the service dry-eyed.

A young woman was escorted past them, and Deborah was momentarily startled by her resemblance to Phoebe. When the woman sat next to Phoebe's mother, Deborah knew that she must be Phyllis, Phoebe's sister.

As the minister took his place and began the service, Deborah felt tears come into her eyes. She held Triage's hand tighter as a choir sang "Blessed Assurance."

After the eulogy was read, it was time for Deborah to speak. Triage stood and walked with her to the altar, then took a seat in the front pew, waiting until she finished.

Deborah had carefully kept her eyes away from where Phoebe's body lay. She straightened her papers on the podium, took a deep breath, then looked into the sea of solemn black, white, and brown faces.

Oh, God, she thought, help me get through this.

"Phoebe was a wonderful friend to me. I met her months after arriving in LA, when I first went on tour. She befriended me and taught me many valuable lessons." She took a breath. "I wanted to pay tribute to Phoebe in a special way, and so I wrote this for her." Deborah lifted the paper and took a deep breath. "This is titled 'My Friend.'

"Such a beautiful lady,
Never knew she was loved, till too late.
She was my friend and I miss her,
So cold and unkind is fate.

"Talented, warm and loving,
She wore her heart on her sleeve,
Only to be taken for granted.
I never thought she'd leave.

"I hope she's smiling down on me.
I'm thinking about my friend Phoebe.

I never thought this day would be
Without her here . . . only memories.

"I can feel her smiling down on me.
I know she's happy finally,
Cradled in God's arms just like a baby,
Yet I'm missing my friend Phoebe."

Phoebe's family thanked her as she stepped down, and she held each of them close before Triage took her hand and led her back to her seat. He put his arm around her and whispered, "Are you okay?"

She nodded, but finally released the tears that she had been holding back.

It had been a long day. After the service, they followed the long line of more than sixty cars to Rose Hills Cemetery. It surprised Deborah that Phoebe's mother had chosen to bury Phoebe in Los Angeles rather than Detroit. But Lavelle explained that Phoebe had made her own arrangements a few months earlier. That revelation made Deborah shudder. Had Phoebe seen this coming, or was she just trying to be responsible and prepared?

After a short graveside ceremony, they went to Lavelle's house. The anguish in the air choked Deborah, and in less than an hour she returned to her apartment with Triage.

As she lay back on the couch, Triage took off her shoes and massaged her feet.

"You did good at church today," he said.

Deborah closed her eyes. "I wanted to be strong for Phoebe. But I'm so tired."

He placed her feet on the floor. "I think I'm going to go home and let you get some rest," he said, kissing her. "I have to be up really early tomorrow for a shoot. I'll call you."

When Triage closed the door behind him, Deborah was surprised at how grateful she felt for the time alone. It had been three emotion-packed days, and she wanted some time to come back.

Lavelle had canceled rehearsals for the rest of the week, and Deborah wasn't sure if he would be able to make it next week. Lavelle was engulfed with grief, and Deborah knew it would take some time for him to recover.

After her shower, she felt restless, so she sat at her piano and hit the keys, playing a few melodies.

"I didn't do right by God."

Phoebe's words had played over in her mind for days, and Deborah didn't know why.

As her fingers moved across the keys, Deborah began to sing. "'Jesus loves me, this I know. For the Bible tells me so. . . .'" As the words flowed from her into the room, she felt the same comfort that she always did when she sang this song.

Her eyes became wet with tears, but she kept singing, louder and with more strength, until she was exhausted.

Finally, she turned off the lights and climbed into bed. But she didn't close her eyes until she thanked God for bringing her through this tragedy.

CHAPTER 45

I T TOOK LAVELLE WEEKS TO GET BACK ON SCHEDULE. Deborah used the time to jump into the meetings, planning, and rehearsals for her own album.

Capricorn had brought in writers to work with Deborah, and now, as she sat with William, she went over the list of songs that had been decided on.

"I think this one is going to be hot," William said. "'I Wanna Love You Down.'"

Deborah glanced through the list: "Freaky, Deaky," "Let's Go All the Way," "You Taught Me How to Cheat." And these were the best of the bunch.

"Deborah," William began as he came around the desk and stood leaning toward her, "Capricorn is so excited about this project. The promotion they have planned will have you in every household in America. Your words and your voice will be heard all over the country."

She looked at the paper in front of her. This was what people would be hearing from her: "Sexy Revenge."

"Deborah?"

Her eyes focused on William, who stared down at her as if something were wrong.

"Deborah, are you all right?"

She nodded.

What can I say? she thought. This is what I've wanted. This is my dream—to be singing under contract with a national label. To be on the verge of making millions. She looked at the list again: "So Hot, So Fast."

She stood and picked up her purse. "William, I just remembered something I have to do. I'll give you a call later."

He didn't have a chance to say anything before she was out the door, running to her car and locking the doors as if someone were chasing her.

She held her face in her hands. "God, what am I doing?"

The list of twelve songs ran through her head again. "But this is my dream, and I'm using what God has given to me. What am I supposed to do?"

She started he car and drove aimlessly for forty minutes, then headed toward her church.

She tried the front doors, but they were locked, so she went around to the side of the building. She rang the bell, and moments later, Clara, the pastor's assistant, answered the door.

"Hey, Deborah."

"Clara, I needed to know if I could just sit in the sanctuary for a few minutes."

Clara frowned. "Sure. Are you all right? Do you need me to find Pastor Clarke?"

Deborah shook her head. "No, I'm fine. I just need to spend some time here."

Clara nodded knowingly. "I'm going back to my office. Just call me if you need anything."

The sanctuary was empty, as it would be on a Thursday afternoon. Deborah sat in the front row and looked at the altar, surrounded by luscious green plants and flowers. Pastor Clarke's and Deacon Jones's two large chairs flanked the oak podium. Deborah's eyes held the large gold cross that hung on the wall behind the altar. For the first time in hours, she felt a bit calm, though a war of emotions raged inside.

"Lord, I don't know what's going on," she whispered. "But something is wrong." She paused, trying to find the words. "Lord, I never want to feel that I'm not doing right by You. But that's what I feel, Lord. I'm lost. You've blessed me with this career; I know it came from You. But now . . . am I just supposed to walk away from what You gave to me?"

She felt hot tears stinging behind her eyelids as she continued. "So, Lord, if You want me to leave this, if I'm supposed to be doing something else, speak to my heart and let me know. I surrender to You. I want to do right by You. I want to hear You say, 'Well done, My good and faithful servant.' Please, God, help me through this."

Deborah sat in the sanctuary until she could feel the shifting light of the sun though the stained-glass windows. Then she walked out into the parking lot, got in her car, and drove home.

CHAPTER 46

TONIGHT'S PERFORMANCE WAS THEIR FIRST SINCE Phoebe's death, and it would also be their first performance without Emerald, who was taking a two-month leave of absence at the Betty Ford Clinic. There wasn't going to be a replacement for Emerald, because she had made her announcement only two days earlier, at the beginning of rehearsals.

"I'm not going to be singing with you guys," Emerald said.

Lavelle dropped the Danish he'd been eating. "Emerald, you've missed enough rehearsals." He sighed. "I'm not going to be able to put up with this much longer. The only reason I've stuck in this long is because we go way back."

Emerald sauntered over to Lavelle and stood so close that they were almost touching. Deborah and Vianca were standing at their microphones, and Deborah took a quick glance at Vianca, who was standing with her arms folded across her chest.

"It's probably because we go so far back that I have this problem now," Emerald said accusingly.

Lavelle held up his hands and backed away from her. "Don't blame that on me. You drink because of you, but you're always wanting to blame someone else."

It was a moment before she spoke. "You're right, Lavelle. I'm in trouble because of me, and I'm finally going to do something about it." She turned to face Deborah and Vianca. "I'm checking into Betty Ford. I'll be away for about two months."

They stood silently for several moments before Deborah walked toward Emerald and hugged her.

"I am so happy for you. I've been praying that you would get well."

"Thank you, Deborah." Emerald glanced over her shoulder at Lavelle and Vianca, who had stayed where they were. When she saw that they weren't going to move, Emerald's eyes turned back to Deborah. "I guess no one else cares," she said, dropping her head.

"That's not true, Emerald. We all care. This is just a shock."

Suddenly, from behind them, Lavelle said, "So, do you plan on coming back?"

The arrogance she had shown earlier had disappeared. "I don't know."

"Well, we're going to have to hold auditions—"

"I understand—"

"And I can't promise that there'll be anything here for you when you get out."

Emerald's eyes were moist as she looked up at Lavelle. "Lavelle, there is nothing here for me now," she said softly, then turned and walked away.

It took Lavelle only a few moments to say, "Okay, Charles, let's get another girl in here."

They hadn't had a chance to audition anyone in time for this show, so Deborah and Vianca would be going out alone— as they had many times in the last few months.

And tonight, at the Anaheim Pond, Deborah would be singing the two duets with Lavelle.

She fanned herself with a magazine as Kim sprayed her hair.

"Stop that," Kim protested, as she pulled back the can.

"It's burning up in here."

"It'll be worse onstage. I don't know why you won't let me put your hair up tonight. You've got to try it at least once."

Deborah stared at her face in the mirror. Even with the concealer Kim had used on her, Deborah could still see the bags under her eyes. In the past weeks she had had little sleep as she went from rehearsals to meetings in preparation for her debut album. But even when she had time to sleep, she found herself roaming through her apartment thinking of Phoebe.

"I didn't do right by God."

She needed to do something different.

She took a sip of her Mountain Dew. "Go ahead, Kim. I need a change. Put my hair up."

Kim smiled into the mirror. "Okay, turn around. I want to surprise you. You're going to look gorgeous."

For fifteen minutes, Kim twisted and twirled Deborah's hair. Deborah used the time to try to relieve the permanent tension that had attached itself to her shoulders ever since Phoebe's death. The curling iron that Kim used added heat to the room, and Deborah had to resist running from the chair.

When Kim stepped back and clapped her hands, Deborah opened her eyes.

"Now this is what I'm talking about!" Kim exclaimed. She spun the chair around so that Deborah faced the mirror. "See how beautiful you look."

Deborah's eyes widened with surprise. Kim had twisted her thick hair into a French roll with long spiral curls along the edges. It was elegant, and she looked just like Phoebe.

"What's wrong?" Kim's forehead had creased into a deep frown. "I thought you'd like it."

Deborah pressed her hands against her face as if this would hold back her tears. "Please, Kim, I need to be alone."

Kim opened her mouth as if to say something, then simply nodded and quietly left the room.

Deborah stared at her reflection, then let her eyes roam to the soda can.

"I didn't do right by God."

Deborah stood up and slipped into the scarlet satin slip dress that looked much like the nightgown Phoebe had given her for Christmas. She didn't pause for a moment as she stepped into her shoes. Without looking into the mirror, she straightened her dress and almost ran into the hallway, because she knew if she slowed down, she might never go on the stage again.

CHAPTER 47

THE RINGING TELEPHONE PULLED DEBORAH FROM the sleep in which she had hidden all day. When she answered, Triage's voice made her smile.

"Hey, baby."

"Hi." She smiled through her sleep.

"You were taking a nap?"

"Uh-huh," she said, wanting to tell him that she'd napped all day. She had not even gotten dressed.

"Well, I was calling to say that I miss you."

"I miss you too. How's New York?"

"Busy. We're moving from meeting to meeting, from deal to deal. I don't have time for anything—except to think about you."

Deborah rolled over on the bed and smiled. "I wish I were with you."

"What's wrong? You sound kinda down. I'd thought you'd still be flying after last night in front of the home crowd. I love performing in Los Angeles."

Deborah wanted to tell him all that she was feeling—that she didn't know what she was doing anymore, that she wondered what she should be doing, that she wanted to do right by God.

"I'm just tired. I've been working so hard."

"Are you still going to start recording next week?"

She hesitated. "It looks that way."

"Great!" She could feel his smile through the phone. "I hope I'm going to be back in time. I really want to be in the studio with you."

"I'd like that."

They chatted for a few more minutes before Triage had to rush to another meeting. After hanging up, Deborah wandered around the condo, playing the piano a bit before she turned to her journal.

She bit the tip of her pen before she began writing down the prayer that she'd been saying inside for weeks.

"Lord, I really thought this was what You wanted me to do. I prayed, but now I feel such a sense of shame. I don't want to do anything to bring dishonor to You, Lord. You gave me this gift, and I want to make You proud. What is it that You want me to do? Please tell me, Lord. Please."

She leaned into the deep, soft pillows of the couch and drifted into the safety of sleep. But less than an hour later, she sat up abruptly, panting and trying to catch her breath. It took several minutes before her erratic pulse steadied.

"Oh, my God," she said aloud, as she stood and paced around the living room. The dream had seemed so real. She was in a coffin, being buried alive. She was screaming, but no one heard her. But she kept screaming—"I tried to do right. . . . I tried to do right. . . ."

Now she trembled despite the warm evening.

She had to make a decision, but she already knew what she had to do. With a heavy heart, she picked up the phone.

"Hey, Willetta."

"Well, if it isn't my superstar cousin! How're you doing?"

"Great, girl," Deborah said flatly. "I just wanted to hear your voice."

"Hey . . . what's up?" Willetta's words came slowly. "You don't sound good."

Deborah tossed a pillow across the room. "I'm fine."

"Well, it's almost eleven o'clock here, and I have to work tomorrow. So instead of me asking you a thousand times what's wrong, let's just cut to the chase."

Deborah paused, her mind a potpourri of all the unsettled thoughts that had bombarded her for weeks. "You know my friend Phoebe passed away."

"Yeah, girl. I left you a message. Didn't you get it?"

"Uh-huh. I've just been busy."

"So you're still feeling bad about that."

"Yeah, but not in the way you think. Since she passed, I've been feeling guilty about what I do, the music that I sing. I think I might have to give this up."

Deborah heard Willetta's intake of breath. "You mean walk away from Lavelle and your solo career? Deborah, you can't do that!"

"That's what I thought. But Phoebe said something right before she died. She said that she hadn't done right by God. Willetta, her words have stayed in my mind as if she glued them there herself. No matter what I do, or where I go, I hear her saying that. And I never want to be in that position where my last words on earth are ones of regret."

"I don't think that would happen to you. You always said that God had given you this gift to use."

"But I'm beginning to realize that I'm not supposed to be using it to sing songs like 'So Hot, So Fast.' Maybe I'm just meant to sing at Mountain Baptist and glorify God there."

"So you want to give it all up?" Willetta's disbelief was evident in every word.

"I don't want to, but I think I have to."

Willetta made a sound before she spoke. "Deborah, why haven't you thought about singing the songs that *you* write?"

Deborah shrugged. "I don't know. I guess because they're spiritual."

"So? You could sing gospel. And not those old fuddy-duddy songs that we do sometimes in church, but that new gospel—contemporary stuff."

"Hmmm."

"I bet you if you looked into all of your journals, you'd see that you'd have enough songs to do a couple of albums."

Deborah sat on the edge of the couch. "But I already have a contract," she said, as much to herself as to her cousin.

"Again I say, so? Just tell them that you're going to do gospel instead."

Deborah chuckled. "It's not like that in this business, Willetta. You can't just change a contract."

"Well, you're thinking about walking *away* from a contract. I'm talking about giving them something that you and the recording company could both live with."

"I don't know—"

Willetta sighed. "I honestly don't think God is telling you to walk away. You're making it sound like it's an all-or-nothing proposition, and it's not. There's a middle ground, and maybe

God put you in Los Angeles to get you started, but now He's telling you it's time to change your course and sing for Him—right there, in the middle of Hollywood. Imagine what you could do if you sang your songs to the same people you've been singing Lavelle's songs to."

"Gospel . . ." Deborah said the word thoughtfully.

"Not just regular gospel—contemporary sounds that young people will listen to. Music with a message."

"There aren't many people who do that." She began to pace the floor again.

"That's all the more reason for you to do it, Deborah Anne. You've got the voice, you've written great songs, you now have an audience—all you need now are the guts to do it right."

A few moments later, Deborah said, "How did you get so smart?"

"It's always easier to see something from the outside in, and this seems so clear to me."

"You know what, Willetta, it's something for me to think about. Listen, I didn't mean to keep you up so late. Go on to bed."

"Okay, but promise you'll call me again before you do anything."

"I promise. I love you, Willetta."

"I love you, and God does too."

CHAPTER 48

DEBORAH SAT UP ALL NIGHT WITH A YELLOW PAD and Tazo tea in front of her. By the time the morning's sun flowed through the large windows, she had six pages written out.

Taking a final sip of tea, she picked up the telephone and dialed her manager's voice mail.

"William, this is Deborah. I need to talk to you as soon as possible. Please call me the moment you get this message."

Filled with surprising energy, she ran into the bathroom. While she would have loved to sit in the center of her Jacuzzi and let the jets massage away the tiredness, instead she turned on the shower. She had to be ready the moment William returned her call.

By the time she got out of the shower, she had a message from William, and she called him back to set up an early meeting.

"What's this about, Deborah?"

"I really don't want to talk about it on the phone, but I promise, you'll be as excited as I am."

She found William pacing in front of the Starbucks on Santa Monica Boulevard. When he offered to buy her a cup of tea, Deborah declined, still filled with the tea she'd drunk all night.

"Deborah, you have me on pins and needles. What's this about?"

She took a deep breath. "I want to sing gospel." She waited for his eyes to focus, letting her know that he had heard her. "And I want to do it now."

"I don't understand."

"I want to fulfill my contract with Capricorn with gospel albums."

"Oh, no, Deborah," William groaned.

She held up her hand. "William, first hear me out. I think when you hear all the facts, you'll change your mind and take this to Capricorn with a big smile on your face."

She spread the papers she'd worked on last night on the small round table and began going over what she'd put together. She showed him lyrics of songs, they reviewed how many African Americans considered themselves Christians, they talked about her audience and whether they would accept this. For an hour, he threw questions at her, and she answered them as quick as lightning.

Through chatting customers and William's ringing cell phone, they addressed Deborah's proposal from every angle William could think of. After another hour passed, William sat back.

"Well, I still think this is going to be a tough sell to Capricorn, but I'll see what I can do. I don't know, Deborah—"

"There's one more thing, William, but I want you to use it as your final ace."

He frowned, but she smiled widely.

"Would they do this if I could guarantee two stars singing with me?" She paused. "I could get Lavelle Roberts and Triage Blue to each sing a song with me on the first album."

William leaned forward with interest.

She hadn't asked either of them, but she had prayed about it last night, and it was what God had dropped into her heart. "Lavelle did it for Phoebe and Triage. . . ." She dropped her eyes. "Well, let's put it this way—he'll do anything for me."

William slapped his hand on the table. "Well, with that, we just might have a deal." He looked at his watch. "I'll make some calls, and try to get there today or tomorrow." He reached across the table and shook her hand. "You've convinced me, but I still think that you're walking away from some money. There's more in mainstream, you know."

"It's not about money for me, William. It's about something greater that I have to do."

He stared at her for a long moment, then shook his head. "I'll give you a call."

Deborah's eyes followed him until he got into his 740i BMW and drove away. There was only one thing she had to do now. She would go home and pray and ask the Lord to work on the hearts of everyone at Capricorn Records, until they were agreeing to things that they never thought they would.

As she pulled her car onto Santa Monica Boulevard, she felt herself shivering. But it wasn't the shiver of distress that had filled her so much recently. It was the shiver of excitement and expectation.

She glanced up at the heavens and smiled. "It's in Your hands now, Lord. I've done my part." When she finally got home, she fell onto her bed, and then, still fully clothed, she slept through the rest of the day.

CHAPTER 49

THE NEXT DAY, DEBORAH SAT BY THE PHONE skimming through magazines while she waited for William to call. But the phone had remained stubbornly silent all morning.

It rang at noon.

"Hello." She was a bundle of nerves.

"Hey, baby."

Though she was glad to hear his voice, she couldn't hide her disappointment. "Hey, Triage."

"You're not glad to hear from me?"

"Of course I am. I'm just . . . surprised. How are you?"

"Missing you."

"I miss you too."

"Really, how much?"

"More than you can imagine," she moaned. "I'm going through something right now, and I could really use your support."

"How bad do you want it?"

She laughed. "Really bad."

"Bad enough to do anything?"

"Like what?"

"Like opening your front door?"

She frowned. "What?"

"You heard me. Open your door, woman!"

She ran to the door and swung it open. Triage was standing with his cell phone in his hand. Her mouth opened wide, and Triage laughed.

"What are you doing here?" she cried.

"You said you missed me!" She playfully pulled him inside, and they kissed passionately.

"I guess you're glad to see me."

She nodded. "This was the best surprise. Why didn't you tell me you were coming in?"

"Because then it wouldn't have been a surprise," he said, and kissed her nose. "So what do you have going on that you need my support for?" He sat on the couch and pulled her onto his lap.

"I always need you," she said softly, and kissed him again.

"You know, I think I'm going to get up and go out again, because I sure like how you greet me."

She laughed.

"But I'm curious. What's going on?"

She got up. "Not so fast. I want to hear all about your trip. Are you hungry? We can order something in."

He frowned. "You're stalling, but I am hungry. Let's order Thai."

He filled her in on the details of his trip as they waited. When the food arrived, Triage said grace, then went toward the refrigerator.

"What do you want to drink?" he asked over his shoulder.

"Just water."

When he opened the refrigerator, he asked, "What happened to the Mountain Dew?"

"I don't drink that anymore. All I have is juice."

Deborah could tell that Triage wanted to ask her about it, but he remained silent.

They sat at the dining room table across from each other and shared the Thai noodles and shrimp tempura.

Finally, Triage said, "So when are you going to tell me what's going on?"

She twirled a thin noodle on her plate. "You know the Bible says that anything that is meant for bad, God will turn it around for good. And I think Phoebe's death is an example of that."

"What do you mean?"

Her eyes were still lowered. "Well, I loved her, and I miss her so much. But I think there was a message in her death."

Triage took a sip of his pineapple-orange juice. "Are you talking about when she said that she didn't do right by God?"

Deborah looked up in surprise. "Yes. I think God used Phoebe to have me ask that question of myself."

"And so—"

Deborah took a deep breath. "I talked to William, and I'm not going to do the albums for Capricorn—"

The glass was halfway to his mouth, and he held it in midair. "What—"

"Now don't get excited." She spoke quickly. "I still want to record for them, but I want to sing gospel."

His face was stretched in disbelief. "Deborah, why would

you change everything now, just when things are beginning to break for you?"

"Because I think this is what I was called to do. I've been using my gift, but not for God. Willetta pointed it out to me."

"I understand, but what you're about to do is a big move. Has Capricorn agreed?"

She shook her head. "No. I thought I would hear from William yesterday, and definitely by now. . . ." Her eyes moved to the phone.

"I wish you had talked to me before you did that, Deborah."

She pursed her lips. She had expected a different reaction from him. "It wouldn't have made a difference, Triage. You wouldn't have been able to talk me out of this because it's not about money or fame or status anymore. I thought I could only do this one way—sing mainstream or nothing at all. But now I see that I can sing *and* glorify God. And I'll probably do better than I ever did with Lavelle."

He held up his hands. "I understand. All I'm saying is that this is a big step, Deborah. Capricorn could say no and decide not to do anything with you."

She shrugged, then stood and sat on the arm of the full chair in the living room. "Well, if they don't go with my plan, I'll just move back to Villa Rica."

Her words shocked them both.

Triage stood, walked to her, then crouched and took her hands. "Deborah, no matter what you want to do, I'll support you. But part of that support means getting you to look at the picture from every angle."

She nodded. "I understand, but there's nothing for us to discuss. After I put this plan together, I felt a peace that I couldn't believe. Triage, I haven't felt this way the entire time I've been singing. So I know it's right. I just have to find a way to make it work. Trust me on this, okay?" she said softly. "But more important, trust God."

He smiled widely. "Now *that* I can do. I love you, Deborah, and I will support you." He kissed her gently on the lips. But when he pulled back, he wasn't smiling. "I just want to ask you one thing—would you really consider going back to Villa Rica?"

There was nothing she could do but laugh at his long, sorrowful face.

CHAPTER 50

DEBORAH FOUND HERSELF STILL WAITING BY THE phone the next day. Though she was tempted to call William, she didn't. If he'd had any news, certainly he would have called her. But the anxiety that she had been trying to keep at bay was sneaking in like a thief in the night. There was only one thing she could do to calm the uneasiness that threatened to overwhelm her. She picked up her Bible.

"There's no need for me to worry about this," she scolded herself, as she turned to Matthew 6:25 and read through to the end of the chapter. As Jesus told the people on the mountain, worry was the opposite of faith. There was no need to worry; if God said to take no thought for your life, surely He could handle a little thing like this contract.

Only it wasn't so little to Deborah. She wanted this badly and didn't know what she would do without this deal. Would she really go back to Villa Rica? She was so different now, and couldn't see herself living in her parents' house on Peterson Road.

When the doorbell rang, she knew it was Triage even before she peeked through the peephole.

"Hey, baby. Sorry I'm late," he said, as he stepped inside and kissed her.

Deborah blinked in confusion. "Were we supposed to do something?"

"We didn't make plans, but you didn't think I would let you sit over here and worry by yourself."

She smiled. "How did you know I was worrying?"

"Because I know you, and . . . that's what I've been doing," he admitted.

She laughed, but their cheer quickly disappeared. "Do you think it means anything that William hasn't called?"

"It means he hasn't called, that's all. We can't read a thing into this."

She nodded.

"Well, get your purse. We're going to get out of here."

"No, I have to wait."

"Deborah, he's your manager. He has every number in the world for you. Take your cell; we'll be fine."

"I don't know—"

"I don't care what you say. It would be too nerve-wracking to sit here all day. And if you make me stay, I'll call William myself right now."

When he lifted her purse and handed it to her, she knew that he wouldn't take no for an answer. Begrudgingly, she followed him into his car.

Deborah didn't ask where they were going. Instead, she

closed her eyes, and tried to imagine all of the scenarios—if Capricorn said yes, or no, or something in between.

"Stop thinking about this," Triage said, as he pulled into a Malibu Beach parking lot. "We're going to have some fun out here."

"Okay." She smiled, though she knew that every cell of her brain would be thinking about the call.

"Let's stop and get something to eat."

"No," Deborah said quickly, feeling the churning in her stomach. "Would you mind if we walked awhile?"

He took her hand and led her to the shore. They took off their shoes and walked where the ocean met the sand. They'd moved less than twenty feet when Deborah pulled her cell phone from her purse and checked to see if it was on.

Triage grabbed the phone from her and stuffed it into his pocket.

She smiled. "I get the message."

They strolled along the almost secluded strand, silently watching the waves crash to the shore.

"You know, I was praying this morning, and I believe this is going to work out for you," Triage said.

She squeezed his hand. "I know it's going to work out. I just want it *settled* so that I know exactly how to proceed. There's so much I have to do—talk to Lavelle, get the songs together. . . ." She stopped and held her head in her hands. "I just want to know."

He took her hands from her face and kissed her palms.

"You'll be fine, you'll see." He put his arms around her, and they held each other. "But you know, Deborah, there are a lot of things in your life that have to be settled."

"There's *nothing* more important than this."

"Really?" He pulled back from her and took a small stick from his pocket.

She cocked her head to the side. "What are you going to do with that?" she asked.

He looked at the small broken branch in his hand. "As I was praying last night, God told me that there were many things that were up in the air with you. Not only your career, but us . . ."

She took his hand. "I don't feel that way, Triage. You're the only thing that I'm sure about."

He rubbed his palm against her cheek. "I want you to be really sure." He knelt down and began writing in the sand.

She laughed. "Oh, another message." She watched as he wrote, and as the message became clearer, her eyes opened wide.

When he finished, he turned toward her and, still on one knee, took a light blue box from his pocket.

Deborah held her hand to her face, but Triage gently brought it to his mouth and kissed it.

"I've been thinking about this for a while now," Triage said, as he opened the box and revealed the glittering jewel. "I bought this for you while I was in New York, though I wasn't sure when I would give it to you. But last night when you said you might have to go back home . . ." He paused and looked into her eyes. "I knew this was the time. I don't want to be without you. I love you." He turned back to the words he had written in the sand.

"You want to marry me?" The words squeaked softly through her lips.

He smiled, then placed the ring on her finger. "Deborah Anne Peterson, will you marry me?"

Deborah had dreamed of this moment all her life, but the joy she felt was nothing like she imagined it would be.

Triage rose from his knee and stared at her. "Deborah, you haven't said anything."

"Oh, Triage . . . yes, yes, I'll marry you."

"Now that's the best news I've had all day."

They kissed as the ocean's water swirled around their ankles.

The call from William was almost forgotten as they sat at Bayside Shrimp sharing a platter of fried shrimp and French fries. An autograph-seeker interrupted them only once, and Triage had proudly introduced Deborah as his fiancée.

"This is so beautiful," Deborah gushed again. She could barely take her eyes from the antique-style platinum band and two-carat diamond.

He took her hand and kissed her fingers. "I was really nervous about this." He looked at the ring. "I wanted to get something that was beautiful and would let you know how much I love you."

She smiled. "I love you too."

They talked through the afternoon, reminiscing about how they got to this point and making plans for their future. It wasn't until Triage parked at Deborah's apartment that the thought of William's call came rushing back to them. Triage handed Deborah her cell phone, and she checked for messages, hoping that somehow they hadn't heard the call. But there was nothing in her voice mail.

Deborah sighed. "Well," she began, taking Triage's hand and leading him into the condo, "I'm not going to let anything spoil this day." She hugged him. "You have made me very happy, and this is all I need."

But a moment later, when the phone rang, they looked at each other.

"Do you think—"

"Go ahead and answer it," Triage yelled.

She laughed, but then got serious when she heard William's voice.

"Deborah, I've been trying to reach you. Didn't you get my messages?"

"I've been checking my cell phone all day."

"Oh, I left you a dozen messages at home. Anyway, it's a go! Capricorn said they would do it."

"Really?" She sank onto the couch.

"What? What?" Triage searched her face for some clue.

"You put together quite a plan, but what sold them was having Lavelle and Triage featured on the album. You're sure they'll do it?"

"Yes." She closed her eyes and said a quick prayer that Lavelle wouldn't have a problem with this. Her plan was that they would sing the duet they'd been singing: "I'm Lost Without You."

Triage squeezed her hand, trying to get her attention, but she was listening to William and agreed with his request to meet in the morning.

Finally, she said, "William, thank you so much."

When she hung up the phone, Triage said, "They're going to do it." His statement was a hopeful question.

Deborah bobbed her head.

He lifted her from the couch and swung her in the air. "Oh, baby. Congratulations. You are going to be so big! I just know it."

"Can you believe it? William didn't give me many details, but he said that it was a go—especially since you and Lavelle are going to sing on the album."

Triage pulled back. "What are you talking about?"

She put her hand over her mouth. "I forgot to ask you. But my ace in the hole was having you and Lavelle featured with me." She put her arms around his neck. "You wouldn't mind, would you, baby?"

He threw his head back and laughed. "Oh, so now you tell me, and now you're begging. But that's okay, because I love a woman who begs."

"I guess that means you'll do it."

"Are you kidding? I'd do anything for you. I keep telling you that I have to take care of the daughter of the woman who took care of my mama!"

She laughed, twirling around in the middle of the living room. "This is a glorious day!"

"I just want to ask you one thing. Which was better—my marriage proposal or the call from William?"

Deborah took Triage's hand and led him to the couch. When she kissed him, there was no doubt of her answer.

CHAPTER 51

TRIAGE PACED THE LIVING ROOM FLOOR. "I DON'T know if we should do it this way. Maybe we should fly to Villa Rica," he said nervously.

Deborah put down the telephone. "Triage, I want my parents to find out about this before it's in the tabloids. Someone from Tiffany's is going to tell that you bought this ring," she said, holding up her hand, "and sooner or later, it'll be front-page *National Intruder* gossip." She put her arms around his neck. "Besides, we don't have time. I have to start on this project tomorrow, and you have your new album. . . ."

He nodded, but his forehead was still wrinkled in doubt.

"You're scared of my father?" She chuckled.

"No, I'm not." He sat on the couch and wrung his hands. "But this is the first time I've ever asked a father if I could marry his daughter."

Deborah laughed. "Well, that's a good thing, honey. My father will be glad to know that."

He grimaced.

"Oh, come on. You're being much too serious about this. My parents like you."

"Yeah, that was before I was trying to become their son-in-law." Triage ran his hand over his head. "You should have heard the way your father talked to me the morning I answered the phone when Phoebe died. He said, 'Milton, is that you?'" Triage had lowered his voice to a deep bass. "I had just fallen asleep, but he woke me right up—scared the daylights out of me!"

"He's that way with everyone—except your grandmother."

"She's another one who's going to be hard to tell."

Deborah sat down next to him. "Why? I think Mother Dobson likes me."

"Oh, she *loves* you. That's what scares me! Suppose she says that I'm not good enough for you?"

Deborah laughed again. "Now you're being ridiculous." She picked up the phone and dialed the number. "Here." She handed the phone to him.

As the phone rang, Deborah wiped a bead of perspiration from Triage's forehead.

He coughed. "Hello, Mr. Peterson. This is Tri . . . this is Milton Waters."

"Hello, Milton. Has anything happened to Deborah Anne?"

"Oh, no, sir! Deborah Anne is fine. I mean, I think she is . . . she's right here, but I wanted to talk to you."

"Well, good," Elijah said. "You know so much stuff goes on out there, that I just worry about Deborah Anne being all alone."

"She's not alone out here, sir. She's with me."

"Well, she's not with you *all night*. But I just pray for her

304

and pray that she doesn't get involved in the wrong things or with the wrong people."

Triage closed his eyes. Oh God, he thought.

"Milton, was there something you wanted to talk to me about?"

He cleared his throat again. "Yes, sir . . . you know, Deborah Anne and I have been . . . well, we've been dating—"

"Yes, I know that—"

"And I've come to love her. Very much." He paused, but when the silence continued on the other end, Triage took a deep breath. "Well, I asked Deborah Anne to marry me, and I would like to ask for your permission to marry your daughter, Mr. Peterson."

The silence continued.

"Mr. Peterson?"

"Virginia," Triage heard Elijah call. "Would you pick up the phone in the kitchen, please?"

Triage closed his eyes and moaned.

"What's wrong?" Deborah whispered.

Triage shook his head and then opened his eyes when he heard Virginia's voice.

"Deborah Anne, is that you?"

"No," Elijah said. "This is Milton. He just asked me if he could marry Deborah Anne."

"Milton, is that true?" Virginia asked.

If he weren't on the phone himself, he never would have believed this was happening. All he wanted to do was hang up, but instead he swallowed and said, "Yes, ma'am. I want to get your permission to marry Deborah Anne?" He didn't mean for his statement to sound like a question.

"Oh, that's wonderful. Isn't it wonderful, Elijah?"

"Well, there are some things I want to know first. Milton, how do you intend to support my daughter?" he asked brusquely.

Triage frowned. Didn't this man know that he was a superstar? "Well, Mr. Peterson, I make a very good living—"

The laughter on the other end of the phone startled him.

"Milton, I was just kidding. And yes, you have our permission."

"Yes, definitely. Is Deborah Anne there?" Virginia said. "We'd like to talk to her."

"Oh, yes. Thank you." Triage quickly handed the phone to Deborah, then collapsed onto the couch.

"Mama, isn't it wonderful? Daddy, I'm so happy."

"Deborah Anne, you'll have to come home. There are so many plans we have to make." Virginia spoke quickly, the way she always did when she was excited.

"Oh, Lord, I think that is my cue to hang up," Elijah said. "I love you, baby. And we want you to be very happy."

"I am, Daddy. I love you too."

Deborah chatted with her mother for a few more minutes and finally hung up after getting her mother's promise not to tell anyone until Triage had a chance to call his parents and his grandmother.

"I won't tell anyone for now. But tell Milton to hurry up. I don't know how long I'll be able to hold this secret."

When Deborah hung up, she leaned back on the couch and grinned at Triage. "Now that wasn't so bad, was it?"

Triage held his hand to his chest. "If it wasn't so bad, why has my heart stopped beating?"

They laughed.

306

❧

They had made a date to meet with Lavelle and Vianca at Lavelle's house that afternoon.

"I'm going to ask you this one last time," Triage said as he drove up the winding driveway. "Are you sure you want to leave Lavelle? You could do this solo album and still stay with the group."

"I know, but I can't do this halfway. I'm trying to make a statement with my music. I can't be onstage doing one thing and saying something else on my album. Now that I know better, I have to do better. In every way."

Triage took a long look at Deborah. "That is why I love you so much. I'm becoming a better man because of you."

"Oh sweetie, what a wonderful thing to say."

When they stopped in front of Lavelle's house, he was already waiting at the door.

"Hey, guys," he said, hugging Deborah and shaking Triage's hand. "It's been a while."

They walked into Lavelle's massive living room. Vianca was sitting at the grand piano, which was in the middle of the floor.

"Hey," she said simply, and continued playing.

Deborah sat next to her on the bench and hugged her. "How've you been? We don't spend any time together like we used to."

There was sadness in Vianca's eyes when she looked up. "I know. I've missed you."

"Well, you've been spending all of your time with Lavelle," Deborah whispered.

Vianca glanced across the room to where Triage and Lavelle stood at the bar. "I know. I'm in love with him. But he doesn't love me, and this isn't going anywhere." She paused. "I'm not going to hang around and end up like Emerald. I'm leaving. I'm going to move to New York and try to make it on Broadway. That's something that I've always dreamed about."

Deborah couldn't hide her shock. "You're leaving Lavelle? Have you told him?"

She nodded, and motioned with her hands. "But look at him. He doesn't care. After I told him, he looked at me, picked up the phone, and called Charles. I had hoped that maybe . . ." She sighed. "I don't know why I thought he'd think I was the one, but I love him, Deborah. I thought that one day, we'd be married."

Deborah looked at her left hand, then brought it down to her side. "Vianca, I am so sorry—"

"Hey, congratulations, Deborah. Triage just told me." Lavelle hugged her as he and Triage stood over the piano. "Did she tell you, Vianca? They're getting married."

Vianca's mouth dropped open, then without a word, she stood and left the room.

"What's wrong with her?" Triage asked.

Lavelle shrugged and sat next to Deborah on the bench. "I don't know. She's been acting weird all day. So have you guys picked the big day?"

Deborah stared at Lavelle. Did he just not know what Vianca felt? Or did he not care? She sighed. There was nothing she could do. Vianca had known all the time what she was getting into. She was just determined to change Lavelle, and everyone knew that kind of thing never worked.

"Well, we're going to have to wait on the wedding for a

little while," Triage said, looking at Deborah for her to continue.

"Uh, yeah, Lavelle, I have some other news. You know, I'm doing this solo album."

Lavelle grinned. "Yeah, girl. When are you going to start recording? I've got to tell you that I was a little disappointed that you didn't ask me to sing something with you." He laughed.

She and Triage exchanged glances. "Well, that is one thing that I want to talk to you about. We've made a change, and I'm going to be doing a gospel album."

He stopped hitting the piano keys and turned toward her. "Really?"

She nodded. "But it's not the gospel that everyone is used to. I want to praise God, but I also want to get His message to people. So it's going to be upbeat, and contemporary, and music that will make people clap their hands and stomp their feet." Her voice got more excited as she spoke.

"Hey, that sounds interesting. Capricorn went for it?"

"It took quite a bit of selling, but the thing that they really went for is . . . I told them that you would do a duet with me."

He looked at her and smiled. "You really want me to do that?"

She nodded.

He leaned over and kissed her on her cheek. "I'd be honored, Deborah." Then he looked up at Triage. "You know, you're a very lucky man."

"I'm a very blessed man." Triage smiled and took Deborah's hand.

"There is something else, Lavelle." She took a deep breath.

"I will always be so grateful for you giving me my chance, but I have to leave the group."

He frowned slightly. "I thought we agreed that you would continue with me. I don't mind that. In fact, I think it would help both of us."

"It would help in terms of sales, but I've been praying about this, Lavelle, and I'm being led to just focus on God. What I'll be singing is really very different from what I do with you, and if I'm trying to get God's message out there, people will begin to wonder, which person am I?"

Lavelle's fingers wandered across the piano keys.

"I'll stay until you find replacements," Deborah explained. "Vianca told me that she was leaving, and I'll do whatever I have to do."

He stood and walked to the large window that was framed with silk curtains.

"I'll help you pick out the new singers, if you want," she continued. Though she felt sad, she didn't feel guilty. It was as if the peace of God had settled over her and was leading her the way she was supposed to go. She would help Lavelle, but under no circumstances would she stay.

Lavelle sighed. "That won't be necessary. With Emerald gone, and now you and Vianca, maybe this is my sign." He turned around and picked up the glass he'd been drinking from. "Maybe God is trying to tell me something too."

Deborah smiled. "Well, you know, you could always join Capricorn with me, and we could use all of our songs to tell people about the Lord."

Lavelle laughed and looked at Triage. "Man, did you know that you're marrying a preacher girl?"

"I'm not preaching, but from now on, my music will be my ministry."

"Well, you go, girl." He put down his glass. "Let me go find Vianca. I'll be back in a moment."

When Lavelle left the room, Triage hugged Deborah.

"I didn't think it would be that hard, but I feel like I'm leaving Lavelle all alone."

"I can't believe Vianca's leaving too."

"We were just backup singers. He can keep going on his own."

Triage looked into her eyes. "Sometimes I think you just don't get it. You guys were more than that for him. Especially you."

Deborah shrugged. "I don't know what we were, but he's at his own crossroads now."

"Well, all we can do now is pray."

CHAPTER 52

EVERY MORNING WHEN SHE AWOKE IT TOOK A FEW moments for Deborah to remember what day it was. The long days turned into eternal weeks, and at night, when Deborah crawled into bed, her eyes closed from exhaustion before her head even hit the pillow.

All plans for the wedding had been postponed, as Deborah's total focus was on the release of her album. From rehearsals to marketing meetings to production reviews, Deborah had chosen to be involved in every aspect of this project.

Capricorn Records wanted to stay with the original first-of-the-year release date, which gave them only a few months to do what normally took a year.

Many of Deborah's rehearsals and recording sessions were spent with Triage and Lavelle looking on. She was grateful to have them—they told her things that she didn't know and showed her things that she couldn't see.

But what Triage and Lavelle couldn't do was sing for her,

and after the first month in the studio, Deborah had to take a week off to rest her throat.

The people at Capricorn kept trying to push her back to the studio sooner, but Triage insisted she stay home.

"Sweetie, if you don't rest, you won't be able to finish the project at all. Take it from me."

The last two songs recorded were her duet with Lavelle and then the one with Triage, which was a song they had written together.

Despite her sore throat and aching body, the album was finally ready two weeks before Thanksgiving. She had planned on leisurely days and weeks of bed rest, but on her first day home, Triage made a big announcement.

"We're having a party, baby!"

"What are you talking about?"

"A celebration—combination engagement and launch party for your album." He put his arms around her. "It'll be great. We'll fly our parents out here—even Grandma. Everyone is so excited about your album."

"But I'm tired," she whined. "I don't have the energy to do this."

"Come here," he said, taking her hand and leading her to the couch. Then he lifted her feet. "See this? This is all you have to do. I have everything under control."

And he did. For the next two weeks, Deborah rested, while Triage worked with a party coordinator to plan the event.

It was hard for the Petersons to leave Villa Rica for Thanksgiving, so they compromised and arrived in Los Angeles the day after Thanksgiving, the day before the party.

They had scheduled their parents' flights to come in at the same time. So while Deborah was at the Delta terminal, Triage waited at United. There would be too many people and too much luggage for one car, so Triage had hired two.

LAX was as empty as Deborah had ever seen it. She was glad they had decided on the day after Thanksgiving. Virginia and Mother Dobson were the first ones off the plane, followed closely by Elijah.

"Mama, it's so good to see you," she said, hugging her mother. Then she turned to her father. "You too, Daddy." Finally, she turned to Triage's grandmother and kissed her cheek. "I am so happy that all of you are here."

"Sweetheart, you look wonderful," Virginia said as she stepped back to look at her daughter.

Deborah had dressed carefully in a navy tunic and pants.

"Thanks, Mama. How was the flight?" Deborah asked, as she took her mother's bag and held Mother Dobson's hand.

"Deborah Anne, I have never flown first-class before," Virginia said. "I could get used to this."

"Yessiree, sweetie, that first-class was something else. They actually had real silverware," Mother Dobson said.

Deborah laughed as she led them through the terminal and then outside, straight to the curb where the driver was waiting.

"We're going by Triage's first to drop Mother off; then we'll go to my house."

"That's fine," Elijah said, as he helped Mother Dobson, then Virginia into the long black car. When just the two of them were standing on the curb, he whispered, "Deborah Anne, is this what you travel in all the time?"

She chuckled. "No, Daddy. I just wanted to make sure there was enough room for all of us."

"All righty now!" he exclaimed, as he slid into the car.

As they maneuvered from the airport onto the freeway,

Deborah pointed out sights that she thought would interest them.

"I've seen all this before," Mother Dobson said, and they all laughed. When they drove up the driveway that was behind the gate and stepped from the limo, Virginia and Elijah gasped with excitement, while Mother Dobson smiled widely.

"Milton lives here?" Elijah asked. "Who in the world needs this much space?"

"Milton told me he bought it just because he could," Mother Dobson said as she tapped her cane on the ground.

As they stood outside marveling at the mansion, another limousine cruised into the driveway behind them, and Triage jumped from the car first. For ten minutes, the families hugged and kissed, before Triage whistled, halting the chatter. "Hey everyone, I paid the mortgage. We can go inside."

They laughed as they made their way into the house, but Triage and Deborah lingered behind.

He put his arm around her shoulders and kissed her cheek. "Well, baby. Here we are with the Petersons and the Waterses. This is going to be the first of many years of family gatherings."

She sighed as she looked up at the house. "It's going to be tough keeping them all entertained, you know."

"Naw! It's going to be a piece of cake. Let's get inside and watch the games begin."

Triage had hired extra staff to help with the evening, and the moment Deborah and her parents stepped through the door, she could feel their presence. One man took their coats, while another asked if they wanted champagne or sparkling cider.

Just as they took their glasses, Triage came over to them.

"Hey, beautiful," Triage said, kissing Deborah on the cheek. Then he kissed Virginia and shook hands with Elijah. "I thought you would've been here a bit earlier, Ms. Guest of Honor."

"I couldn't get these women out of the house," Elijah grumbled, then he smiled. "But I couldn't be too mad when I took one look at them."

Deborah smiled. She had chosen a simple black halter jumpsuit trimmed in rhinestones, while Virginia wore a gold, crinkled-gauze floor-length dress that Deborah had picked out for her.

"We do look good, don't we?" Virginia said, as she placed one hand on her hip.

They laughed.

"I have to go into the kitchen for a moment. Take your parents into the den—everyone's in there." The first person they saw was Lavelle, who greeted Virginia and Elijah as if he'd known them his entire life.

"I know you're proud of your daughter. Have you heard the CD yet?"

"Not yet," Virginia said, sipping her cider.

"You're going to love it." Lavelle smiled brightly. "I couldn't believe it when she said she was leaving me." He pouted playfully. "But when I heard the entire CD"—he stopped and

316

fanned his face—"I knew she was going to the top with this one. And to think she's doing it all for God."

Elijah beamed. "I understand you sing a song with Deborah Anne, Lavelle."

He nodded. "Yes sir, and I was happy to do it."

"Maybe we'll hear more of that from you," Elijah boomed, and stepped away from where they were standing.

"Excuse us." Virginia smiled.

"Don't pay any attention to my father, Lavelle," Deborah said. "He's like that with everyone. And he's really protective about my music. He never said anything, but he didn't like what I was singing before."

Lavelle swallowed what was left in his glass. "After listening to you, I think your father is right."

"Let me go find my parents. I'll see you in a bit."

Deborah wandered through the room, smiling, waving, and chatting with all the people she'd met over the past year. When she found her parents, Virginia whispered excitedly, "I saw Patti LaBelle. And then we saw that actor from that show . . . I can't think of the name, but we watch it sometimes on Thursdays. Deborah Anne, did these people all come to hear your new album?"

Deborah nodded. "I've had so much support with this—things have happened that should never have happened."

"That's when you know it's nothing but God," Elijah said.

Deborah hugged her father. "I hope you guys like the album."

"Honey, when you exalt the Lord, you know we're going to love it."

Deborah walked with her parents through the crowd, introducing them to the Capricorn executives and others. When the Petersons found the Waterses, Deborah couldn't tear the parents apart.

She was standing on the balcony when she heard Triage call her name. He had set up a small stage in the corner of the living room. She joined him as the crowd of over seventy guests gathered around.

Triage took her hand and said, "I want to thank all of you for joining us tonight. This is an exciting time in our lives. First, and the most important thing, is that we are here to celebrate our love. In case you don't know, in case you missed every headline in America, Deborah and I are engaged." The crowd cheered, and Deborah and Triage kissed. Triage raised his hand, signaling that he had more to say. "But while that is the most important reason to me, there is another reason, near and dear to my heart. My baby is going solo!" The crowd cheered again. "But this is not an ordinary album. As Deborah says, this one is for the Lord. I'm going to let Deborah tell you more about it. So please, put your hands together for the love of my life, Deborah Anne Peterson."

Deborah was trembling when she kissed him. She had learned to stand and sing before thousands, but this was her toughest crowd yet.

"First, I want to give glory and honor to God because He is the reason that I'm here." She was surprised at the cheers that came from the group. "Second, I want to say that this album is my future, but you don't have a future without a past. And I have been blessed with an incredible history, and overwhelming love from my parents, whom I want to thank tonight." She stretched her hands toward her parents, and they beamed. "I love you, Mama and Daddy."

"I feel like I'm standing at the Grammys giving my award speech." She laughed.

"You will be!" someone from the crowd yelled out, and the cheers continued.

"Over a year ago, I was a little country girl, being blessed with the opportunity to sing with Lavelle Roberts. It was beyond my wildest dreams. And it was an important thing for me to do, because it led me to this place. There is nothing wrong with what I've been doing," she said, looking directly at her parents. "It's just that where I want to go now is on a different path. I could go on and on, but I think now, it would be best for us to introduce the album."

With a background tape, Deborah sang "The Secret Place," one of the songs she and Triage had written, but the guests went crazy when she and Triage did a duet, "Ordained by God."

"My love for you is real,
So powerful, consuming and oh, so true,
I've found happiness that I never knew
Because it's been ordained by God. . . ."

Deborah was sure that the ovation they received was the longest she'd ever gotten. Triage hugged her, and their parents joined them on the stage. But as the crowd continued their applause, the thing that touched Deborah the most were the tears that had filled Lavelle's eyes.

A week later, the album was released, and the reviews were immediately positive. The single, "Ordained by God," had made three *Billboard* charts, and several times she and Triage heard it being played on the radio.

But it was the call that came five days later that made Deborah drop to her knees.

"Deborah, where have you been?" William asked. "I tried calling you on your cell phone too, and there was no answer."

"I didn't know you were trying to reach me. What's up?"

"What's up? What's up is that the single has just gone platinum! This is incredible, Deborah. Congratulations."

The moment she hung up, she dropped to her knees, lifting her hands and praising God for success beyond what she could have ever imagined. "Lord, this is what You wanted me to do. Thank You, Father, for Your guidance and Your patience and Your goodness and Your mercy. . . ." She continued to pray through tears of joy, and she was still crying when Triage came to her door.

"What's wrong, baby?"

She was trembling with the excitement of the news.

"Did something happen? Is it your parents?"

She shook in his arms. "William called . . . I . . . he wanted to tell me that the single has gone platinum."

He pulled away to look into her eyes. "Are you serious?"

She nodded as tears still fell from her cheeks. "Triage, this is all about the abundant blessings of God."

He squeezed her close again. "Oh, baby, you're right. We are truly blessed, because this *has* been ordained by God. And there's one more blessing He has for us. It's time for us to get married."

CHAPTER 53

DEBORAH AND TRIAGE HAD ARRIVED IN HAWAII A day before their families and other guests. No one had been told the location of the wedding until their tickets were delivered to them by Federal Express.

"Deborah, this place is really beautiful," Willetta gushed as she stood in the open lobby of the Hyatt Regency, overlooking the Pacific Ocean.

"Wait until you see it in the daytime. Now you should get up to bed, Willetta. With the time change and all, you've got to be ready for the breakfast rehearsal in the morning."

They chatted as they went up to their rooms, and once she was alone, Deborah went over a mental checklist. Everyone had arrived, with the exception of Pastor Duncan and the photographer from *Ebony* magazine who was covering the event for an exclusive story. They would arrive in the morning. Deborah had purposely purchased most of the tickets so that everyone would arrive at night—which would give her one more day to get things in order.

As she stood on the balcony of her suite and gazed into the blackened, star-filled sky, Deborah thanked God for her blessings. In two days, she'd be marrying a man she loved and who knew the Lord. She was blessed with a career that had taken off from the moment the album hit the stores. It had become impossible for her to walk the streets without people stopping her, and now even she wore disguises when she and Triage went out. It was a different life, but it was a blessed one, and she would be forever grateful.

The ringing phone brought her in from the balcony, and she smiled when she heard her soon-to-be husband's voice.

"What are you doing?" he asked softly.

"Thinking of you."

"Ah, that's just what I'm doing."

"You're thinking of you too?"

They laughed.

"Do me a favor and go out to your balcony," Triage said.

"I was just out there—"

"Well, go back out there."

Deborah took the cordless phone outside.

"Now look to your left."

Her head turned, and she saw Triage, wrapped in a white terry cloth bathrobe, standing two balconies away. She smiled.

"I thought your room was on the other side of the hotel."

"It was, but I had to be able to say good night to the woman I love." He blew her a kiss. "Good night, my love."

"Good night."

She stepped back into her room and crawled into bed. Her smile remained on her face through her peaceful sleep as images of her wedding danced through her dreams. When she awakened, she showered and dressed quickly, wanting to be the first in the banquet room for breakfast. But when she arrived, Triage was already there, speaking with the hotel waiters.

"Why didn't you come by my room and get me?" Deborah asked after they kissed.

"I wanted you to get some rest, and I have this under control."

She shook her head with delight and said a quick prayer that Triage would always be this way.

Slowly, the room began to fill. Their parents arrived together, saying that they had been up for a few hours and had already explored the expansive grounds of the luxurious hotel.

"Deborah Anne, you should see the flowers around this place," Virginia said. "Your father wants to plant some of these in our garden."

"I don't think they'll grow in Georgia, Mama."

"That's what I tried to tell him."

Deborah looked toward the door and excused herself from her parents. "Vianca," she said, hugging her friend. "It is so good to see you. When we didn't hear back, I wasn't sure if you were going to come."

Vianca smiled. "I'm sorry. I couldn't decide, and then yesterday I knew that I just couldn't miss my friend's wedding," she said softly.

They hugged again, and Deborah stepped back and looked at Vianca. She had let her hair grow out a bit and had layered it with blond highlights.

"Congratulations on your CD." Vianca smiled. It's playing everywhere in—" She stopped as Lavelle came into the room.

He looked at them and then walked over, a smile on his face. He kissed Deborah first, then turned to Vianca.

"It's good to see you."

Vianca smiled, but lowered her eyes.

"Listen, you two," Deborah began, "I have to get everything started. Are you going to be all right?" she asked Vianca.

When Vianca nodded, Deborah made her way to the head table, where Triage was sitting between their parents.

When everyone was seated, Triage and Deborah stood.

"First of all, we would like to thank all of you for coming so far to celebrate this special time with us. It means a lot, especially since we couldn't tell you anything about the wedding. So thank you for understanding our desire to avoid any disruptions or distractions from the media."

Deborah smiled as she looked out into the crowd. Her cousins weren't listening to a word Triage was saying—their attention was on the back of the room where Lavelle and Vianca sat.

"Before we eat, I would like to ask my future father-in-law to bless the food," Triage continued.

Elijah stood, and there were moans from half the room.

Virginia laughed. "Now y'all behave. Your uncle Eli promised that he wasn't going to preach this morning."

It took a moment for the laughter to simmer down, and it was only then that Elijah asked them to bow their heads. As he prayed, Deborah thanked God with her own silent prayer. But she was thanking God for much more than the food. There was so much she had to thank Him for that if she spent every minute of every day making a list, it would never be enough.

After the breakfast rehearsal, Deborah and Triage had

planned an entire day of entertainment for their guests. First, there was the chartered glass-bottomed boat that was going to cruise along the Kona Coast to the Kealakekua Bay Marine Reserve.

While everyone ran to change quickly, Lavelle and Vianca walked toward Triage and Deborah.

Triage kissed Vianca and shook Lavelle's hand.

"Hey, we wanted to tell you guys that we're not going on the cruise," Lavelle said.

Deborah eyed the two of them. "Anything wrong?"

"No, we want to spend some time talking." Lavelle took Vianca's hand.

"Talking?" Deborah looked from one to the other. "About—"

"No problem," Triage interrupted Deborah, and began pulling her away. "We'll see you later. Just remember the dinner tonight."

"Wait, Triage," Deborah said, when they were several feet away. "Don't you want to find out what's going on with them?"

"No." He grinned. "Let them work it out."

Their guests were amazed at the boat cruise and the fish that came right to the glass bottom. When the boat docked for lunch, Triage took a few cousins snorkeling, while others sat on the beach.

Willetta and Deborah sat together, watching as others romped in the water.

"Deborah Anne, you deserve all that is happening to you, and a whole lot more."

"Thanks, Willetta. You know, the only thing that makes me sad is that we won't be living next door to each other. I'm going to miss that."

"Girl, you didn't expect that to last forever, did you?" Willetta chuckled. "And anyway, I'll be moving out soon. I think Steven and I will be the next ones walking down the aisle."

"Willetta, that's terrific."

She grinned, then put her finger over her lips. "But don't say anything yet. Steven wants to ask my dad, like Triage did. Your man caused quite a stir in Villa Rica. Uncle Eli told *everyone* how Triage called him up!"

Deborah laughed. "You should have seen Triage that day! It was quite a picture."

For the rest of the afternoon, guests split into groups. Some went shopping, some went hiking, and others stayed at the beach. As Deborah dressed for dinner, she hoped that everyone would make it back for the special banquet they planned.

By the time the traditional Hawaiian feast began with the arrival of torchbearers via canoe, everyone who had come for the Peterson-Waters wedding was in attendance.

The conch shells were blown, and the torchbearers began to light the pathway surrounding the area where the luau would be held.

There was an audible gasp when the roasted pig was lifted from the underground oven.

"What's that?" Maxine asked Deborah.

"That's part of the dinner."

Deborah chuckled as Maxine turned green; then the buffet table was opened. Some of the children began running toward the food, but they stopped when Elijah held up his hands.

"No matter where we are, we must give thanks to the Lord."

The children slumped back to their parents, and everyone

held hands while Elijah prayed. But the moment he said "Amen," hungry folks flanked the buffet table.

As Deborah and Triage watched the crowd flow past the buffet, she could see some of her cousins talking to Lavelle, and she smiled. He was being so gracious to her star-struck family, and she made a mental note to thank him for it. But a moment later, her smile turned to a frown when Vianca walked up to him and they kissed.

"Hey, did you see that?" Triage whispered.

Deborah frowned. "Yeah, but I don't know if that's a good thing, Triage."

"Well, good or bad, it's none of our business." Triage took her hand and led her to where their parents were sitting. But Deborah continued to look over her shoulder, watching Lavelle and Vianca as they sat with their heads close together.

Deborah sat next to her mother, while Triage sat at the opposite end of the table between his mother and Mother Dobson.

"Deborah Anne, this is so incredible." Virginia squeezed her hand.

She smiled.

"Do you know how much I love you and how proud I am?"

"Yes, ma'am, but I love hearing you say it." Deborah kissed her mother's cheek.

Then Virginia glanced down at Triage. "You have a good man there, Deborah Anne. Be good to him, and I pray that you have as many loving years as your father and I have."

"I plan on that."

Virginia patted her daughter's hand. "You know, Milton's family is so pleased that you children are getting married.

Mother Dobson said this was the best decision that Milton ever made."

Virginia and Deborah laughed as Triage came to their end of the table. "What's so funny?"

"Nothing, honey," Deborah said. "My mother was just telling me how smart she thinks you are."

He grinned. "You noticed already?"

Virginia laughed again as Deborah took his hand and led him to the buffet. "I have to make sure you eat tonight so that you can have your strength for tomorrow."

"Oh, you think I'll be too weak at the wedding?"

"No, silly. I'm talking about tomorrow *night*. I want to make sure you keep up your strength for that."

It took him a moment before his lips pulled into a wide grin. "Well, move out of my way . . . there's a lot of food I have to eat!"

CHAPTER 54

THE PETERSON GIRLS, ALONG WITH CYNTHIA, Triage's sister, were in the dressing room of the beachside chapel. While the bridesmaids jabbered in front of the dressing table as they put the finishing touches on their makeup, Deborah stood in front of the full-length mirror.

The image that stared back was stunning. She had chosen a gown by Tracy Rae, and up-and-coming African American designer. The cup-sleeved Italian silk gown had an opulent, hand-beaded bodice with a detachable six-foot train. Her tulle veil fell just below her waist.

Deborah turned from side to side, surveying her reflection. The cream color complemented her copper complexion.

As she stood in front of the mirror, there was a knock on the door, and when she turned around, Elijah walked into the room.

"Hey, Uncle Eli," Maxine said.

Willetta glanced at her uncle, then her cousin, and said,

"Ladies, let's get our flowers." She closed the door behind them.

In the silent moments that followed, thousands of thoughts ran through Deborah's mind—from when she was a little girl sitting on her father's lap as he read stories to her, to when he sat next to her on the piano bench and taught her how to play. She remembered the nights when she had sat with him in the dark house while her mother slept, talking about her dreams and desires. And then there was the image she had imagined—on her wedding day, when she would stand before her father and accept his words of wisdom.

"Deborah Anne . . . oh, baby." He paused and swallowed. "You are beautiful."

"Thank you, Daddy."

"You know there is so much I want to say—how much your mother and I love you, how we are so proud of you and how we want you to be happy."

"I know, Daddy."

"But there is something else that I have to say," he said, taking her hands. "We've given you the best foundation we knew to give, and now your mother and I have to let go and let you start this new part of your life. But first I have to say that I pray that you've invited God to this wedding and into your marriage. That's the only way it's going to work."

She smiled. "Yes, Daddy. God is the head of my life, and I know that I can't do anything without Him. And Triage feels the same way."

He nodded, then hugged her. They both turned at the knock on the door.

Willetta peeked inside. "Are you ready? It's time." She

stepped into the room with Deborah's bouquet, and the scent of the lilies filled Deborah's nostrils.

Elijah took his daughter's hand. Then they strolled through the narrow hallway to the double doors that led to the sanctuary.

As the organist began to play, Pauline walked down the aisle, then Maxine. Before Willetta began to walk, she turned toward Deborah with wet eyes and mouthed, "I love you."

Instantly, hot tears stung Deborah's eyes, and she scolded herself. She couldn't start crying now.

When Elijah heard the first note from the Wedding March, he turned so that he and Deborah stood in front of the door. Deborah took a deep breath as they stepped forward, and her eyes focused on Triage.

He had never looked more handsome, and she hoped she was what he expected. By the time she got to where he was standing, his smile told her that he was pleased.

Elijah lifted Deborah's veil, kissed her cheek, then took her hand and put it into Triage's.

"'Therefore shall a man leave his father and his mother, and shall cleave unto his wife: and they shall be one flesh.'"

As Pastor Duncan began the ceremony, Triage squeezed Deborah's fingers, but she kept her eyes forward, trying to still her shaking legs. Pastor Duncan's words continued to strike her ears, but she couldn't focus. Instead, she was trying to hold on to each second of every minute that passed, pressing it into her memory to be recalled years from now. It wasn't until Pastor Duncan told them to face each other to pledge their love that Deborah moved.

They had decided on the traditional vows, repeating the same words that couples had said for hundreds of years.

Deborah's hand shook as Triage placed the platinum band on her finger, and she was surprised that his hand trembled as much as hers did when she put the matching band on his finger.

Pastor Duncan looked down on them. "Both of your mothers have requested to do a reading from the Bible. Each has chosen one of her favorite scriptures as a gift to you, to lead you, to help you in your marriage."

The pastor nodded toward Virginia and Erlene, and they both stood.

Virginia clasped her hands in front of her and recited the scripture from memory. "'But seek ye first the kingdom of God, and his righteousness; and all these things shall be added unto you.' All you have to do is put God first, and He will take care of you. He will take care of your needs, your wishes, your desires." Virginia then took two steps up to the altar and kissed Deborah, then Triage.

After Virginia sat, Erlene looked down into the small Bible in her hand. "Psalm 46:10 says, 'Be still and know that I am God.'" She looked up. "You don't have to search for the Lord. As long as He is part of your life, part of your marriage, He will be there. The hardest thing for us to do is to be still. But once you learn that, all will be well."

Deborah smiled. Her mother-in-law's favorite scripture was the same one that she herself loved so much. There were no coincidences with God.

"Let us bow our heads," Pastor Duncan directed. After the prayer, he said, "I now pronounce you man and wife. Milton, you may kiss your bride."

The fifty-three guests stood and cheered.

Pastor Duncan said, "May I be the first to present to everyone: Mr. and Mrs. Milton Waters!"

⁓

Even though they were a small group, Deborah and Triage had rented the Grand Ballroom in the Hyatt. On one side of the room were the tables, decorated in white and gold, with gold hearts as centerpieces. On the other side was the keyboard, dance floor, and a small stage.

Before the food was served, Elijah stood. "May I have everyone's attention, please?"

Immediately, the Peterson family began to bow their heads.

"No, that's not what I'm doing," he said gruffly, then laughed. "I want to make a toast."

Laughter filled the room as Elijah raised his glass. "I want to welcome you, Milton, into our family. You are now the husband of the most precious person in my life, and we know that you will take complete care of our child. Isn't that true, Milton?"

"Yes, sir."

Elijah lifted his hand high above his head. "To Mr. and Mrs. Milton Waters. May you always be as happy as you are today, and may God always be a part of your life."

The guests took a sip of their cider.

Then Walter Waters rose to his feet. "Like Elijah, I would like to welcome Deborah into *our* family. And to say, like everyone has already said today, keep the Lord at the center of everything you do, and you will have many years of happiness." When he raised his glass, the guests sipped again.

Then waiters dressed in colorful flowered shirts and tan shorts began to serve the six-course dinner, beginning with pineapple soup. Before eating, Deborah and Triage walked from table to table, chatting with their guests.

When it was time for the couple's first dance, Lavelle took the stage.

"Deborah and Triage asked me to sing the song for their first dance as husband and wife. They told me to keep it a surprise, and I'm glad I did, because I changed my mind. I'd like to sing the duet that Deborah and I have sung so many times."

Everyone clapped.

"Deborah and I sang this onstage and on her album, but I always knew that she wasn't singing to me—she was singing to the Lord. But what's great about this song is that I think it epitomizes Triage and Deborah's relationship too. Since Deborah moved to Los Angeles, they've been inseparable, even when they were 'just friends.' That's what they told everyone, but we all knew what was happening between them—a very precious love was brewing.

"The best part was that they were friends first, and that's how it should always be. So I dedicate this song to two people who mean so much to me." Lavelle picked up the microphone. "But there is one thing—a duet needs a partner." He stretched out his hand, and Vianca came onto the stage.

Her smile was so bright that Deborah couldn't help but smile too.

As the music began playing, Lavelle said, "Enjoy."

The guests applauded as Triage took Deborah's hand and led her to the center of the dance floor. But the room could have been silent, and they could have been alone, for in that moment, all Deborah saw was the man she had married. And while she had been able to contain herself all through the ceremony, now she felt the first tear stream down her cheek.

"What's wrong?" Triage asked.

She shook her head. "Nothing. I'm just happy."

He chuckled and pulled her close. "You are no happier than I am. This is the best day of my life."

Minutes later, Elijah and Virginia, then Triage's parents, joined them. Before the song was over, the entire dance floor was filled.

Deborah waltzed through the throwing of the bouquet and garter, speeches of good wishes from family, and even the traditional glass-clicking that begged the couple to kiss.

At seven, Deborah and Triage rushed to their rooms to change and pack for the short flight to Maui, where they would be spending their three-week honeymoon.

The limousine was already waiting as the guests filled the hotel lobby to wish them well. Deborah hugged her parents, and then Triage pulled her into the car as they were sprinkled with rose petals.

On the private plane, they sipped sparkling cider and cuddled. When they landed twenty minutes later, another car was waiting to take them to the Carlton on Maui. They were whisked to the hotel, then whizzed through the lobby to their suite. As they rode up in the private elevator that would take them to the penthouse, Triage kissed Deborah.

"I've been looking forward to this night for a long time."

She ran her hands along the muscles in his back and took in his scent. "Me too."

Deborah took a final look at herself in the bathroom mirror. She straightened the thin straps of her silk nightgown, took a deep breath, then turned out the light.

She slipped into the bedroom and was greeted by the flicker of candlelight. Her eyes moved to the king-size bed where Triage was raised up on his elbow. He was naked to the waist.

He lifted his hand, reaching for her to come to him, and slowly she moved forward, struggling to hide her nervousness.

Triage took her hand as she got to the bed and gently pulled her down. When she lay back, she pulled the covers to her chin.

He ran a finger along her cheek. "There's nothing to be afraid of, baby. I promise."

She nodded. "It's not that I'm afraid." Her voice trembled. "It's just that we've waited. . . ."

He kissed her hand. "I'm so glad that we waited," he whispered. He slid his finger under one of the straps of her nightgown and pulled it from her shoulder. "Are you going to take this off?"

She smiled. "I thought you'd like it."

"It's beautiful—"

"But right now, you'd rather see it on the floor," she teased. Then she stood, and let the gown slide from her body. It was her husband's sharp intake of breath that finally made her relax.

When he took her hands and pulled her onto the bed,

Deborah fell into his kisses. And she knew this was where she was supposed to be.

❧

They were still awake hours later, and Deborah leaned back into Triage's arms. He squeezed her to his chest.

"I just want you to agree to one thing," Triage said softly.

"What's that?"

"If you get pregnant tonight, I want to name the baby Hallelujah!"

She laughed and lifted his hands to her lips. "So are you saying that I was okay?"

"Okay is not quite the word I would use to describe what happened with us tonight." He rolled onto his stomach and looked into her eyes. "You were so right; you were worth the wait. And we would have never had the chance for a night like this if you didn't stand by what you believe." He took her hands into his, and kissed them. "Thank you for this."

He turned over and pulled her back into his arms.

"When I saw you singing in the choir that Sunday, I had no idea it would lead to this night."

"You had no idea? Imagine me, just a country girl with big dreams, meeting this big-time superstar. Now here we are . . . in bed together, and you won't let me sleep."

He laughed. "Oh, you're blaming this on me. I've been trying to sleep for hours."

She turned onto her stomach and kissed him. "Okay, you can go to sleep now, if you want to."

But as she moved away, he pulled her back to his chest. "Where do you think you're going?"

She shrugged. "I don't know . . . if you're going to sleep, I'll have to find something else to do."

He grinned. "You know, I'm not that sleepy after all."

"Oh, really?"

"Yeah," he said, and turned her onto her back. "And there are still a few more things I want to show you."

"Oh, really? Well, *show* me, Mr. Waters."

"I will, Mrs. Waters."

Reading Group Guide

SINGSATION

1. Deborah Anne had dreamed of a singing career all of her life. How did she sense a calling in her dream? A God-given dream does not mean there is no human preparation involved. Think about a dream that God has placed in your heart.
How are you preparing yourself for that dream to become a reality? **Read Genesis 37:6–7 and Proverbs 16:3.**

2. When Triage first approached Deborah Anne about singing backup for Lavelle, should she have considered it further? Did it seem that she automatically assumed that the opportunity was from the Lord? Have you ever had an experience that made you feel as though you mistook Satan answering your prayer before the Lord had a chance to get around to it? **Read Matthew 4:1–10.**

3. Imagine how difficult it must have been for Elijah to withhold his reservations about the direction in which Deborah Anne's career seemed to be headed. Did he do the right thing by not vocalizing his objections? **Read Prov. 17:27 and Eccl. 3:1, 7.**

4. Deborah Anne's relationship with Triage began as a friendship that only later blossomed into romance. What qualities and behaviors did Triage exhibit to demonstrate his readiness to be a husband? **Read Ruth 2:1, 3:11.**

5. How does the way that Deborah Anne entered into a career as a professional singer demonstrate that God's plans for us are not necessarily the plans that we have made for ourselves or that others have made for us? **Read Genesis 45:1; 50:20 and Isaiah 55:8–9.**

6. How did Deborah Anne demonstrate her willingness to go wherever God was leading her? How did her behavior with the group show that she sought to find the Lord at every turn of her career? **Read Genesis 12:1–3; 13:5–11; 22:1–3 and Hebrews 11:6, 8, 17–19.**

7. Beyond her relationship with her parents, what incidents in Deborah Anne's life demonstrate that she came from a loving support system of family and friends? Recall some of the other persons in her life and how they showed support and concern for her. **Read Ruth 1:16–18; 3:1, and Luke 1:39–43 and 2 Timothy 1:5.** How did her solid support system help her through the demands of a professional singing career?

8. Deborah Anne's dream became real for her as she sat in the studio for her first day of rehearsal. She acknowledged her dream and promptly thanked God for it. When the Lord fulfills the desires of our hearts, how should we respond? **Read Genesis 12:7; Exodus 15:19–32; Luke 1:67–79.**

9. Deborah Anne had longed to be a professional singer, but the physical and mental demands began to wear on her. Still, she did not give up. Have you ever been tempted to believe that a dream was not divinely inspired simply because the going got a little rough? **Read 2 Kings 4:13-28 and Exodus 5:22.** What should we do when the road to achieving our dreams gets a little bumpy? **Read Habakkuk 3:17–18.**

10. Consider the cycle that moves us away from the Lord: (1) we may get too busy to pray; (2) Bible study tapers off; (3) church attendance declines; (4) we begin to accept certain worldly ways into our lifestyle. **Read Luke 11–14.** What steps/actions did Deborah Anne incorporate into her lifestyle once she moved to Los Angeles to insure that she maintained her relationship with the Lord? **Read Genesis 8:18–20; 33:18–20; Exodus 23:33; Joshua 22:5; and Psalm 119:165.**

11. What was a major sign that Deborah Anne would be working with people who did not share her beliefs and values? **Read Joshua 24:15.** How do you cope with situations that require you to work with unchurched or unsaved persons? **Read Psalm 40:8; 119:29.**

12. In what ways was Deborah able to impact the persons she encountered in pursuit of a singing career? **Read Acts 5:15** (Consider Triage, Vianca, Emerald, Lavelle, Phoebe.)

13. What do you believe sparked Deborah Anne's interest in having a friend like Phoebe? What does the friendship of these opposites indicate about friendships between godly persons and worldly persons? **Read Luke 7:36-48; 19:5–10.**

14. What does Deborah Anne's influence on those persons reveal about the power of being a living testimony for the Lord? **Read Mark 1:44 and John 4:28-29.**

15. If Deborah Anne had accepted the condominium from Triage, do you believe she might have been tempted to have sex with him out of gratitude? How do you think her response to Triage's offer affected him? **Read Ruth 3:11 and Proverbs 31:10–11.**

16. Deborah Anne was willing to hold out for the kind of solo career she believed God wanted her to have. **Read Genesis 32:24–30.** What does her decision, as well as her actions in the days following, reveal about how believers should deal with a calling from the Lord? **Read Proverbs 16:3–4.**

Reading Groups for African American
Christian Women Who Love God and Like to Read.

BE A PART OF
GLORY GIRLS READING GROUPS!

THESE EXCITING BI-MONTHLY READING GROUPS ARE FOR THOSE SEEKING FELLOWSHIP WITH OTHER WOMEN WHO ALSO LOVE GOD AND ENJOY READING.

For more information about GLORY GIRLS, to connect with an established group in your area, or to become a group facilitator, go to our Web site at **www.glorygirlsread.net** or click on the Praising Sisters logo at **www.walkworthypress.net**.

WHO WE ARE

GLORY GIRLS is a national organization made up of primarily African American Christian women, yet it welcomes the participation of anyone who loves the God of the Bible and likes to read.

OUR PURPOSE IS SIMPLE

- To honor the Lord with <u>what we read</u>—and have a good time doing it!

- To provide an atmosphere where readers can seek fellowship with other book lovers while encouraging them in the choices they make in Godly reading materials.

- To offer readers fresh, contemporary, and entertaining yet scripturally sound fiction and nonfiction by talented Christian authors.

- To assist believers and nonbelievers in discovering the relevancy of the Bible in our contemporary, everyday lives.